Absolution

A Medieval Romance

By Kathryn Le Veque

Part of the Guard of Six series

KATHRYN LE VEQUE
NOVELS

ARE YOU SIGNED UP FOR KATHRYN'S BLOG?

You'll get the latest news and information on exclusive giveaways, exclusive excerpts, coming releases, sales, free books, cover reveals and more.

Kathryn's blog followers get it all first. No spam, no junk.

Get the latest info from the reigning Queen of English Medieval Romance!

Sign Up Here

kathrynleveque.com

Sir Torran de Serreaux is the leader of Henry III's personal guard. Known as the Guard of Six, they are an elite group made up of knights from the finest and oldest families in England. They have a reputation for being powerful, fearless, and dedicated.

They are also mortal men with demons, and Torran has more demons than most.

It has been three years since the fall of Simon de Montfort and, still, there are lingering de Montfort supporters in England that are being systematically rooted out and subdued. At a particularly nasty battle at Kennington Castle, Torran and the royal army manage to raze the castle and kill all but two members of the oppositionist's family—a lovely young woman and her excitable younger brother.

Torran is introduced to Lady Andia St. Albans.

The family of St. Albans were great supporters of de Montfort. Torran takes Andia and her brother to London as prisoners. Henry, as punishment to the St. Albans family, orders the siblings thrown in the vault. Torran, who is fighting a great attraction to Andia, has other ideas.

Keeping them at his family's London townhome.

Torran keeps them as his personal prisoners because the truth is that there's something about Andia that intrigues him. She's reserved, but very intelligent, and he is coming to suspect that Andia is hiding something. He can't help but feel she's harboring secrets, much as he is, and as he tries to figure him out, she is trying to figure him out as well. But all of the suspicion in the world can't dampen the sparks that fly between them.

Passion that roars like a wildfire.

In England's complex political world, Torran and Andia are major players. When the truth of Andia's involvement in her family's support of Simon de Montfort is revealed, Torran must make a choice. Can he forgive a woman he's fallen in love with?

Or is he the one who must seek absolution?

GUARD OF SIX

Fortitudo in unitate

Motto: Strength in Unity

We are protectors.

Defenders.

The shield between the king and those who threaten him.

We are the Guard of Six.

Fortitudo in unitate

Strength in unity.

Author's Note

Welcome to the first in the Guard of Six series!

I'm actually really excited about this series. I've had to put it off because I had other big series to write, but I have finally managed to start it with this book—and what a book. We're in the middle of political intrigue and kingly drama once again!

To be clear, the Guard of Six aren't just a normal group of royal bodyguards. These guys are kind of Henry III's death squad. They do whatever he wants them to do. If Henry says jump, they jump, and each one of them has a bit of a dark secret that Henry holds over them. They're really a bunch of misfits, unlike other groups I write about. These guys have secrets and scandals in their past. The Guard of Six comprises (their families/house name in parentheses):

- Torran de Serreaux *(The Unholy Hour—a contemporary novel)*
- Aidric St. John *(The Warrior Poet)*
- Dirk d'Vant *(Tender is the Knight)*
- Jareth de Leybourne *(Lady of the Moon)*
- Britt de Garr *(Lord of Light)*
- Kent de Poyer *(Netherworld)*

These are all families from some of my older or lesser-known books, so I love the fact that they're coming to the forefront again. Do you recognize them? The names of the books their families are originally featured in have been put in parentheses.

De Serreaux, who is the hero of this novel, has an interesting familial path. The name actually comes from a contemporary novel I've written—originally, it was called *Resurrection*, but that was quite some time ago. I added content and re-edited the book, retitling it *The Unholy Hour*. The prologue is a Medieval scene where the ancestor of the hero—and possibly a descendant of the hero in this book—is in the middle of the fall of the Knights Templar. So, that's where de Serreaux's family comes from, and I have to say that I really love the family—they are all knights or (in the case of the contemporary book) FBI agents and firefighters, so they are a family of public service.

Torran is the de facto leader of the Guard of Six, and although I write about groups of knights all the time, the Guard of Six is a little different. They're not linked by family ties, or spy networks, or a training guild, but are rather six highly trained knights that Henry has selected to be his personal guard. That's their connection. They have a relative amount of freedom when Henry doesn't need them, but when called into service, they are a circle of men that cannot be broken. Fortunately, they all like one another, and the truth is that they are loyal to each other over the king. That can be a bit of a conflict at times, so watch for that in the books. Not surprisingly, they are not entirely fond of a king who would use their secrets to force them into service, which isn't very smart if you think about it. Henry is trusting the Guard of Six to keep him safe, so they don't serve him out of love. It's out of duty, pure and simple.

Something to note here is that the Guard of Six came before the position of Lord Protector, offered to Patrick de Wolfe (*Nighthawk*) and Thor de Reyne (*One Wylde Knight*), and also to the sons of Patrick de Wolfe (*the de Wolfe Pack Generations tales*). Lord Protector is a position of right-hand military man to the king, his personal protector, and while the Guard of Six are very much his protectors, they are also more. They transcend the position of "just" bodyguards. Torran does call himself Lord Protector, but it's a position that eventually evolves into something else.

Now, on to the cameos in the book…

You know I always have a lot of cameos. We've got a few in this one. The opening scene has Daniel de Lohr (*Shadowmoor*) and Davyss de Winter (*Lespada*). Interesting that those two are contemporaries. In fact, during this period of the thirteenth century, there were many of my heroes who were contemporaries. In addition to Daniel, his son Chad, and Davyss, there are the Lords of Thunder, Patrick de Wolfe, and a few others. The thirteenth century happens to be one of my favorites, so I've got a lot of books crammed into that one-hundred-year span. Also, in this book, Davyss de Winter is designated for the first time as the Earl of Radnor. That comes from his father's side. In Davyss' book, it was never really spelled out that he had a title, only that he hated titles and politics, but the truth is that he is the Earl of Radnor, so we are using it formally for Davyss in this novel (and he is probably hating it).

Last but not least, here are some fun facts about a character in this novel—he appears briefly and goes by the name of Styx. He has a real name (which is revealed later, so I don't want to spoil it), but his parents are none other than Achilles and Susannah from the Executioner Knights novel, *Starless*. And here's another tie-in: I'll bet you didn't realize that Achilles is the youngest brother of Brickley de Dere, a major secondary character in *Steelheart*. Poor Brickley didn't get the girl (she belonged to David de Lohr), and, of course, David de Lohr is Daniel de Lohr's father (*Shadowmoor*), and Daniel is a major secondary character in this book along with his cousin and friend, Roi de Lohr.

Nothing is coincidence in my universe!

The usual pronunciation guide: (and we've got some great names in this one!)

De Serreaux – duh Sir-ROW
Andia – ON-dee-uh (her nickname, Andie, is pronounced ON-dee)
Aidric – AID-rick (Aid, as in first aid)
Desiderata – des-uh-der-RAH-da
Gaubert – basically, go-BARE

Davyss – another spelling of Davis

Ó

Happy Reading!

PROLOGUE

Year of Our Lord 1268
Kennington Castle

"MERCY, MY LORD!"

"I cannot show you mercy."

With that, the knight rammed his enormous broadsword into the man's neck, straight down so that it carved into his chest cavity.

He was dead before he hit the ground.

The knight who had killed him made the sign of the cross over his victim.

"I give you Absolution, my son."

From his right, a man charged him, tripping over the bodies that were already littering the ground. As he faltered, he was close enough that the knight was able to slice him through the neck with his bloodied broadsword. As the man fell to the ground, the knight made another sign of the cross over him.

"I give you Absolution, my son."

Absolution was a legend that day. The longsword of Torran de Serreaux had a reputation almost as much as the man who owned it. The enemy knew about the knight who was moving through the battle and killing with a sword that was as long as it was sharp and deadly.

Absolution was its name.

And the knight was giving his enemy Absolution.

Overhead, a nasty storm had blown in. Thunder rolled and lightning flashed as Torran worked his way through piles of the dead and dying. He wasn't interested in those men—the dead because they were beyond help and the dying because they would have to explain their loyalties to God, and he didn't want to interfere with that. Absolution was for the able-bodied, men who were still fighting in a futile situation. Those were the men who needed Absolution the most because they didn't know that they had been beaten.

Torran would absolve them for the sin of pride.

It had been a nasty battle at the mighty bastion known as Kennington Castle, and it wasn't over yet. The lord of Kennington was a supporter of Simon de Montfort, who had been killed about three years earlier. Henry, King of England, was fully in control of his country and of his destiny with the death of de Montfort, and he had ordered those loyal to the Earl of Leicester to seek out the warlords who had opposed him and punish them.

Kennington was part of that directive.

The royal army had been busy over the past three years, rooting out the enemies of the Crown. They had been systematic in their destruction and on a cool October day, they had marched north from London, gathering more troops at royal outposts as they went, before they finally ended up at Kennington. They were joined by several other allied armies that had been summoned, including the Earl of Canterbury, Daniel de Lohr, and the Earl of Radnor, Davyss de Winter. The unfortunate fact was that Anselm St. Albans, Earl of Ashford, had been a de Montfort supporter. A *big* supporter. His family, a very old family, had made its money in import and export. They weren't merchants, but they owned ships that merchants paid to have their goods transported on, so Ashford had a good deal of wealth to put behind de Montfort, something Henry was particularly upset about.

Therefore, Kennington had to be taught a lesson.

Henry wanted what Ashford had.

That was the punishment.

Although the royal army had a commander in an older knight by the name of Luc de Lara, Henry had sent his entire personal guard into the battle as well. Torran and five of his closest companions, only these weren't just any companions. They were Henry's private attack force, men who not only protected him, but who also acted as spies and assassins, leaders of armies, and anything Henry wanted them to do. They were some of the most elite knights in England, highly skilled, highly experienced, and they were involved in Henry's business perhaps more than even Henry himself.

The Guard of Six, as they were known, took Ashford's support of de Montfort personally. Ashford had been a supporter of Henry at first, but somehow, de Montfort got to him and extolled the virtues of a country managed by men and not simply by a king. Ashford fell for those dreams, like a snake charmed by a snake charmer, and he'd taken his army and his money to de Montfort's side. Ashford had been a friend the men in Henry's circle, so when he went to de Montfort's side, every one of those men felt betrayed.

Now, Ashford was paying the price for that betrayal.

Kennington Castle was the heart of Ashford's earldom. It was the target set by Henry himself and it took three days to not only decimate the countryside, but to weaken the gatehouse. Kennington was a concentric castle, meaning it had two sets of walls—an enormous exterior curtain wall and then a smaller interior wall. The portcullis for the exterior wall had been partially breached because they'd managed to heat the iron with a pyre of flaming debris that softened it up so much that they were able to twist it. That created an opening through which the royal army was able to slip, but when they were through, they saw that Ashford's army had retreated to the inner ward.

That started the siege all over again.

The inner gatehouse did not have the iron portcullis that the outer gatehouse had. The inner gatehouse had two enormous wooden gates that were made with great iron rivets holding the wood together. There was also an iron frame built around the gates but it wasn't nearly the strength of the exterior portcullis and, therefore, when they started a pyre against those gates, it was only a matter of time before the wood caught fire and the iron began to soften.

In a panic, Ashford's men had come over their own wall, descending into the outer bailey to stave off the complete collapse of the inner gatehouse. That had been a sight to see as soldiers lowered themselves over the inner wall and attacked the royal army. Unfortunately for them, the royal army was much larger than they were and that mode of defense was over before it really got started. But, somehow, Ashford's men still kept coming and the royal army realized it was because they were coming from the postern gate. All of them, flooding out to defend the inner gatehouse.

Torran wasn't exactly sure who was leading the battle for the Earl of Ashford because it seemed that in the beginning, someone who knew what they were doing was handling it, but into the third day, it seemed as if there was little organization at all. Anyone with any manner of military training would not have allowed men to go over the wall into the enemy, or open the postern gate, so as the third day began to wane, the royal army could sense victory.

But it was victory at a cost.

There were many wounded and many dead, and most of them were from Ashford's army. As the storm overhead let loose, pounding the earth with sheets of rain, the blood from the dead and the wounded mingled with the mud and created rivers that looked like rust. This rusty mud was all over Torran's boots as he stood just inside the outer gatehouse, watching that activity on the inner wall. He was determined that the battle would be over by sunset because it was clear that Kennington was falling. He didn't want to risk any more men than he had to if the battle was almost over, but he also wanted decisive victory, so he'd ordered his men to charge the inner gatehouse. One way or the other, they were going to capture the castle.

"Torran!"

A shout came from the behind him, and Torran turned to see one of his dearest friends in the world approaching. Sir Yancey de Mora, a knight with the House of de Winter, was coming through the twisted iron, lifting a hand to Torran as he approached. But Torran waved him off as if disgusted by the sight of him.

"So you come when victory is assured?" he teased. "Get out of my sight, Yance."

Yancey grinned. He was tall and lithe, a bright mind and an even better sword arm. "Who do you think burned that portcullis?" he demanded, turning to point at the smoldering ruins that were now being pounded by the rain. "Who do you think inspires the men? Not you, de Serreaux."

"Not *you*," Torran said, pushing back. "They see you and laugh."

"They see you and drink."

Torran quickly conceded the point. "True enough," he said. "Fear will do that sometimes."

"Fear *and* annoyance."

Torran cocked a dark eyebrow at him, watching Yancey chuckle. "You think you're so clever," he said snidely. "Very well. Show me how clever you are. Get through that gate and claim this place in the name of Henry. I am tired of waiting and would genuinely like to sleep tonight, and I cannot do that if this castle does not fall."

Yancey grinned brightly. "So you call upon me?" he said. "Of course you would. Only I can force this place to its knees. Well? Get out of my way, you dolt. Let me show you how this is done."

Torran snorted at the man when he moved past him and shoved him in the chest, not hard enough to really move him but enough to be irritating. He stood there, shaking his head at Yancey as the man slogged over to the inner gatehouse in about six inches of orange mud and began shouting at the men trying to keep the flames going in the rain. As Torran watched Yancey redirect the men, he caught a glimpse of someone standing beside him.

"So he's trying to take the inner gatehouse once and for all, is he? I have to see this."

Torran turned to Kent de Poyer. He was part of the Guard of Six, a very big man with dark hair, dark eyes, and a brooding personality. As Torran nodded in resignation to Yancey's antics, more of the Six joined him.

All of them, in fact.

Torran found himself looking at men he had lived with, and killed for, for several years. Men who were closer to him than brothers, all of them with intrepid spirits, honorable hearts, and souls that were perhaps more tortured than most.

But he wouldn't make a move without them.

Aidric St. John was the first one he saw, tall and blond and with fists that struck an enemy like hammers. Dirk d'Vant was by Aidric's side, another big blond knight with a full beard, a quick wit, and a voice that could boom commands across half of England. Jareth de Leybourne came strolling up, carrying a longsword that his father had given him long ago, one that was allegedly hundreds of years old and stolen off a Celtic demigod. Jareth was their diplomat, but even he hadn't been able to negotiate any manner of surrender with Ashford.

The last member of the Six was Britt de Garr, a knight with curly brown hair that flowed down his back. He kept it tightly bound up for battle, which was a good thing considering he was always in the heat of a fight and hair would only get in the way of his flying sword and vicious tactics. With his addition, now all of the Guard of Six were standing in front of the inner gatehouse, watching Yancey work the men into a frenzy as they began smashing through the burned sections of the gate.

"And now we are at the end," Britt said, watching the battle for the inner gatehouse. "Has anyone seen Ashford? He was on the outer wall when we arrived, but no one has seen him since."

Torran shook his head. "Nay," he said. "I was thinking the same thing earlier—I've not seen him since we arrived."

"Mayhap he is dead," Jareth said. "There would be no other reason for a man to disappear like that."

"Possibly," Torran said. Then he began to look around, noting a group of Ashford soldiers that had been subdued by royal troops. "Speaking of a missing Anselm St. Albans, it seems to me the tactics changed for Kennington midway through this fight. Did anyone notice that? At first, they were tightly bottled up, and then…"

"And then they came rushing out," Jareth finished for him. "I saw it, though I genuinely have no idea why they should do that. They opened themselves up to defeat when they came forward. When one's castle is being attacked, one does not open the gate and invite the enemy in."

Torran nodded. He found himself looking up at the inner wall, where soldiers were moving around frantically. Perhaps Ashford was up there, somewhere, keeping himself concealed. Rain was pounding him in the face and he had to wipe his eyes more than once. He thought he saw a child, or children, on the wall, but with the rain, he couldn't be sure.

But no Ashford.

"All I know is that I am increasingly weary of this," he finally said. "Aidric, where are the rest of the commanders? De Lohr and the others?"

Aidric looked over his left shoulder, down the long curtain wall of Kennington. "The last I saw Canterbury, he was to the rear of the castle, at the postern gate," he said. "De Winter was with him."

Torran returned his attention to the inner gatehouse. "And de Nerra is up with Yancey at the gatehouse," he said, referring to yet another earl in their midst, Becket de Nerra, Earl of Selbourne. "Aidric, send for de Lohr and de Winter. I want them here when we breach the gatehouse. But make sure they station men at the postern gate to catch anyone who runs."

Aidric nodded, heading off down the long wall. He always moved as if he were hunting something or someone. As Aidric went to find the Earl of Canterbury, Daniel de Lohr, Britt, and Jareth strolled toward the gatehouse as Yancey screamed orders. That left Dirk with Torran, watching the activity.

"Jareth is aching to use that sword on someone again," Dirk said. "He says Annihilation needs blood to keep it alive."

Annihilation. The name of Jareth's ancient sword. Every member of the Guard of Six had a sword with a name, something that defined the weapon, giving it a sentient soul that was hungry for warfare. Some men called it superstition, some a curse. But the Six believed that the swords they carried were partners in positions they found themselves in. Guarding a king was serious business.

It required a serious partner.

Torran grinned to Jareth's comment.

"So I've been told," he said. "Annihilation requires blood, Obliteration requires flesh, Insurrection requires fear, and so on. It's what feeds the steel beasts."

Jareth looked at him. "What does Absolution require?"

"Souls."

A smile played on Jareth's lips. "Then it has been fed well today," he said. "Now, shall we join de Mora and the others at the inner gatehouse? I suspect it is time to breach the inner sanctum of Kennington."

Torran nodded. "Breach it," he muttered. "Purge it, control it. It is time. I grow weary of fighting in this weather, seeking a man who would have done us all a favor had he died at Evesham with Simon. A pity he did not."

Jareth couldn't disagree. Together, they moved toward the gatehouse just as some of the men were able to wrench some of the smoldering wood from the iron frame, widening what was already becoming a man-sized gap. There were men on the other side of the gate who very much didn't want anyone to get through, so there were swords poking through the gap at the invaders.

That brought the Six.

It became a sword fight at the inner gatehouse as more of it was wrenched away. There was now a significant gap, and Yancey was the first man through, using his sword on any resistance. The lure of the inner ward and the keep were in his line of sight. In fact, he was hypnotized by it. He managed to fight his way through soldiers who were crumbling to him and those who came behind him, clearly already sizing up the keep because that was the last holdout.

"Torran!" he shouted, turning to see if his friend had come through the gap. When he spied the man slicing through yet another Ashford soldier, he waved him on. "Come with me! Hurry!"

Torran had to shove a dead man out of his way, stepping over another one in his path, before he was able to get through the gap.

"Wait a moment," he called. "There may be more resistance waiting. Wait until we have more men."

Yancey laughed at him. The man turned to the keep once more and began to walk toward it. In doing so, he came out from the protection of the gatehouse, out into the very small inner ward. Torran was looking at him when something came down from the wall, straight onto Yancey's head.

The man fell like a stone.

Startled, Torran shoved his fist into an Ashford soldier to move the man out of the way so he could get to Yancey. He could hear Britt and Jareth behind him, mostly because they were ordering Ashford soldiers to stand down. Torran went right to the end of the gatehouse where it opened up into the small inner ward and reached out a hand, grabbing Yancey by the foot. That's how close the man was. He pulled him back into the shelter of the gatehouse before flipping him over so he could get a look at the man.

What he saw shocked him.

Yancey's head was grossly distorted on the top and in the front where the projectile hit him. Shocked, Torran looked at the object that had come down on the man where it rested several feet away and realized it was an iron pot that had been filled with something. It had hit Yancey, fallen to the ground, and then tipped over. It took Torran a moment to realize that he was looking at a spill of dirt and rocks.

The dirt and rocks had made the pot quite heavy.

Fighting down his panic as men began to move past him into the inner ward, he put his fingers under Yancey's jaw, feeling for a pulse, but he couldn't find one. He quickly moved to assess the damage to the man's head and, after a few sickening seconds, realized that his skull had been crushed where the pot had hit him.

Yancey de Mora was dead.

"Torran?" Britt was beside him, reaching down to grasp Yancey's arm. "We must take him back to the wounded. The men are starting to enter and there will be another fight here shortly with the remaining Ashford men."

Britt was pulling, but Torran stopped him. "There is no need," he said, his tone dull with shock. "He's dead."

Britt's eyes widened. "What?" He dropped Yancey's arm and went to his knees, checking for breathing, for a pulse, a heartbeat. Anything.

But he, too, came up empty and looked at Torran in horror. "Christ's Bones, Torran. What happened?"

Torran was quickly reverting to the efficient knight he'd always been. He wasn't one given to emotion, not even with his friends, and especially not in battle. Men died in battle. Friends died in battle.

Weeping wasn't going to bring them back.

"An object came down off the wall and hit him in the head," he said, pointing to the pot. "That iron cauldron, full of dirt and rocks. Enough to smash his skull."

Britt closed his eyes briefly in horror at the realization. "And he was not wearing his helm."

"I doubt his helm could have saved him."

"Do you want me to find out who did it?"

Torran almost declined. After all, it didn't really matter, did it? Yancey was dead. Finding the culprit wasn't going to bring him back. But there was something in him, perhaps the part of him who had loved Yancey like a brother, who wanted to know. The more he thought about it, the more enraged he became.

Rage that turned deadly.

"Aye," he said, standing and heaving Yancey's body up. "Find out. Slay anyone who lies and tells you they do not know. I shall return him to de Winter and then come back to see how you have fared."

Britt helped Torran put Yancey over one broad shoulder. Men were pouring in through a big gap in the broken gates now, so Torran pushed through as men were rushing in. Britt watched him go for a moment, feeling a genuine stab of grief because he genuinely liked Yancey, before forcing that down and resuming his battle mode. Kennington was almost won and he wanted to be part of it.

But first, he was going to find out who had killed Yancey de Mora.

CHAPTER ONE

I T HAD NOT gone as she had hoped.

After her helping Aeron drop the only real weapon they had on the head of the knight after the inner gatehouse had been breached, the situation had not taken the direction she had intended. As the rain whipped and the wind howled, she'd found herself manhandled off the wall by enemy soldiers, listening to her brother scream and fight as they grabbed him, too. Aeron was only seven years of age, but he had fought fiercely.

If their father had been alive, he would have been proud.

But that was the problem.

Their father *wasn't* alive.

Now, the children of the Earl of Ashford found themselves being dragged into the great hall of Kennington, a place that was normally full of comfort and laughter, but a place that was now their prison. Around them, men were being slaughtered until there were heaps of dead bodies cluttering the inner ward. She didn't see one living Ashford soldier.

The smell of death was everywhere.

That greasy, putrid smell. She was hauled into the great hall alongside Aeron, who was kicking and biting at his captors, so much so that one of them clobbered the lad on the side of the head and he went limp.

Dazed, he still tried to strike out, but Aeron ended up in a pile on the floor next to his kneeling sister.

Big knights with big swords were all around them.

"Now, lady," a big knight with an equally big sword said. "You will tell me the truth. Are you Ashford's daughter?"

Her head came up, eyes of a pale golden-brown color, fixing on the knight with the long hair tied up at the top of his head. "Who told you that?" she demanded.

The knight lifted an eyebrow at her. "I am asking the questions," he growled. "You will answer me. Are you Ashford's daughter?"

After a brief hesitation, she nodded. "Aye," she said. "I am Andia. This is my brother, Aeron."

The knight doing the questioning studied her for a moment before his gaze moved to Aeron, who was starting to come around enough that he tried to push the man behind him away. The boy evidently didn't like to be caged in. But the knight's focus returned to Andia.

"Where is your father, Lady Andia?" he asked.

Again, she hesitated, but only briefly. When she spoke, it was with resignation. "Dead," she said. "The first day of the battle, he caught an arrow in his neck."

"Where is he?"

"In the vault. We've not had the time nor the men to bury him."

The knight looked to another knight next to him. "Do you know Ashford on sight?"

The other knight, with a blond beard, nodded. "Aye."

"Then identify him. Henry will want to know."

The knight with the blond beard fled. As he did so, more men pushed into the hall, men bearing tunics of red and gold, and blue and gold, and also crimson with lions. Andia recognized the crimson tunic with the three lions.

The royal crest of Henry of England.

On her right, Aeron kicked the man behind him in the shins and the man growled, reaching down to grab Aeron by the neck. The boy began to howl, and Andia reached over, trying to pull her brother away from the man even as she calmly spoke to him.

"Please do not hurt him, I beg you," she said. "He is a child who has just lost his father. He is not himself these days."

The soldier wasn't happy. Still holding Aeron, he frowned at her before looking at the knight standing in front of them. The knight nodded, once, and the soldier immediately let the boy go. Aeron's response was to try to kick him again, but Andia grabbed him by the ear and forced his head down.

"Cease this stupidity or we all die," she hissed at him. "Stop or I will beat you myself!"

The boy stopped kicking, but his sister had him by the ear and he was wincing. Still gripping her brother's ear, Andia looked up at the knight in front of her.

"I think it is reasonable to say that we neither one of us is ourselves today," she said. "We have lost our father and our home. I am not condemning you for your actions because you did as you were ordered to do, but I beg patience from you, my lord. We were doing what we were ordered to do, too."

A big knight with graying blond hair separated himself from the group that had just entered the hall. He went to stand in front of Andia, crouching down so he would be more at her level. He was handsome, and fair, but also older than he should have been to have been actively engaged in a battle. After a moment of studying her and Aeron, he smiled faintly.

"You pinch his ear as if you have done this before, my lady," he said.

Andia nodded. "I've boxed his ears, too."

"Spoken like a true sister."

"I have had some practice."

The man's eyes crinkled with humor. "I see," he said. "My name is Daniel de Lohr. I am the Earl of Canterbury. Do you remember me?"

Andia peered at him more closely. "I believe I do recognize you," she said. "You have been to Kennington before."

"I have."

The more she looked at Canterbury, the more she realized that she did know him. Realizing the man had been a guest in her father's home undid her, and her eyes suddenly filled with tears as she looked at all of the heavily armed men standing around. Her bravery had held out only so long. She wasn't a warrior by nature, but much more delicate in her pursuits, so the entire siege had been a nightmare for her from the outset. She didn't like to fight with weapons or kill men with pots dropped on their heads. Not that she was weak, because she wasn't. Andia St. Albans had a steely grace about her.

But this was more than she could take.

The entire siege had been more than she could take.

"My father extended the hospitality of Kennington to you," she said as the tears began to come. "Yet you came to kill him?"

Daniel's smile faded. "Politics are complicated by nature, my lady," he said gently. Having daughters of his own, and a wife, he was adept at dealing with women. "You know your father has been entrenched in the fight of Leicester against Henry for quite some time. Don't you?"

Andia nodded, wiping the tears that were falling faster than she could dash them away. "Aye."

"And you know that Leicester was killed about three years ago."

She sniffled. "I know."

"And I am certain you have heard, more than likely from your father, that Henry is punishing those who opposed him."

Her lower lip was trembling and the tears were running freely. "I have heard."

"Then our appearance should be of no surprise."

Andia continued to wipe the tears. "My father wanted to have a voice in government," she said. "He did not wish to do anything evil. He simply wanted his opinion to be heard in de Montfort's Parliament. He loves this country like you do, but he does not like how it is governed. Can a man not have a say in his own country?"

Daniel clearly wasn't going to debate anything with her, but he wasn't unsympathetic. Reaching out, he pulled her hand away from Aeron's ear.

"Let go," he said softly, in a very fatherly way. "Leave your brother alone. He has had a trying day, as have you. I will have you both escorted to your chambers for the night."

Andia gazed up at him with watery eyes. "Has Kennington fallen, then?"

Daniel looked around at all of Henry's knights around him before nodding his head. "It has, my lady."

"I saw Ashford men being killed."

"That is the nature of war."

"It is the nature of war to murder?"

"It is the nature of war that men die. Death is part of war."

"Even men who have surrendered?"

Daniel merely shrugged. He hadn't given the order to kill Ashford soldiers, and it wasn't something he particularly agreed with now that the castle had surrendered, but it was done. As he'd told her, that was the nature of war. When Andia realized that he wasn't going to answer her question, she looked at the boy who was rubbing his ear.

"Does that mean Aeron will lose his legacy?" she said. "Because of my father's actions? My brother is the Earl of Ashford."

Daniel knew that. In fact, they all did. That feisty, kicking boy was the new earl in the wake of his father's death.

"That is for Henry to decide," he said, standing up and pulling her to her feet. With a hand on her, he held out his other hand to Aeron. "Come along, lad. It has been a long day. It is time for food and sleep."

Aeron was still rubbing his ear where his sister had twisted it. But he didn't want anything to do with the hand Daniel was holding out to him, going so far as to jerk away when Daniel tried to grasp his arm. Given that Daniel had several grandchildren, he knew how to deal with disobedient little boys, so he grabbed him by the head, clamping down on top of it like a vise, which Aeron didn't take kindly to. He twisted and complained, trying to pull away, as Daniel took the pair to his son, Stefan, who had accompanied his father on this campaign because Daniel's eldest son and heir, Chadwick, had remained at Canterbury. The man's wife was due to give birth any day and he didn't want to miss it.

But Stefan was very capable. He was very big, like his grandfather—the great Earl of Hereford and Worcester, Christopher de Lohr—and had his grandfather's height. He stood about a head taller than his father. He looked, and fought, like any other de Lohr relation, but Stefan was harboring a secret.

He was going deaf.

His hearing had been fine as a lad, but over the years he was slowing losing it. The physics told Daniel and his wife that Stefan had been born with the condition. He was hell on the field of battle, an excellent knight among knights, but he couldn't hear the commands very well these days. It was something he had difficulty acknowledging, but Daniel didn't treat him any differently. Stefan was still the same knight he'd always been, but the loss of hearing was also doing something to his manner. He could be sullen and bitter these days.

A man about to lose a part of himself.

Daniel presented Andia and Aeron to Stefan.

"Take them to their chambers," he said. "Let no one take them from you or harass them. Lock them in and stay there until I send for you. Is that clear?"

He'd said it rather loudly for Stefan's benefit, who wasn't exactly thrilled at being the nursemaid of the pair.

"Can't someone else?" he asked.

Daniel shook his head. "I must entrust them to you," he said. "They are valuable prisoners."

Stefan didn't question his father again, though he wanted to. With an unhappy sigh, he took them both by the arm. Even Aeron, who kept trying to pull away, but Stefan was having none of it. Daniel watched Stefan escort the pair away before turning to the other men in the room.

The Guard of Six.

He found himself facing five of them.

"Where is Torran?" he asked quietly.

"He took Yancey back to de Winter," Jareth said. "He will be here soon."

Daniel shook his head with regret at the mention of Yancey. "De Mora is a big loss," he said. "Davyss depended on him a great deal. It will be difficult for him."

"He was a knight, and a foolish one that that." Torran suddenly appeared, pushing through the men still gathered in the great hall. When everyone turned to him, he remained focused on Daniel. "I stand by what I said. He was being reckless when he charged into the inner ward, so I am not surprised it cost him his life. If he were standing in front of me at this very moment, I would tell him the same thing."

Knowing that Torran and Yancey had been great friends, Daniel didn't think the comment was distasteful. In fact, he knew it was the man's grief talking. Torran was one of those men who kept everything bottled up, never speaking of his feelings, never acknowledging them. In that regard, Torran and Stefan had a good deal in common and, in fact, were good friends. They were very much alike.

But sometimes they were also too arrogant for their own good.

"Are you the one who ordered the soldiers in the inner ward killed?" Daniel asked.

Torran nodded. "Aye," he said. "I told Britt to discover who had killed Yancey. If they would not confess, they were put to the blade."

Daniel grunted in disagreement. "That was unnecessary," he said, scratching his head. "You said yourself that Yancey was being reckless."

"Someone dropped an iron cauldron full of rocks on his head."

"This is war, Torran. A man has a right to defend his property."

The great Earl of Canterbury had issued a rare rebuke. Torran wasn't pleased with the man's comment but didn't say so. He knew Daniel well and knew the man had a better moral compass than most.

That was where Torran blurred the lines at times.

With a sigh, he turned to his comrades.

"Did we discover who committed this act?" he asked.

Jareth shook his head. "Nay," he said. "We questioned every soldier we could find in the inner ward, but if they knew, they would not tell us. However, there are two left that are not soldiers."

"Servants?"

"Ashford's son and daughter," Jareth said. "They might know."

Torran started to say something, but Daniel cut him off. "Leave them alone," he said with a distinct hint of hazard in his tone. "The son is a child and the daughter is a young woman, quite upset by this siege. You will not interrogate them and you will not be cruel."

Another order that Torran wasn't fond of. "I will not be brutal," he said. "But if they know—"

"What does it matter?" Daniel said, cutting him off as he motioned to his men and headed for the door. "Yancey is dead. Crucifying a young woman and her brother will not bring him back, so your quest for vengeance is at an end. Let the dead lie, Torran. And let your bloodlust be satisfied because enough men have died this day. You do not need to add more."

It was both an admonition and a warning. Daniel came from a warring family, so he knew about bloodlust. Probably more than most. That meant he knew what he was speaking of, and Torran was quite aware of the fact. He also knew that the man was right—in all likelihood, the person or persons responsible for Yancey's death were lying outside in the inner ward, guts spilled out in the rain. Therefore, his bloodlust really *should* be at an end. As Daniel and his men departed the hall, Torran remained with the Six, wallowing in moody silence.

It was Kent who finally spoke quietly.

"Does he know that your orders from Henry are to return Ashford and his family to London?" he asked.

Torran nodded. "He knows," he said. Then he seemed to let his guard down for the first time since the battle started, going to the nearest table and laying his sword across the top of it. Wearily, he sat. "He knows, and his message is a warning to me not to interrogate them on the trip to London. If I do, and news of my actions get back to him, I am certain he will have words with Henry—and Henry would probably throw me in the Tower if I caused trouble between him and the House of de Lohr. They are some of his biggest supporters."

"Then we are at an end finding Yancey's killer?" Kent said.

Torran looked at the group around him, at the exhausted faces of men he knew so well. He was starting to feel some grief now that the rush of battle was over and reality was setting in. Three very hard days had brought them to this point.

Removing his helm, he set it on the table.

"We are at an end," he muttered. "I suppose Canterbury is right. It does not matter now. I will admit that I had a taste for vengeance after it happened. Every soldier in the inner ward is dead, anyone who contributed to Yancey's death, so the vengeance… it must be satisfied."

Jareth unsheathed his sword and put it on the table near Torran's.

"*Must* be?" he said. "*Should* be, you mean. But is it truly?"

Torran ran his hands through his dark, damp hair. "Aye," he said with resignation. "Men die in battle every day. This was simply Yancey's time. Forgive me if, for a time, my actions suggested otherwise. I know Canterbury did not approve of my actions. But know that if it had been any one of you, I would have done the same thing."

No one contradicted him. They knew he spoke the truth, in all things. Torran was the first one to close off his feelings so it wouldn't affect his judgment like this little incident had. He'd let his emotions dictate the order to show no mercy to those who had caused Yancey's death. Now, he was reverting to his usual, stoic self.

He would simply move on.

"Will you send word to Henry that the battle is over and we have been victorious?" Aidric asked.

Torran nodded. "Truthfully, I think Canterbury or Radnor should do it," he said. "They are the ranking warlords in this fight, so it should come from them. But I will send him word that I am bringing Ashford's children to London. That will give him time to decide what to do with them."

"He risks much if he seeks to use them as an example to others who continue to support de Montfort's ideals," Aidric said. He had a low, distinct way of speaking. "Not many, including Canterbury, will admire a king who punishes the children of an enemy."

Torran nodded. "I know," he said. "So does Henry, I am certain. But I do not think he means to make an example of them as much as he simply means to imprison them as political hostages. Some of those prisoners live quite well. It is not a terrible life."

"The boy is in more danger than the sister," Jareth said quietly. "Torran, that boy is the Earl of Ashford. Henry could make the child his prisoner for the rest of his life simply to keep control over the Ashford properties and assets."

Torran thought on that before finally grunting at the irony of that statement. "There are not many assets now," he said. "I do not know what is left of the army, but it would be fair to say that it is not much. There is this castle, of course, and Ashford made his money from sheep, or so I've heard, but I've also heard the man was very rich. *Where* is the money?"

Instinctively, the knights looked around the hall. "Here, some-where," Jareth said. "Surely Ashford hid it."

Torran sighed heavily before standing up, weaving on his feet. "I am certain he did," he said grasping his helm and his sword. "But let that be a problem for Henry to solve. I care not about a treasure hunt. I would like to return to return to London and get away from this battle altogether."

"We will be transporting prisoners," Dirk said. He was the quietest of the group, only speaking when he genuinely felt the need. "What do you propose we transport them in, Torran? In the back of the provisions wagon?"

Torran shrugged. "Possibly," he said. "Will you see to it, Dirk? If Kennington has a carriage, we shall use it. I would prefer to transport them in something a little more secure than an open provisions wagon."

As Dirk nodded and headed out to see about transportation for the prisoners, Torran sheathed his sword and donned his helm. "And now, good lords, it is time to assess what Kennington has become," he said. "Henry will want a firsthand account in addition to whatever Canter-bury or Radnor sends him, so let us go about our business smartly. Aidric, you and Britt assess the Kennington dead and wounded. Jareth, return to Canterbury and be of service to the man. He may need your diplomacy skills. Kent, you will see to our own wounded. We will need an assessment of how many able-bodied men we have and who can make the journey back to London. As for me... I intend to speak with

Radnor about returning Yancey home, but when I am finished, I will join Kent."

With their assignments given, the men headed from the hall and out into the driving rain. Torran brought up the rear of the group, adjusting his gloves, pausing before he departed the hall because he was fussing with the left glove. The lining in it had torn. Frustrated, he did the best he could with it, stepping outside and lowering his visor so the rain wasn't hitting him in the face. But as he did so, he caught sight of the keep and Canterbury's words came back to him.

The son is a child and the daughter is a young woman.

Ashford's two children. Canterbury had told him not to interrogate or harass them, but he didn't tell Torran that he couldn't speak with them. Moreover, they were his prisoners now, so he should probably introduce himself and inform them of their impending future. Given what happened to Yancey, perhaps he wasn't beyond taking some pleasure in their defeat. It wasn't exactly vengeance, but if the daughter wished to weep at the course her life had taken, he wouldn't be displeased. It might give him some satisfaction. Perhaps he simply needed to see the faces of the family that had caused the death of one of his closest.

He needed to look into their eyes.

With a lingering look at the keep, Torran finally headed in that direction.

CHAPTER TWO

THE BIG KNIGHT was standing on the landing.

Andia was in her chamber, back in the place that had given her the most comfort throughout her life, but this time, it was markedly different. Aeron was in his chamber across the landing and she could hear him shouting insults to the knight standing outside.

Terrible insults.

She wondered how long the knight was going to take it.

Oh, if she could only get over to Aeron's chamber, she'd not only twist his ear, but sew his mouth shut as well.

You are a shag-haired varlet!

Knight? Do you hear me? You are an onion-breath cock!

That one had Andia slapping a hand on her forehead in dismay, terrified that the knight was going to kick Aeron's door down and cut his tongue out. She huddled against her door, listening to Aeron's tantrum, and he was becoming particularly creative with his insults.

You are a mumbling, measle-face dog!

Did they boil your brains at birth? Is that why you are so stupid?

Andia was beside herself. Aeron was more than a handful at the best of times, thanks to her father's lack of discipline on his only son, but this went beyond what she thought Aeron was capable of. The lad was staring death in the face and, still, he was harassing the enemy. At seven years of age, he had no restraint at all because any restraint she'd tried to put on him had been met with resistance from her father.

Now, that lack of discipline might have terrible consequences.

You! You, there! You are a soulless, deformed ninny-head!

That had Andia yanking open her door.

The knight, taller than a tree, was standing right at the head of the landing, looking down the stairwell. He had his back to her and didn't turn around when she opened the door. In fact, he simply stood there, staring. His lack of awareness concerned Andia, but her concern for her brother took precedence. Quietly, she scooted across the landing and opened her brother's door just as he was shouting out another insult.

"You, knight, are a hag-born whelp!"

"Silence!" Andia hissed at him. "One more word and I will put a gag in your mouth!"

Aeron, ever ready to fight, weakly lashed out a foot at her as he balled his fists. "Try it," he said. "I'll not make it easy!"

Andia rolled her eyes as her brother proceeded to throw punches and kick at an unseen enemy. He moved around the chamber, kicking and punching the air, as she watched with frustration.

"Aeron, cease this instant," she said. "Do you not understand the position we find ourselves in? The army who captured Kennington has killed our army. Papa is dead. We are the last ones left and if you keep this up, they could very well kill us, too!"

Aeron paused in his punch-and-kick fest. "They would not dare," he said. "I am the Earl of Ashford. They must obey my commands."

"They are not your men," Andia said. "Only your own men must obey you. These men were sent by the king and they only listen to the king, but if you upset them enough, they will run you through. Do you understand me?"

"I can fight."

"With what?" Andia asked, cocking an eyebrow. "What do you have to fight with? Did you see the broadswords those men were carrying? One more insult and they will slice you in half."

Aeron sneered at her. "You are trying to scare me."

"I am telling you the truth."

He shook his head. "Andie, I am the earl now," he said. "I will fight for Kennington and you should not stop me."

"Kennington has fallen, Aeron. There is nothing left to fight for."

He frowned deeply. "You take that back!"

"It is true."

"I am going to fight you for saying that!"

He rushed her, which he'd done in the past, and Andia simply stepped aside as he charged so that he ran right into the wall. He hit his knuckles on the stone, which infuriated him, and he ran at her again only for Andia to trip him. Once he was down, she kept kicking him in the arse or in the arms to keep him down when he tried to push himself up.

"Stop that!" he commanded. "You cannot say such things about Kennington. It's mine!"

"It belongs to Henry now."

That caused him to kick at her even though he was on the ground. Andia's patience was gone, and she grabbed a sash from where it had been haphazardly tossed on the bed, a sash used to secure clothing, and immediately put it over Aeron's mouth. He was muffled but not completely silent as she proceeded to push him onto his stomach, securing the sash behind his head as she used her legs to pin his arms and torso down. He managed to get a hand free, trying to slap at her, but she grabbed it and tied it up with one end of the sash, lashing it to the other hand.

Soon enough, Andia had her brother trussed up, but the sash had slipped away from his mouth and he was screaming murder. He was angry that she had subdued him, but she'd done it before and knew his weaknesses. He was in the process of calling her a hag, a cow, and anything else he could think of, when she grabbed his straw-colored hair and yanked.

That subdued him quickly.

"Listen to me," she hissed. "Stop all of this foolish posturing, for it will not help you against a knight three times your size. Do you know what it feels like to have a sword shoved into your belly? It will be pain such as you have never known. You will wish for a quick death, but it will not come. You will bleed on the ground and grow weaker and weaker. They might even cut you open and pull your guts out, all while you are alive, and they will laugh at your pain. Keep your mouth shut, Aeron, and you will live longer. If you do not, you will not live to see your destiny as the Earl of Ashford. Do you understand me?"

"That was quite an explicit description."

The voice came from the doorway. Andia gasped, startled, as she turned to see a very broad man standing in the opening. In fact, he had shoulders that were almost as wide as the door, supporting enormous arms and a thick neck. But his face… The moment she looked into his blue eyes, she felt a jolt. Something ran through her, like a tremor. He had a square jaw, dimpled chin, and a scar on the right side of his face. He also had dark hair, cut short, but she could see the wave to it—perhaps ordinary hair on anyone else, but on him, it framed that extraordinary face and she was having a difficult time getting past that.

But she had to.

The man was her enemy.

"Who are you?" she asked warily.

The knight scratched his ear before speaking. "I serve Henry," he said. "I am addressing Anselm St. Albans' daughter?"

She nodded once. "Aye," she said. "I am Andia. This is my brother, Aeron."

The knight's bright gaze lingered on her for a moment before shifting over to the boy on the floor, now sitting up.

"Lord Ashford," he greeted the boy.

Aeron's face lit up. "You see, Andie?" he crowed. "He does know me! He will obey me!"

Andia hissed at him. "Hush," she said. "Keep silent!"

Aeron frowned. "I will not," he said. Then he twisted violently, trying to slip free of the ties that bound him. "Knight, remove these restraints. Take them off!"

The knight didn't move. He remained in the doorway, watching the child twist around on the floor like a fish out of water.

"Alas, I cannot," he said. Then he looked at Andia. "Why did you bind him?"

Andia took a deep, frustrated breath. "Because he was trying to fight me," she said. "He was being naughty and rude, so I bound his wrists. Unfortunately, sometimes it must be done until he calms himself."

Torran's gaze moved back to the boy. "It is unseemly to fight a woman, my lord," he said. "Being that she is your sister, that makes it worse. That is shameful behavior."

Aeron didn't care. He was still flopping around, trying to free himself. "Free me!" he demanded. "Free me or I will punish you!"

Andia rolled her eyes in horror. "He did not mean it, my lord," she said. "He would not move against you."

"I would!" Aeron insisted. "I am a killer of enemy knights!"

Terrified at what was about to come out of his mouth, Andia put herself between her brother and the enormous warrior. "He is young and foolish," she insisted. "He is simply angry."

"Angry?" Aeron spat, finally managing to free one of his hands. "I am *not* angry. I am speaking the truth!"

Andia turned to him. "Aeron, *please*," she said. "Not now. This is not the time."

Unfortunately, Aeron was young. He didn't understand the gravity of the situation, nor his sister's cues as she tried to defuse whatever he was building. All he knew was what he wanted, at that moment, and nothing else. Danger never entered his mind. Ignoring his sister's pleas, he focused on the knight who stood just a few feet away.

"If you do not obey me, I will punish you," he said.

The knight almost seemed amused. "I am certain you will try."

"You do not believe me?" Aeron said, incensed. "I will drop a cauldron on your head, too!"

There it was.

Those terrible words that Andia had been trying to prevent.

She'd had a feeling that was where Aeron was going with his wildly reckless conversation, and now he'd said it. The very thing he shouldn't have said, to an enemy who probably knew the man they'd dumped the pot on.

They were fighting on the same side, after all.

Men died in battle all of the time, but usually, they were hit by random bolts or fighting men they didn't know. There wasn't a name or a face associated with those who did the killing, and that was what Andia had been trying to prevent, because now that Aeron had revealed that he, indeed, had been one of the killers, that gave a face to the enemy. Someone to blame for the rebellion and damage.

Horrified, she closed her eyes tightly, praying that admission didn't get them both killed. She had participated in it, too, after all, and she was terrified that Aeron's boast might just be his last.

She could see it in the knight's face.

God help us!

Any hint of compassion or neutrality in the knight's expression vanished. Before Andia could plead for her brother's life, he moved around her and grabbed the boy by the scruff of the neck. As he lifted him up, heading for the door, Andia threw herself at the knight and latched on to his right arm.

"*Nay!*" she cried. "Nay, he did not mean it! Please do not kill him!"

The knight had Aeron pinned with his left arm, holding the boy against his torso so his arms were trapped, while he dragged Andia toward the door. She was holding on to him with a death grip, begging for her brother's life, but the warrior wasn't listening. As he got to the door, the knight who had been guarding the landing was suddenly there, having heard the commotion.

"Remove her from me," the knight struggling with Aeron commanded. "Lock her in her chamber and do not let her out."

The knight who had been guarding the landing took hold of Andia, who refused to let go of the first knight as he hauled the kicking, screaming boy out of the chamber. Between the two of them, they were creating quite a ruckus until the knight guarding the landing managed to break Andia's hold—and nearly broke her hand in the process. As she cried out, holding her stinging hand, he picked her up and carried her back to her chamber. As Henry's knight headed down the stairs with Aeron in his grip, he heard Andia's door slam.

He could also hear her screaming.

But Torran didn't care.

Nay, he didn't care at all.

In a shocking twist, he had the culprit who had murdered Yancey. He wasn't going to allow himself to be swayed by the lady's lovely sister, and she was indeed quite lovely. Beautiful, even. But Torran wasn't a sucker for a pretty face, so he was able to push her out of his mind and focus on the task at hand.

And he had one.

A big one.

Once he came down the stairs with Aeron, Torran headed for what looked like a solar off the entry. He could see a table and chairs, and the clutter that was usually associated with a solar and the business of the castle. In he went, slamming the door behind him before finally letting Aeron go. The boy was twisting and fighting so much that he ended up throwing himself on the ground once he was released. As the child came up and opened his mouth to yell, Torran grabbed his face with one hand and used his thumb to essentially prop the boy's mouth open. He couldn't close his mouth and he couldn't speak, and Torran's grip on his face was uncomfortable but not painful. But the look in Torran's eyes implied the situation could become much, much worse if Aeron didn't behave.

And neither one of them was sure he would.

Especially Torran. He'd seen enough of the boy, in the brief few moments that he'd known him, to tell him that Aeron was a spoiled lad who lacked respect for anyone or anything. To think of a child like that murdering Yancey ate at Torran. In his mind, Yancey should have had the dignity of a worthy opponent, and this child was no worthy opponent. He had been given an opportunity to kill and he'd taken it. Nothing more. Torran was quite sure that the lad had no grasp of the finality or the severity of what he'd done.

None whatsoever.

It was appalling, really. Appalling and ironic and infuriating. Yancey deserved so much better in death, but instead, death had come to him by the hand of a child. A child that Torran was now looking at, seeing fear and defiance in his eyes. Nay, the lad had no idea what he had done. In his mind, he was simply defending his property, as hundreds of his men were, so this was nothing more to him than a fight to save what was his.

But the castle was no longer his.

Henry's Six and the royal army had prevailed.

That was, perhaps, the only thing that kept Torran from truly punishing the child. He was able to keep his rage at bay by telling himself that, ultimately, Yancey's death contributed to a victory and that was an honorable death for any man.

But it was still a struggle for composure.

"I want you to listen to me," Torran finally said. "Are you listening?"

Aeron tried to say something but the position of Torran's thumb prevented it.

"A nod is sufficient," Torran said.

Aeron's response was to struggle against him, so Torran began to squeeze. When Aeron realized that, and the fact that it was starting to hurt, he seemed to lose some of his fight. He yelled.

Torran stopped squeezing.

"Do I have your attention now?" he asked, his tone low and threatening.

Aeron was proud. Foolish and proud. But not so foolish that the little hint of pain Torran had given him hadn't produced a sense of self-preservation that he didn't usually have. He'd gone through life doing what he pleased, when he pleased, and hadn't learned to deal with a man who was standing up to him. But Torran was. And it was clear that he could hurt him if he wanted to.

That brought about a change in attitude.

When the boy stopped fighting, glaring at him balefully, Torran loosened his grip, but not completely.

"Good," he said. "Now, you and I are going to have a conversation. I am going to ask the questions and you are going to give the answers. Is that clear?"

Mercifully, Aeron nodded. "Aye," he said, mumbling because Torran's thumb was still on his jaw.

"Very well," Torran said. "I am going to let you go, but if you kick, curse, fight, or scream, then I am going to tie you up and throw you on the fire. Do you understand me?"

Aeron muttered something else, an affirmative of some kind, and

Torran watched him for a moment to see if he really meant it before releasing the lad's face. Even as he did it, he wanted to grab it again. He wanted to punish this terrible boy. There were so many emotions swirling in Torran's chest that it was difficult for him to single out just one. Rage, grief, despair, anger... All of them were moving like a maelstrom. Being edgy by nature, he knew what he was capable of should the boy further enrage him. What was it Aidric had said?

Not many will admire a king who punishes the children of an enemy.

And not many would respect a knight who did, either.

Therefore, he proceeded with restraint.

"You spoke of dropping a pot on a knight's head," he said. "Tell me what you did. Tell me everything so I may hear it from your point of view."

Aeron was rubbing his face where the knight had squeezed. "He burned my gate," he said. "He was coming in and I killed him."

"Where did you find the pot?"

"Andie found it," he said, no longer entirely angry and defiant because Torran had genuinely struck some fear into him. "Only the soldiers had weapons and most of them were gone or dead, so she said we should swing it at anyone who tried to mount the walls, but I said we should fill it with rocks and drop it on someone's head."

"And you did."

He nodded solemnly. "I put dirt and rocks in it and dropped it on a knight's head when he came through the gatehouse."

"Did your sister help you?"

"She had to because it was too heavy for me to lift."

So there it was, in simple terms. But it also shed new light on the subject. The children of Lord Ashford found themselves on the battlements of the inner wall because, as the child had said, most of the soldiers were either dead or gone. The children were fighting a losing battle and, without any other weapons, found a pot to use any way they could. He could accept that.

Almost.

But it had been Yancey who paid their price.

"Did you aim for him?" he asked. "Or were you aiming for the first man who came through the gate, no matter who it was?"

Aeron thought on that. "The first man through the gate is the man who is trying to take my castle," he said. "He would kill me if he could, so I had to kill him first."

Torran digested that. In doing so, he averted his gaze but ended up looking over the solar. It was a rich solar, no doubt, but things were scattered on the floor, on the table. It was in disarray. It looked as if a tempest had swept through the chamber, leaving everything upended. No doubt, Lord Ashford had been here during the battle and certainly before it, perhaps contemplating the approaching army and what he was about to lose. Perhaps speaking to his young son, telling him to defend the castle to the death. Torran could see all of it as if he'd been there to witness it.

The boy had done what his father had instructed him to do.

He could feel himself calming.

Sort of.

"What happened to your father?" he finally asked, his gaze still on the chamber.

He hadn't been in the hall when Daniel had asked the very same question, so he didn't know what had become of Lord Ashford.

"He took an arrow in his neck," Aeron said.

Torran looked at him then. "Where was he when this happened?"

The boy gestured toward the window and the ruined castle outside. "On the wall," he said. "The arrow went straight through his neck and he died."

"And that left you and your sister defending the castle."

Aeron nodded. "Some of the soldiers ran after Papa died," he said.

"Some remained to help. But I swore to my father that I would kill the enemy and I did. My father believed he should help govern England, and as long as I live, I will do what my father wanted me to do. He wants me to kill the enemy and I did. I would do it again!"

He sounded like a frightened little boy, but also like a spoiled little boy. Torran let his gaze linger on the lad, sensing that the child would be a problem when he grew older. He would remain in opposition to the king purely based on his father's beliefs unless someone changed his mind. But Torran didn't have the patience or the inclination to try to change the boy's mind in a polite, reasonable way. He suspected that wouldn't have worked anyway. Aeron was a lad who had been raised a certain way and probably saw a man with reason as a man with weakness. Torran had known the Earl of Ashford, distantly, and knew he was a hard man with a hard soul. He was raising his son the same way.

Henry would probably throw the boy in the Tower and keep him there.

But not before Torran sought to change his mind in a way the boy could understand.

"Mayhap you did kill a man, but he was a man worthier than you'll ever be," he said, unable to keep his mouth shut because a surge of grief washed over him. "Your father was worthless and you are too. Now a worthless earl with a worthless title and a worthless castle. From this day forward, young Ashford, you are a worthless man."

Aeron's face turned red. "You cannot say that to me."

"I can and I will."

"I told you that I will kill you, too, and I will!"

"I would not say that if I were you."

"Why not? You cannot stop me!"

As fast as lightning, Torran's hand shot out and he grabbed Aeron by the arm, yanking the boy over to him. Aeron began to fight and yell again, but Torran had something in mind that would stop all of that.

Something Aeron would understand.

He had to be punished for Yancey's death, after all.

Torran threw the lad over his knee and began to spank him within an inch of his life. He was a big man with a big hand, and Aeron began to yell. He kicked and tried to twist away, but Torran held him firm. Ten full blows to his buttocks with an open palm and Aeron's shouts of anger and threat began to turn into wails of pain. The spanking bloody well hurt, but that was what Torran had intended.

He swore he could hear Yancey laughing.

After giving the boy a total of twelve sharp spanks, he finally released the child, who tumbled onto the floor in a flood of tears. Tears of pain, of shock, and of humiliation. Finally, spoiled Aeron got what was coming to him, and Torran leaned over the boy as he sat on the floor and wept.

"Remember this moment," he hissed. "I could have done to you what you did to the knight with your pot full of rocks, but I showed you mercy. Remember that mercy and behave yourself. Your father is no longer here to protect you, Aeron St. Albans. You are living in Henry's world, by his good graces, and bad behavior will not be tolerated. You have been warned."

With that, he pulled Aeron up by an arm and returned him to his panic-stricken sister. Torran's last vision of the pair before he shut them up in the sister's chamber was of a grateful embrace, both of them weeping, both of them thankful to be alive.

Time would tell if the warning would be heeded.

CHAPTER THREE

T HEY HAD BEEN on the road for three days.

Three long days of being treated no better than animals. Andia never thought in her lifetime that she would ever experience anything like this, but unfortunately, she'd also never believed that Kennington Castle would fall.

But it had.

She was now at the mercy of the king.

The day after the castle had collapsed completely, the knight who had spanked Aeron had headed up an escort to take her and her brother to London. As it had been explained to her, Henry had wanted her father as a hostage, but given the fact her father was dead, the next best thing was his children. Even three years after Simon de Montfort's death, the man still had supporters throughout England, and Henry was smart enough to know that there was a network of them who were probably already aware that Kennington had fallen and the Earl of Ashford had been killed. That meant taking the children hostage because Henry wanted to ensure that those determined to seek vengeance for Ashford's death might think twice before doing so.

Andia and her brother were going to serve that purpose, a political purpose. That meant they were to be taken to London immediately, but the only reasonable mode of transport was a heavy provisions wagon.

That was where Andia and Aeron found themselves today.

Lurching about in a wagon.

Evidently, Henry's men had hunted for a carriage of some sort, but there was no such conveyance at Kennington, so they had to settle on the wagon. Andia's father didn't believe in comfort when one traveled, so the only transportation at the castle had been horses that the conquering army had already seen fit to confiscate. Andia recognized several of her father's finer horses being ridden, or led, by the escort around them.

And they'd confiscated everything else, too. Andia had seen the looting from her chamber window. Throughout the night, she had seen men going in and out of the keep carrying items with them, and she'd hardly gotten any sleep realizing that her father's curated collections and valuables were being looted. The only thing she took comfort in was the knowledge that his coin had been well hidden. She had seen to that herself. Nothing short of a demand from God was going to force her to reveal the location.

At least the money was safe.

Not even Aeron knew where it was.

Sitting beside her in the wagon, her brother had been strangely silent since the spanking dealt to him. Truthfully, Andia was grateful that the knight with the big shoulders had only spanked him. She had been quite certain that he had been taking the boy off to kill him, but he hadn't. The blood-covered knight had shown mercy, even if that mercy had been in the palm of his open hand as he'd paddled Aeron's skinny bottom.

But it could have been so much worse.

Andia glanced over at Aeron, who was sullen as he watched the road pass behind them. The road from home, leading to from the things they knew into a world they didn't. They were prisoners, Andia understood that, and, all things considered, she was grateful that their confinement wasn't worse. In fact, her guards seemed to show an inordinate amount of concern for their comfort. Their wrists were bound, but on the second day of their travel, Andia's skin was chafing so badly that one of her guards had found a softer strip of cloth to wrap around the rope to ease the irritation. They even had her and Aeron sitting on a bed of straw that was covered with a blanket so there was some comfort as they bumped and jerked over the road.

Odd behavior from men who, at first, had been so cruel.

Cruelty in not only the battle, but their behavior afterward. Andia had only been given about an hour to pack before they left Kennington, rushed by knights wearing Henry's tunic, so she had a satchel with her that contained what were now the only possessions she had, and that included her only cloak. During the day when the sun was high, she'd been allowed to wear the cloak with the hood over her head to protect herself from the sun, while Aeron had developed a nice sunburn on his forehead. He was quite fair as it was, with his straw-colored hair and freckles, so the sunburned forehead and sunburned nose had him looking like a farmer's child, which he didn't like one bit.

But still, he kept quiet.

That was perhaps one of the most disorienting things about the entire journey. Aeron, who had little restraint when it came to his mouth or his actions, had been inordinately quiet. The spanking he'd been dealt seemed to have done something to him, and Andia had to admit that she was relieved. A little brother who was quiet and obedient was so much better than a little brother with a damning tongue and an even more damning sense of his own mortality. She wasn't exactly sure what that knight had said to her brother when he'd spanked him, but it was enough to keep Aeron subdued.

The third day of travel had been a little different from the previous days because a storm was blowing in from the sea and the wind had picked up a great deal. They were traveling through farming villages and the fields around them were being battered by the wind. Seabirds flew overhead, riding the drafts, and Andia would watch them swoop into the fields looking for something to eat. She'd heard some of the men talk about staying the night at Rochester Castle, a place that she had visited before with her father. Anselm had known the steward of Rochester Castle, and they had stayed there once overnight on a trip from London. Since her father had supported de Montfort, however, the relationship with the Rochester steward had cooled, as Rochester was a Crown property.

Thoughts of Rochester brought about thoughts of her father. Aeron missed him a great deal, Andia could tell, but she didn't share the same sentiment. Anselm had been a cold man to the women of the family, only warming to his only son because he felt the boy was the sole person of value. Once Aeron had been born and her mother had died in childbirth, Anselm sent his confused and grieving daughter to foster simply to get her out of the way. Andia had spent several years at Okehampton Castle in Devon before finally coming home a couple of years ago. It seemed that her father only wanted her as chatelaine, and perhaps even as a servant to her young brother who was now incorrigible and demanding, so her return home hadn't been a pleasant one.

That was the truth of it.

But she'd had nowhere else to go, thanks to her father, who had turned down two marriage offers for his daughter from knights at Okehampton. One offer was from the commander of Okehampton, an older man who had lost his wife years ago and had a special fondness for Andia. He was nice enough and Andia liked him, certainly preferring him over the other knight, who was from a very fine family but only wanted a beautiful wife to show off to everyone. He had no care for her other than her beauty. But Anselm had turned both of them down, wanting his daughter to remain at Kennington to be subservient to her brother.

And that had been her life until a few days ago.

Now, Andia had no idea what was going to happen, but there were some strange dynamics going on within the escort. She recognized several of them from the day Kennington fell, men who had been in the great hall when she'd been questioned by the Earl of Canterbury. Canterbury himself wasn't with the escort, having remained behind to secure Kennington for the Crown, but his son had come, the same knight who had guarded her door. A very big, very blond and brawny knight with a stylish mustache, named Stefan. She'd heard the others call him by name. There were also men by the name of Kent, Aidric, and Jareth, but she couldn't see the faces of any of them because they were riding with their helms on. Names for the faceless men who now held her life in their hands. Quite honestly, traveling to London made her feel as if she was traveling to her execution.

And she probably was.

By the time night fell, it had begun to rain. Lightning lit up the sky as the escort entered Rochester's city walls through the east gate. Fatted torches lit up the city and the streets, and the heavy smell of human sewage filled the air. The castle, perhaps one of the largest in England, loomed ahead. Rochester Castle was an enormous bastion on the banks of the River Medway, and Andia wasn't sure if she felt better or worse as she envisioned it. She remembered her father speaking fondly of the castle steward, but she was certain there would be no reciprocation this time.

She braced herself.

As soon as the wagon entered the castle grounds, it seemed that the entire population of the fortress had come out to meet them. Soldiers were rushing about, closing gates, and the escort moved into the enormous outer ward before coming to a halt. The rain was pounding at this point, and both Andia and Aeron were quite wet. One of the knights reached over the side of the wagon and pulled Aeron out as another knight leapt onto the wagon bed and helped Andia to her feet. She walked stiffly to the rear of the wagon, where still another knight reached up and lifted her off. As the wind and rain howled around them, they quickly headed for Rochester's great hall.

The stale warmth of the hall hit Andia like a slap to the face. There were people all around, including the steward of Rochester, whom she recognized. She also recognized his wife. Of course, she'd been quite young when she first met them, many years before Aeron was born, so she didn't expect them to know her. Lifting her bound hands to pull back her hood, she heard Lady Penden's voice.

"Why is she bound?" the woman asked, pointing to Andia. "That is Lord Ashford's daughter?"

The knight she was speaking to was the same one who had spanked Aeron, and he nodded. "Aye, Lady Penden," he said. "That is Lady Andia and her brother, the current Earl of Ashford."

Lady Penden's eyes widened and she immediately went to Andia, reaching out to take her bound hands. Without asking permission, she began to untie them.

"You do not remember me, do you?" she said, smiling at Andia. "I am Lady Penden. You visited here when you were no more than your brother's age. The cook made apples dipped in honey and cinnamon and you ate them until you became ill."

Freezing cold, with blue lips, Andia tried to smile in return. "I remember you, my lady," she said with a quivering voice. "The apples were delicious."

Olivia's smile grew. "I will have them make more for you tonight," she said. "You are most welcome, Lady Andia."

"My love?" Riggs Penden, Lord Penden and the steward of Rochester Castle, called politely to his wife. "Olivia, dearest? Please do not break those bindings. Lady Andia and her brother are Henry's prisoners."

Olivia, a small woman with red hair and a lovely, round face, went from sweet to steely in a split second. "Nonsense," she hissed, turning to her husband and the knight standing with him. "A young lady will not be treated like this in my home. Tell Henry if you wish, but I am taking her with me. She needs dry clothing and food. Her brother, too."

"Not me!" Aeron said, finding his voice after three days of silence. "I want to stay here, with the men."

Lady Penden looked at the young boy who also had his hands bound, but he was already moving toward the very large hearth that was belching smoke and sparks into the hall. That was his idea of drying out, evidently, so she didn't argue with him. She would relent when it came to the boy.

But not when it came to a young woman in distress.

The remainder of the bindings came off Andie's wrists and Lady Penden handed them to the nearest knight. "There," she said, looking to her husband and the knight standing with him. "The lady will be well tended for the night. I will see to her myself."

She took Andia by the hand, but a low, firm voice stopped her.

"Lady Penden, if I may." The knight who was their chief jailor very nearly blocked her path. "I am afraid that I am under orders from Henry. You may take Lady Andia with you, but a guard goes with her. If you do not agree, then I will take her from you and keep her with me. I am very sorry, but I must insist."

Lady Penden frowned. "And who are you?"

"My name is Torran de Serreaux, my lady," he said. "I am Henry's *seigneur protecteur*, commander of his personal guard. I am under royal orders that cannot be changed."

Lady Penden was still frowning. "I am not trying to change them," she said. "I am merely trying to help a young woman in your charge."

"She is a prisoner, my lady."

"She is a delicate young woman and must be treated with care."

"Forgive me, my lady, but she is being treated as well as her being a prisoner dictates."

Lady Penden was beside herself. "What has she done?" she demanded. "If she is a prisoner, what has she done to warrant this terrible treatment?"

Torran shook his head. "It is not what she has done, but her father," he said. "Her father's actions have dictated her treatment."

Lady Penden was aghast. "How unfair," she said. "How terribly cruel. What if this was your own sister being treated this way? Or, God forbid, your wife? Would you not protest?"

It was clear that Torran wasn't going to argue with her. He looked to the woman's husband, who quickly stepped in.

"Olivia, my love," he said as gently as he could. "This is not our affair. You must let Sir Torran do as his duties dictate."

Lady Penden wasn't going to back down. "Look at her," she said, sweeping a hand in Andia's direction. "This tiny child is a threat? She is such a threat that she should not be afforded any consideration?"

Torran cleared his throat quietly. "My lady, it is not that she is a threat," he said. "But her father is an enemy of the king and—"

"There is no need for this debate," Andia said, interrupting him. When all eyes looked at her, she focused on Torran. "Have no fear, my lord. I will not go with her, though she was most gracious to offer."

Before anyone could stop her, Andia quickly moved toward the hearth where her brother was trying to dry out. Lady Penden watched the cold, wet young woman move away, disappointment in her expression, before returning her attention to Torran.

"Does Henry truly have such heartless and cruel men?" she asked seriously. "Where is your soul, sir knight? You took an oath to protect the weak, yet you have treated this young woman so poorly?"

"My love," Lord Penden said before Torran could reply. "Sir Torran is not being cruel by choice, but she *is* a prisoner. You must not question his motives."

"Why?" Lady Penden demanded. "What should I not question how she has been treated?"

Torran's patience with the bold woman was at an end. "Her father was a supporter of Simon de Montfort," he said, not as polite as he could have been. "Henry's allies laid siege to Kennington Castle and Lord Ashford was killed during the fight. My orders are to bring the lady and her brother to Henry as prisoners of war, and that is exactly what I am doing. In spite of what you must think, there is no malice on my part. I am simply following my orders."

That explanation did nothing to ease Lady Penden. She pointed a finger in Andia's direction. "That young woman is soaked through to her skin," she said. "If she does not get into dry clothing, she will catch her death of chill and Henry will have no prisoner. If you allow that to happen, then there *is* malice on your part. Cruel and unnecessary malice."

Torran's gaze lingered on Lady Penden for a moment before he looked at Andia. She was in the process of removing her cloak, which was sopping wet. He could see the water on the floor. He could also see, even from where she stood, that she was quivering with cold. Something told him that not only was Lady Penden going to harp on this and cause problems, but she was right and she knew it. Torran wasn't so blinded by his sense of duty that he couldn't see it for himself.

Without another word, he made his way over to the hearth.

"Lady Andia," he said, watching her look up from her cloak like a startled deer. "I think it would be best if you went with Lady Penden. You need dry clothing and she is determined to help you, so you may go with her."

Andia shook her head and looked back down at her cloak as she spread it out in front of the hearth. "That is not necessary," she said. "I will dry out here."

Torran watched her position the cloak on the hot stones. "You would probably be more comfortable if you went with her."

Andia's jaw twitched faintly as she finished with her cloak and stood up. Taking a few steps, she ended up closer to Torran than she'd ever been. Her eyes, a pale brown that was almost gold, were glittering at him.

"I am going to stay here with my brother," she hissed. "You are so determined to treat us like animals that I would feel uncomfortable accepting Lady Penden's hospitality. You want everyone to see us in our shame, so let them see us. Let all of Rochester see us because, certainly, tomorrow all of London will see us. Let everyone point and jeer at the children of a supporter of Simon de Montfort. That is what you want, is it not? Do not show me kindness now, sir knight, for it would not be in your character. It would be a deception and I will not fall for it. Let everyone see how you treat enemies of Henry. I am staying here."

With that, she went back and sat down next to her brother in front of the hearth, refusing to look at Torran as she sat there and shivered. He should have been annoyed by her words, but she, too, was right. He had treated her and her brothers like prisoners because they were. Lady Andia understood that even if Lady Penden didn't. His gaze lingered on her a moment before returning to Lady Penden.

"She will not go with you," he said. "She is choosing to stay with her brother at this time."

Lady Penden was greatly distressed. "But… but she must be dried off," she insisted. "And where will she sleep?"

Torran gestured at the hearth. "There, where she is sitting," he said. "She says she will stay there."

As he spoke those words, Andia abruptly stood up and marched over to the knight who was still holding her bindings. She snatched them out of his hand only to walk over to Torran and hold them out to him.

"Here," she said through clenched teeth. "Lady Penden should not have removed these. You may replace them."

Torran's eyes locked with Andia's and he swore, at that moment, that he'd never seen a stronger or more stubborn woman. He began to realize that she was turning the tides on him somewhat, pointing out his cruelty in front of witnesses, making sure everyone understood just how he had behaved. The spanking he'd dealt Aeron didn't matter now, but his most recent actions did. Perhaps he'd shown the boy mercy, but that was the last time he had shown anything like that. Since departing Kennington, he'd treated the brother and sister like captives, because they were. How else was he supposed to treat a captive?

Even a captive as lovely as Andia St. Albans.

Aye, she was lovely. More than lovely, actually. He'd seen it from the moment he met her, but somehow, at this very moment, she was the most beautiful woman he'd ever seen. He had no idea why that was, but that petite woman with the golden eyes and skin like cream was the strongest thing in that room at the moment. And she was trying to make a point.

He would let her.

Taking the bindings from her hand, he proceeded to tie her wrists again as Lady Penden gasped with outrage. He looked her in the eye as he did it, looping them around her wrists, pulling them tight against skin that had already been chafed by the ropes. But she was calling his bluff and he had obliged. The expression on her face suggested that he was doing everything she had expected.

Cruelty.

Duty.

Torran de Serreaux would do nothing less.

When he was finished, Andia returned to the hearth and sat next to Aeron, who was drowsy from the heat. She refused to look at Torran any longer, instead choosing to stare off into the great hall as if wishing herself off into another world, while Lady Penden stood there and worried. In fact, it was too much for her to take, so she went over to the hearth and stood in front of Andia.

"Please, my lady," she begged softly. "Let me take you to a chamber where you may dry off and rest. Surely you do not wish to remain like this all night."

Andia was cold, hungry, and exhausted, which made for a bad combination. She knew Lady Penden was only trying to be kind, but she didn't want kindness right now. She didn't want anything. She was a captive of Henry and, quite frankly, was resigned to it. She was afraid that any behavior that wasn't submissive might cause her and Aeron more trouble than they were already in.

"My lady," she said without looking at the woman. "I realize you are trying to be hospitable, but I have no need of your hospitality. Please go away and leave me alone."

Lady Penden looked as if she might weep. Deeply upset, she backed away from Andia, looking at the woman's defeated expression and knowing there was nothing more she could do. She couldn't force her, and Andia had already made it quite clear that she didn't want help. Verging on tears, she quit the hall as her husband watched her go sadly.

That didn't sit well with him.

"Torran," he said, "I am only going to say this once, but I feel that I must. I realize you are doing your duty, but have you considered the deeper implications of this task?"

Torran had no idea what he was talking about. "Deeper implications, my lord?"

Lord Penden nodded faintly. "Aye," he said, gesturing toward Andia. "That young woman is the daughter, and sister, of an earl. She is a noblewoman of great breeding. I knew her father, and his mother was a Baldwin, a descendant of the House of Flanders. He was related to

Queen Matilda, wife of the Duke of Normandy. That makes Lady Andia a distant cousin to Henry. You *do* know that, don't you?"

Torran looked at him with surprise. "I did not."

"Henry did not mention it?"

Torran shook his head. "Nay," he admitted. "But it makes sense now that he was so distressed by Ashford's change in loyalty, especially since the Dictum of Kenilworth came about."

Lord Penden knew very well what he was talking about. "The decree that allowed for de Montfort supporters to keep their lands if they paid hefty fines," he said. Then he shook his head. "That was not meant for St. Albans. He is a cousin. Even a king should be able to trust family."

"And if he cannot, then he must punish them."

"Destroy them, is more like it."

That was all news to Torran. He'd been around Henry for a few years and never heard anything about the Earl of Ashford being a distant cousin. But it did explain why Henry's orders for Ashford had been so absolute.

Ruin the castle.

Bring me prisoners.

Truthfully, he felt rather peeved for not knowing that very key fact, and it was difficult not to feel like an idiot.

"If I remember my history correctly, Queen Matilda was a descendant of Charles the Great," he said. "*Charles le magne.*"

Lord Penden nodded. "Indeed, she was," he said, looking at the woman and her brother huddled by the hearth. "Great blood flows through them, Torran. Though that should not make a difference in the way you treat them, you should be aware all the same. More than likely, they have more ancient royal blood in them than Henry does."

Considering Lady Andia looks like a queen, that is not surprising.

That was Torran's first thought. It was on the tip of his tongue and, thank God, he didn't say what he was thinking. But it did make him rethink allowing Lady Andia to make decisions about her health, remaining in wet clothing as she was. It wasn't the fact that she had ancient blood in her, or the fact that her beauty had him increasingly interested, but that she was a cousin to the king. He didn't want the woman getting sick and dying, because it would be his fault.

That strong, stubborn woman with the golden eyes.

Aye, that changed things a bit.

Without another word to Lord Penden, he went over to the hearth where Aeron was now sleeping on his sister as she sat against the stone next to it. Her sopping cloak was spread out in front of it, steaming into the hall, and around them, servants were starting to bring in supper. Rochester soldiers were coming in from the outside, and soon it would be noisy in the hall and impossible to sleep.

He was going to tell her so.

"Lady Andia," he said, "they are preparing to serve supper in the hall and soon it will be full of drinking, shouting men. You cannot sleep here tonight."

Andia heard him but refused to look at him. "Then put us in the vault," she said. "We are prisoners, after all. That is where we belong."

"I am not going to put you in the vault."

"We are captives. That is where captives belong."

"Why are you being so stubborn when someone is trying to show you some consideration?"

She did look at him then. "'Tis not stubbornness, I assure you," she said. "I am simply obeying your wishes. Prisoners do not ask for special consideration."

He resisted an urge to roll his eyes at her because she was most definitely being mulish. "You are wet and undoubtedly uncomfortable," he said. "Lady Penden was being quite kind to you, and you were rude in return."

"She shouldn't be speaking to a prisoner, anyway."

Torran sighed heavily. "I will again ask you why you are being so stubborn."

"Because I am a captive. How else should I be?"

"Captives are compliant."

"How am I not being compliant?" she said. "I asked for my bindings restored. I am sitting here where you told us to sit."

"That is not what I meant."

She was finished speaking to him. Standing up, which made Aeron fall backward because he'd been sleeping on her, she went straight to Lord Penden, who was still standing near the door.

"My lord," she greeted him. "I know you and my father were friends, but since you know he turned against Henry to support de Montfort, I am certain you do not wish to acknowledge your friendship with him, and I accept that. Thanks to his actions, however, my brother and I are now prisoners of Henry. Will you please have one of your soldiers escort us to the vault?"

Lord Penden looked at her with a mixture of sympathy and disappointment. He could see Torran coming up behind her and, in all matters, knew that he needed to defer to the knight, but before him was the daughter of a man he'd known for years. It was true that Anselm had decided to support de Montfort, but it was also true that Penden wasn't a rabid supporter of the Crown. He'd thought—privately, of course—that de Montfort's idea for government had some merit, but he wasn't willing to risk generations of his family's position over it.

And he wasn't willing to condemn a young woman for her father's actions.

"Do you remember my daughter, Lady Andia?" he asked, completely avoiding her request. "Desiderata was her name. You remind me of her, in fact. She had your strength. She married last year, if you had not heard."

Andia shook her head. "I had not heard, my lord," she said. "And I do remember her. She was very kind to me when we visited."

"She died in childbirth last month," Penden said bluntly, the warmth in his eyes fading at the memory. "I have lost my daughter and you have lost your father. I understand something about grief, my lady, and mayhap that is why Lady Penden wished to help you so much. She no longer has a daughter to assist."

Andia lost some of her stubbornness as Lord Penden shared his tragedy with her. In fact, she could see the terrible agony in the man's eyes as he spoke of his daughter, a girl that Andia had only met a couple of times, but who had been very sweet during those encounters. Andia was a woman of deep feeling and was quite sympathetic to the man's grief.

"I am so very sorry to hear that, my lord," she said, the hardness gone from her voice. "I did not know."

Lord Penden tried to smile again. "I know," he said. "I simply thought you should know why my wife was so eager to assist you. Desi was our only daughter and Olivia has felt the loss deeply."

"I can understand that," Andia said, sounding much more like herself and not like the hard, stubborn woman she'd been portraying. "I did not mean to be rude to Lady Penden."

Lord Penden's dark eyes twinkled. "Then you would do her a great kindness by allowing her to dote on you as she would have doted on Desi and her child," he said. "I would consider it a great favor if you would allow my wife to tend to you while you are here."

Andia hesitated a moment, turning to look at Torran, who was standing a few feet away. He was watching her carefully to see what she was going to decide, more than likely expecting her to remain stubborn. As much as Andia wanted to, the truth was that she couldn't refuse two grieving parents.

"If Sir Torran will allow it, then I will go to her," she said quietly before turning to Torran and holding out her hands. "Will you please releasing my bindings?"

Torran's gaze lingered on her a moment before he reached out and untied the ropes. Andia watched him, his lowered head, studying the man's face at close range as he focused on her bindings. He had very dark hair, shaggy and wavy, and the longest eyelashes she had ever seen. His jaw was set, square and unmovable, and he was sporting a few days' worth of beard growth. If he hadn't been her enemy, she would have thought him handsome.

Very.

But there was no use in thinking that.

He was her jailor and nothing more.

"Come with me," Lord Penden said once the bindings fell away from her wrists. "Torran, you will come also. I want you to see that I am not helping the lady escape, but genuinely taking her to my wife for care. I believe Henry will be pleased with that. Come!"

He was waving a hand at Torran, who dutifully followed the man out of the great hall and into the rain. Andia wasn't wearing her cloak, having left it back in the hall, but she was soaked through anyway, so a little rain didn't matter. Lord Penden took her into Rochester's enormous keep where he could already hear his wife as she called to one of the servants. When he finally located her near the door that led out to the kitchens, Lady Penden was quite surprised to see that he'd brought Andia along.

But also quite pleased.

The evening, for Andia, was about to get interesting.

CHAPTER FOUR

A S IT TURNED out, Lady Penden took care of Aeron, too.

Lord Penden had brought the boy over from the great hall, and Lady Penden ensured that her maids removed the wet clothing from his body, put him in a bath, and then re-dressed him in some of Lord Penden's clothing, which was too big for him, but it was dry and warm and comfortable. Aeron had stuffed himself on stew and bread before passing out in one of the chambers on a lower floor where visiting guests were housed. It had been a simple night for Aeron, but not for Andia.

Her night wasn't over yet.

Removing her from her wet clothing had only been the start. Lady Penden was eager to tend to her, driving the servants like a zealous wagon master, and all Andia had to do was essentially let the woman have her head. She did what she was told to do, when she was told to do it, and that had meant a hot bath, a hair washing, a body washing, and dressing in the most glorious sleeping shift and robe she'd ever seen. It had belonged to Desiderata, she was told by one of the servants, because Lady Penden couldn't speak of her daughter without collapsing.

Therefore, she wasn't mentioned.

Truthfully, if Lord Penden hadn't told Andia about his daughter, she might not have ever known from Lady Penden's behavior. The woman seemed strong and in control, but it was just an act. Even Andia could see that. She was *too* kind and *too* helpful, anything to keep her thoughts away from her shattered world. She doted on Andia in every aspect, even combing her hair and drying it mostly before rolling it in strips of linen.

That was when she finally brought up Desiderata.

Desi, as she was called, liked to have a curl to her hair, and Lady Penden spoke of the nights she would wind her daughter's hair in pieces of linen before bed so when morning came, she had a glorious head full of waves. The funny thing was that she didn't even ask Andia if she wanted her hair rolled—she simply did it. Then she wrapped a white scarf around her head to keep the curls in place and gently tucked Andia into bed.

But that wasn't all.

Andia could see Torran out on the landing, holding the door open as copious amounts of food were brought in. Andia tried to get out of bed to sit at the table where the food was placed, but Lady Penden ordered her back to bed and then brought the food to her. Andia ate her supper while sitting in bed, surrounded by luxury and a woman who did everything but personally spoon food into her mouth. Andia was somewhat uncomfortable with it all, to be truthful, but it seemed to bring Lady Penden a good deal of joy, so she didn't speak her mind. She allowed the grieving woman to stuff her with stew, bread, and little pies filled with apples and cinnamon and honey.

When Andia couldn't eat another bite and there was nothing left for Lady Penden to do, she forced Andia to lie down and proceeded to cover her up with heavy blankets against the chill of the stormy night. Andia let the woman do what she needed to do but found herself praying Lady Penden would leave her alone. The entire evening had been a little much, and, unused to such attention, Andia was hoping the woman had gotten it out of her system and there would be no more.

When Lady Penden was finally finished washing, dressing, combing, rolling, and feeding her charge, she quit the chamber and blew Andia a kiss.

The door shut softly behind her.

Lying on her back and nearly burning up from all of the covers, Andia waited a nominal amount of time before tossing everything off. The room was inordinately warm because Lady Penden had had her servants stoke the fire to a roaring blaze. It was almost cloying. Getting out of bed, she went over to the table where there was still plenty of food and two pitchers of mulled wine. As if Andia was going to drink both of them—but given the rigorous evening she'd just endured, she very well might. She poured herself a cup, in fact, because the wine was quite good. Just as she lifted the cup to her lips, a thought occurred to her and she paused, her attention moving for the door.

Curiously, she went to the panel.

Quietly, she opened the door to find what she suspected—or, more correctly, *whom* she expected.

Torran was sitting on the floor of the landing.

"I thought you might be sitting out here," Andia said. "Truly, there is no need. If you think I am going to try to flee on a night like this, you would be mistaken. I would not flee in any case. If you wish to go about your business, rest assured you will find me here in the morning."

Slowly, and perhaps a bit stiffly, Torran stood up, stretching out his big body. "If I did not know it was you, I might not recognize you at all," he said as he slowly made his way over to her. He was looking her over, from the top of her scarf-wrapped head to the bottom of the elaborate robe. "It seems that Lady Penden took great care of you."

Andia looked around, almost fearfully. "Is she nearby?"

He shook his head. "She went down the stairs and told me to stay away from your door," he said. "Shall I send someone for her?"

Andia shook her head. "Nay," she said quickly. "I was simply asking."

"Why?"

Andia grunted uncomfortably. "I fear she's gone off to find more food or clothing or balms or salves," she said, watching Torran's dark brows lift questioningly. "Do not misunderstand me, my lord. I very much appreciate her kindness, but it has been rather... overwhelming."

Torran understood. "As Lord Penden said, she has just lost her daughter."

"I think she was pretending I was the child she lost."

"I suppose you cannot blame her."

"I suppose." Andia's thoughts moved from Lady Penden back to Torran, who was still dressed in the clothing he'd been wearing all day. She could smell the mildew from him, as his wet clothing had been unable to completely dry, so she extended the cup of wine in her hand. "Here—take this. Have you eaten yet?"

He hesitated a moment before taking the cup, peering at it. "Nay," he said. "What's this?"

"Mulled wine," Andia said. "There is a barrel of it in here."

He tossed the wine back in one swallow, handing her back the cup. "Thank you."

Andia took the cup, studying him for a moment. "Are you going to sit on the landing all night?"

"Probably."

She sighed. "Truly, my lord, you do not have to guard the door," she said. "I swear to you that I shall not go anywhere. I would certainly not flee and leave my brother behind. You do not have to watch me like a hawk."

He didn't move. He continued to look at her, almost appraisingly, his blue eyes glimmering in the weak light emitted from her chamber.

"You seem more agreeable than you did earlier," he said. "I assume you must be feeling better."

She knew what he meant. That testy exchange in the great hall when he asked her why she was being so stubborn. The problem was that she wasn't entirely sure why she had been so irritated, only that fear and hunger and exhaustion had driven her to it. Punishing Torran for doing his job. But she was feeling better now, and her mood had much improved to the point of her feeling somewhat forgiving toward him.

"I *am* feeling much better," she agreed. Then she made a sweeping motion with her hand in the direction of her chamber. "Lady Penden brought enough food to feed four people, so if you've not yet eaten, I would invite you to share what was brought to me. If you do not, it will simply go to waste."

Torran looked at her open chamber, the table and hearth beyond. He could see bowls and cups and pitchers upon the table.

"I think not," he said after a moment. "It would not be proper for me to go into the chamber, but your generosity is noted."

Andia turned and headed back into the chamber. As Torran watched curiously, she picked up a tray on the table and brought it out onto the landing.

"Here," she said. "You can eat it out here, then."

She went and put it over where he had been sitting, backing up to her door to give him some room. Torran eyed her for a moment before moving over to the tray, sitting back down on the floor and leaning against the wall as he inspected what was on it.

"You did not poison this, did you?" he asked.

Andia cocked an eyebrow. "With what?" she said. "I did not bring any poison with me, de Serreaux."

"So you say," he said, picking up a spoon and scooping up a good portion of the cooled stew. Taking a bite, he chewed a couple of times before nodding his head. "It is not poisoned, fortunately for you."

Andia shook her head slowly. "What a suspicious mind you have."

His mouth was full. "A mind that has kept me alive all these years."

"How long have you been a knight?"

"Sixteen years."

"Always with Henry's army?"

He shook his head. "Not always," he said. "And I am not with his army. I am with Henry's personal guard. But if there is a battle, he'll usually ask us to fight it."

He was well into his food by now, and Andia ended up sitting on the floor next to her open doorway, watching him eat as if he hadn't in days. The man was positively starving. But he did seem slightly evasive toward her, his professional persona never wavering. Even so, she was increasingly curious about him.

"May I ask a question?" she said.

He shoved bread into his mouth. "What is it?"

"Did you know my father?"

He glanced at her. "I was never formally introduced to him, but I knew of him," he said. "I knew him enough to identify the body in the storage vault."

She nodded faintly. "You fought against him, then?" she said. "During the wars with de Montfort, I mean."

"Probably," he said. "I fought with Henry's army in several battles."

"Then you are not a pampered knight who simply guards prisoners."

He snorted softly. "Nay, I am not," he said. "Who do you think commanded the siege of Kennington?"

"You?"

"Me and Canterbury and Radnor. We all had different roles in the siege."

"Canterbury is de Lohr, but who is Radnor?"

"Davyss de Winter," he said. "The Earl of Radnor."

"And these men are friends of yours?"

He shook his head. "My lady, I am a knight," he said. "Knights like me are not friends with warlords like Canterbury and Radnor. We serve them, as we serve Henry."

"But you said you helped command the battle," she said. "Surely you must be a ranking noble for that."

He glanced at her. "How would you know that?"

"Because my father was the Earl of Ashford," she said. "I know quite a lot about how things work."

"In battle?"

"In battle and in the nobility of England."

He eyed her a moment. "Where did you foster?"

"Okehampton Castle."

"Built by Baldwin FitzGilbert."

"How do you know that?"

"Because my family came to these shores with the Duke of Normandy," he said. "So did FitzGilbert's family. Okehampton is a de Courtenay property now, strong supporters of Henry."

Andia thought fondly of the warlord in whose castle she had fostered. "John de Courtenay was a good lord," she said. "Lady de Courtenay was quite kind. I appreciated them both, very much."

The conversation faded a little as Torran wolfed down the rest of his meal and Andia's thoughts wandered to her days at Okehampton Castle. Such carefree days she missed a great deal. It seemed like a million years ago. Her days were no longer carefree.

And an uncertain future awaited her.

Feeling depressed, she eyed Torran as he continued eating. He didn't seem like the talkative sort, and clearly there was no reason to keep up a conversation with her, since she was his prisoner, so she picked herself up off the floor.

"I will leave you to your evening, my lord," she said. "I will be ready to depart before dawn, or sooner if you wish. Oh, and one more thing, if I may. I wanted to thank you for sparing my brother's life. You did not have to, but you showed mercy. You have my deepest gratitude for that."

He looked up from his food. "Your brother is Henry's prisoner," he said. "It is not my privilege to end his life."

Andia paused by the door. "But it is Henry's," she said quietly. "Is that why we are going to London? To face our deaths because of our father's actions?"

Torran could hear something in her voice, something between terror and resignation. Up until this moment, he'd been completely professional. He hadn't exactly been warm, nor had he been cold, but somewhere in between. But he had to admit that lovely Lady Andia had his interest more than he wanted her to. She had such a beautiful voice, a sweet and sultry way of speaking. She was articulate and soft spoken when she wasn't being so stubborn, but he could already tell that stubbornness wasn't inherent to her. Strength, yes, but not stubbornness.

It was difficult not to feel some compassion for her.

"His intentions were not conveyed to me," he said. "But I would be lying if I did not tell you that Henry intends to keep you and your brother as his guests for a time."

"You mean his captives."

"Aye."

She sighed sharply. "But to what purpose?" she said. "Aeron is a child even if he is the new earl, but he is lord over a smashed castle with no army. Quite honestly, I have no idea how we will survive if we are returned to Kennington. Your army took everything of value and I am quite sure there is nothing left. How are my brother and I a threat to the Crown?"

Torran swallowed the bite in his mouth and brushed off his hands. "That is not my decision, my lady," he said. "My duty is to take you to London. That is all."

Andia sighed again, heavily this time, and leaned against the door-jamb. She began rubbing her arms as if cold, even though she wore clothing that was heavy enough to make her sweat. But her thoughts, her mind, were a thousand miles away, thinking of the life she knew as it came to an end.

"Lady de Courtenay is a musician," she said softly. "Did you know that? She taught all of her charges to play instruments and sing, and I learned to play the harp and sing quite well. I even had the idea that I would form a group of other young women who liked to play and sing, and we would travel the world playing and singing for kings and great lords, and they would pay us with gold and fine horses. My father thought it was a silly dream, of course, and he expected me to serve my brother as a slave would serve a master. Even so, I still had that dream. He could not take it away from me. But I suppose Henry will, once and for all."

Torran stood up, tray in hand, as he listened to her reminisce about her future. There was something sad about her words, about the course her life was taking. He'd refused to acknowledge that, but in her moment of vulnerability, he was unable to avoid it. He knew it wasn't healthy to let his guard down with a prisoner, but he found that the walls were weakening. And he had very strong walls of professionalism, of self-protection.

But Andia's soft words had shifted his foundation a little.

"My lady, I am fairly certain that the king has no intention of executing you," he said. "Your brother might be another matter, but he has no reason to rid himself of you. I would not give up on your dreams quite yet. You must have faith."

She looked at him, a shadow in the darkness of the landing. "Faith." She snorted softly. "I gave up on faith years ago. The day my mother died in childbirth and my father decided I was a burden to him was the day I lost my faith in God. He has no regard for me, so I return the favor."

Torran came closer, holding out the tray to her. "Then if you hold no regard for faith, then at least believe in hope."

"Even hope is a struggle sometimes."

He could well understand that. And it wasn't as if he disagreed with her because, once, he'd had his own struggle of hope. Andia took the tray from him and turned for her chamber as Torran watched her go. He wanted to give her some encouragement, but he couldn't. He'd already said too much. She was his captive, his duty, and he'd already blurred that line a little. He wasn't going to make it worse.

Without another word, Andia shut her chamber door, and Torran heard her throw the bolt.

There was no mistaking the weeping he heard.

CHAPTER FIVE

IT WAS A rainy morning after a rainy night, a storm that didn't seem to want to let up, and Torran was soaked to the skin because he'd been outside with his men ensuring that the escort was ready to depart for London. More than that, Lord Penden had loaned him a carriage for Andia and her brother at Lady Penden's insistence. It was barbaric, according to Lady Penden, for Andia to be traveling in the back of an open wagon, so her personal carriage had been brought out to complete the trip to London.

Heavily muscled horses to pull it were also part of the bargain, a matched set of four, all of them dark in color with white stripes down their faces and tails that had been docked to keep them out of the wagon wheels. Torran himself made sure to check the harnesses along with Kent and Stefan. Jareth was in conversation with Lord Penden, who was also up at this predawn hour, while Aidric, Dirk, and Britt made sure the men were assembled and at least moderately protected from the rain with oilcloth cloaks that they had borrowed from Penden. Although the soldiers usually traveled with their own cloaks, several of them simply weren't adequate, so replacements were found.

"'Tis a sturdy conveyance," Kent said as he finished checking the front wheels. "Fit for a king, I might add."

Torran blew water out of his lips. "Indeed," he said. "But I do not want a soldier driving it. One of us should."

"I will," Kent said. "However, in weather like this, someone will need to check the road ahead very carefully or this thing will end up on its side. And it's heavy enough that we might not be able to right it."

Torran nodded, stepping back to look at the horses and their finely tended hooves. This was a team meant strictly for this carriage, and they were clad in rain cloaks of their own, from their ears to their tails. Lord Penden had seen to that. They were expensive animals and he wanted them well protected. Torran checked the legs of the horse nearest him, patting the animal on the neck when he was finished.

"This is a sturdy lot," he said. "Penden must have spent hundreds of pounds on these animals, so we'll want to be very careful with them. Let's make sure we have men assigned to the road at least a quarter of a mile ahead of the carriage. Roads, bridges—I want all of it checked in this weather before we cross it."

Kent nodded and headed off to gather a few men to assign to the task. As he did so, Stefan approached Torran, wiping water out of his eyes as he moved.

"The escort is mostly ready," he told Torran. "Shall I fetch the boy?"

Torran pointed to the keep. "He is in a lower chamber under guard," he said, loudly for Stefan's benefit. "Go to the entry level. You'll find him there."

Stefan glanced up at the keep. "And the girl?"

"I will fetch her."

Stefan headed into the keep in search of Aeron as Torran finished his inspection of the carriage horses, leaving a royal soldier to watch over them as a peal of thunder ripped across the sky. Lightning flashed. He was turning for the keep when he caught sight of people emerging. Servants were holding up a canopy against the rain as Lady Penden, Andia, and Aeron began descending the stairs, and Stefan, seeing them coming, stopped at the bottom of the steps.

Lady Penden had hold of Andia, who was dressed in something glorious. The closer Torran came to her, the more he could see that she was clad in a traveling dress with a matching cloak, all of it made of the most glorious white wool. He knew she'd brought a small satchel with her, and presumably more clothing, but the satchel had been left in the wagon last night, so the garments she was wearing must have been more of Lady Penden's items. Andia had a hood on, but he could see curly tendrils peeking out from the edges, and as he drew close, Lady Penden called to him.

"Sir Torran?" she said, holding Andia by the arm. "We require your assistance, please."

Torran headed over to Andia as Stefan took charge of Aeron. Truthfully, Torran wasn't paying any attention to the lad because the magnificent image of Andia had his focus completely.

He struggled not to be obvious about it.

"What is your wish, Lady Penden?" he asked.

Lady Penden, bundled up against the gloomy morning, pointed to Andia. "Will you please carry her to the carriage?" she asked. "I am afraid her feet and legs will become soaked before she even gets there."

Torran didn't hesitate. He bent over and scooped Andia into his arms quite easily, heading for the carriage without a word. In truth, he was feeling rather odd because he seemed to be unable to speak at the moment. Something about her golden eyes fixing on him as he picked her up had rendered him strangely speechless.

That wasn't usual for him.

Puzzled by his reaction, and the bizarre thumping of his heart, he carried her all the way to the carriage as Stefan, who had already put Aeron into the cab, held the door open. Stefan helped him get Andia into the cab because she was wearing so many heavy layers that he needed help to push the cloak in as she slid into the cab. Both Stefan and Torran were forced to tuck in the long train of her garments before they could even close the door, but it remained open as Lady Penden handed over some other items for the cab. Not only did she have a packed satchel for Andia, which she instructed to keep it as a gift, but she also had a basket of food for them to take along. That was put on the floor of the cab near Aeron, who eyed it longingly as the cab door was shut.

And with that, they were ready to depart.

As the rain whipped and the wind howled, Lord and Lady Penden said their farewells from the inner ward, with Lady Penden blowing kisses at Andia, until Lord Penden finally forced her to go back inside. The escort, now with the expensive carriage adorned with the red and gray of the House of Penden, left the safety of Rochester's enormous bailey and headed out into the stormy dawn.

From Rochester, it was about a day's ride to London, and Torran expected them to arrive sometime in the early evening because the weather would slow them down somewhat. He rode next to the carriage, which Kent was driving quite ably, and he had the Six spread out around it while Stefan remained on point.

As the sun rose and gray light illuminated the land, the road remained soft but passable. There was a small ferry crossing at the River Medway, which they made without incident, and then a larger crossing lay ahead across the Thames. Torran could only hope that the weather would let up a little because the ferry crossing could be dicey even on a good day. It was a big, wide river with a strong current. He was looking forward to getting through it and on into London. As Torran planned out the remainder of the journey, inside the carriage, something quite different was going on.

It had all started, for Andia, before dawn. She'd awoken because she was coughing and climbed out of bed to drink some of the mulled wine that was still on the table. That had satisfied her enough to return to bed, but within the hour, she had a sore throat and her eyeballs felt warm. In her world, that told her she had a fever, something she'd been fearful of since suffering through a terrible illness a few years earlier. She'd contracted a sickness of the lungs and been ill with it for about three weeks before she saw any improvement.

Therefore, when her eyes felt hot and even the heavy coverlet wasn't enough to keep her warm, she knew that she was ill. Fearful of Torran's reaction, however, she didn't tell anyone, least of all Lady Penden. She didn't want to be the reason why the entire escort was delayed. Therefore, when the woman came to dress her about an hour before dawn, Andia did her best to not cough or give any indication that she was ill. Lady Penden didn't notice anything strange, and here she was, in the carriage bound for London.

But she was feeling worse.

The cough returned and she couldn't stave it off. Lady Penden had given her a basket full of food and watered wine, and she sipped on the wine, trying to keep the cough at bay, but her head was aching now and she knew her fever was worse. Huddled on the seat of the cab, she leaned against the cab wall and ended up falling into an exhausted sleep as Aeron ate nearly everything out of the basket.

In truth, Aeron may have been frightened into behaving, at least temporarily, but he wasn't a fool. He was an astute young man, an intelligence hidden behind his spoiled behavior, and he knew his sister well enough to know that something was wrong. Her cheeks were too pink, her nose red, and she was trying desperately not to cough. She wouldn't eat, but she'd had some wine and was now sleeping against the side of the carriage.

She didn't look well to him.

But he kept his mouth shut. He ate the food in the basket and pre-tended not to notice his sister's condition. The fear of the knight who had paddled his bottom kept him telling anyone. He knew the knight, Sir Torran, was riding next to the cab because he'd seen the man through the gaps in the oilcloth that covered the window. But he watched his sister for a few hours, listening to her cough and breath heavily as she slept, and he knew she was becoming more ill as time passed.

Perhaps she really did need help.

Summoning his courage, he peeled back the oilcloth.

Another knight was there, riding alongside the carriage. It took Aeron a moment to realize it was the knight who had escorted him out of the keep. It was still raining quite heavily, a noisy rain, and he called to the knight twice with no response. The man simply looked ahead. Aeron didn't want to speak too loudly because he didn't want to wake his sister or, worse, have her tell him to mind his own business. Therefore, he began waving his hand at the knight, hoping to catch the man's attention.

Finally, it worked.

The knight flipped his faceplate up.

"What is it?" he asked.

Aeron stuck his head out of the window because he didn't want Andia to hear him. Rain pelted him in the face as he pointed inside the cab.

"My sister," he said.

"What about her?"

"She's ill."

The knight reined his horse closer to the cab. "Ill?" he repeated. "Is the motion of the carriage making her sick?"

Aeron shook his head. "Nay," he said. "She is coughing. She cannot breathe."

That had the knight dismounting his horse even as the escort continued to move. He opened the cab door to see Andia huddled in the corner, flushed and sleeping. Quickly, he shut the door and mounted his horse, charging up to the front, where Torran was now at point. As

Aeron tried to see what was going on up front, the knights exchanged a few words, and suddenly, the very knight that Aeron was afraid of was ordering the carriage to a halt. He climbed off his horse, followed by the other knight, and two others. All of them converged on the carriage as Torran opened the door.

Aeron's wide-eyed gaze greeted him.

"What is wrong with Lady Andia?" Torran asked.

Aeron pointed at her. "She's coughing," he said.

That was about all he could manage to the man he was scared of, so Torran pulled his helm off, handed it to the nearest man, and climbed inside the cab. It wasn't made for a man his size and leaned dangerously as he sat next to Andia and pulled off his right glove. As she started to wake up, he put his hand to her face and hissed.

"She's burning with fever," he said, turning to the men outside. "Didn't anyone notice that she was ill?"

Heads shook. Torran knew he should have been asking himself that very question because he was the one who had put Andia in the carriage. He should have noticed something. But he'd been so over-whelmed with his reaction to her that he was fearful to truly look the woman in the face.

That was his fault.

"Well," he grunted, looking at Andia again, who was now rubbing her eyes. "We should find a physic. Surely there must be a town nearby with one?"

The knight holding Torran's helm handed it over to another man. "I'll ride on ahead and see what's up there," he said. "I am not entirely sure where we are, but we should be close to Dartford."

"Good," Torran said. "That is a big town and there will be a physic. Go find one and take Britt with you. He can secure a room at a tavern for the lady to rest while you locate the physic."

Two knights headed out, mounting their horses and charging on ahead. Meanwhile, Andia stopped rubbing her eyes. She was groggy and, truthfully, a little drunk from the wine she'd been drinking. When she realized Torran was sitting next to her, very closely, she pulled back from him in confusion.

"What has happened, my lord?" she said sleepily. "Why… What is…?"

"You are ill, my lady," Torran said with surprising gentleness. "You have a fever."

It took her a moment to realize what he was saying, and when she did, she put a hand to her cheek to feel that it was quite warm.

"My apologies," she said, her eyes unnaturally bright. "I did not want to be any trouble. I am certain that if you just let me sleep, I will be well by the time we reach London."

"You were feeling poorly this morning?"

She looked at him fearfully. "I… I thought it would go away," she said. "I did not want to delay your departure for London."

He sighed, with some regret, and turned to the knight in the cab doorway. "Get the men moving," he said. "We must make it to Dartford."

The knight nodded and began to shout to the men around them. Torran backed out of the cab so it could move more swiftly without his weight in it. Already, it was lurching forward as he shut the door and collected his horse. Everyone seemed to be moving very quickly.

Inside the carriage, Andia was still trying to figure out what was going on. The knights were concerned, de Serreaux was touching her face, and now the carriage was moving quite quickly. She looked at Aeron.

"How did he know I was ill?" she asked before coughing into her hand. "Did you say something?"

Aeron shrugged weakly. "You were coughing," he said, avoiding her question for the most part. "He… he must have heard you."

Andia was feeling quite miserable and wasn't sharp enough to realize that her brother was lying. With a heavy sigh, she leaned against the cab wall again, closing her eyes.

"I do not want to be any trouble," she mumbled. "He should just continue to London. I will get well soon enough."

Aeron watched her fall back into a fitful sleep, hoping he'd done the right thing by telling the knights that she was ill. He didn't want her to be in trouble, but he also didn't want her to die. In spite of their sometimes-contentious relationship, he did love his sister. She was the only one who had ever been truly kind to him. At that moment, Aeron did something he seldom did.

He prayed.

❦

"WE'VE PASSED DARTFORD some time back."

The escort was still moving quickly, but Stefan and Britt had returned to inform Torran that they'd missed the turnoff for Dartford. The rain had been so bad that it had washed away the sign on the intersection. Everyone had been traveling with their heads down to keep the rain out of their eyes and completely missed it, and that included Stefan, who had been on point.

Now they were in a quandary.

"Damn," Torran muttered. "How long ago?"

"More than an hour," Stefan said, wiping water from his eyes. "Blackheath is ahead of us, and then—"

Torran cut him off quietly. "And then Southwark," he said. "We're practically to London."

"Should we simply continue, then?"

Torran glanced back at the carriage rolling along the muddy road. "Aye," he said reluctantly. "We may as well. But we will not be in London until after sunset, at the very least."

"And then on to Westminster?"

That question lingered for a moment as Torran thought on an answer. Would he take a sick woman, a woman he was charged with, no less, to the king in that condition? That didn't reflect well on him in the least. And if she died, it would be looked upon as his fault. He didn't want something like that blemishing his record.

But there was more to it.

The truth, though he was having difficulty admitting it to himself, was that he felt concern for the lady's condition beyond what it meant for him and his reputation. That woman who spoke of dreams, who had been strong against him and then shown him her vulnerability, had his curiosity. His attention, actually. She was unearthly in her beauty, but there was much more beneath the surface.

"Lockwood is closer," he muttered after a moment. "We'll take her there."

Stefan, who didn't serve with Torran, wasn't quite sure where he meant, but Britt had been listening. Standing next to Stefan, he leaned in on the conversation.

"Are you certain?" he said. "Henry wants the lady and her brother delivered to Westminster."

"And I am to deliver a sick woman to the king?" Torran snorted ironically. "Not bloody likely. That would be a tremendous failing on our part, a slight on our abilities as knights. Nay, we'll take her to my family's townhome near Southwark and let her recover."

Britt cocked an eyebrow. "She would have the finest physics in England at Westminster."

"But it is also an hour and a half from Lockwood, if not more," Torran said, irritated. "You may go ahead to Westminster and inform Henry of the situation. Tell him Anselm St. Albans is dead, but we are bringing his children, including the new Earl of Ashford, as soon as the lady has recovered."

"You'll keep the brother?"

Torran sighed in a way that suggested he didn't want to, but had to. "We had better not separate them," he said. "The lady will worry and the boy will probably do or say something terrible in Henry's presence, so we shall keep them together."

"As you wish."

The matter seemed to be settled, and Torran pointed up the road. "Please ride ahead and have a physic waiting for us when we arrive at Lockwood," he said. "And notify the servants that we will be arriving before sunset."

Britt nodded, glancing at the carriage before spurring his horse up the road. He picked Stefan up and the two of them took off in the rain, splashing mud as they went. That brought the rest of the Six, gathering where Torran was as he explain the situation to them. The decision was made that Torran and Kent would remain at Lockwood while the rest of Henry's Guard of Six went on ahead to join Henry and report on the fall of Kennington.

The situation was decided.

Unfortunately, the roads weren't cooperating. The closer they came to Southwark, the worse the roads seemed to get, and more than once they'd had to use hands and any small tools they had on them to fill in holes or ruts so the carriage could pass over. Torran himself helped fill one particular rut, south of Blackheath, so Kent could drive the carriage onward. The sides of the road were out of the question because the water was pooling and the puddles were deep, so their only choice was to stay the course.

Torran kept checking on Andia, but she never moved from her huddled position against the wall of the cab. Surprisingly, Aeron offered to help the soldiers fill in the holes on the road, but Torran convinced the lad that he was most needed watching out for his sister, so reluctantly, the boy stayed inside the carriage. What should have taken three hours at most ended up taking almost six, and when the entry to Lockwood Tower, the official name of the de Serreaux fortified manse, came into view, those who were supposed to continue on to Westminster decided they'd had enough travel for one day.

Everyone headed in the direction of Lockwood.

A long day was about to become a long night.

CHAPTER SIX

Lockwood Tower
Southwark, London

"I NEED YOUR help, my lord."

Torran had been sitting in the solar that belonged to his father when he heard those grim words. It was near dawn and he'd been up all night, monitoring the situation with Lady Andia because her fever had rendered her semi-delirious. She was coming in and out of a deep sleep, and when she did have moments of being awake, she spoke nonsense.

Aeron had long since gone to bed, sleeping heavily, as a physic from Candlewick Street in London, who had been brought back by Britt and Stefan, closely tended the ill young woman. Torran had told everyone else to go to bed, also, knowing what a long day it had been, but he had remained awake. Or, at least, he thought he had been awake, but when he heard those words from the physic, his head shot up from the table he'd been sitting at. He'd been dead asleep and didn't even know how he got there.

"Why?" he said, standing up and struggling to stay alert. "What has happened?"

The physic motioned for him to follow. "The lady's fever has grown worse," the man said. He was small and wiry, and smelled like cheese.

"You have only a few servants here and your men are sleeping. I need assistance."

Torran rubbed his eyes. "That is because my family does not spend a great deal of time here, so we only have a handful of servants in the house when we are not in residence," he said. "You have failed to tell me what you need."

They were out in the cavernous entry now. Lockwood was built in the shape of a U, with a two-storied entryway and common room, and then a dozen chambers in each wing. The kitchen was under the south wing, a vast complex of rooms that were constantly wet due to the water table from the nearby river, and a great dining hall that faced the placid waters of the Thames. Torran had practically grown up here, so it was the one place he could truly call home. Rubbing his eyes again, he grabbed the physic with one hand before the man could head up the mural stairs.

"Christ upon his mighty throne, man, *what* do you need from me?" he demanded.

The physic paused. "I need your help with the lady," he said, still trying to get up the stairs. "You have two female servants and one male servant, and I have them quite busy filling a tub with tepid water. I must get the lady into the water and get her fever down."

That woke Torran up immediately, and he began to run up the stairs along with the physic. "Is it that bad?" he asked, concerned.

The physic led him up the stone steps, onto the landing, and turned down the corridor on his right. "Bad enough," he said. "It is quite high."

Torran didn't ask any further questions. He was dressed in the clothing he had traveled in and, in fact, had fought the battle of Kennington in. Stained tunic and all, he was emitting a horrific odor that he himself could smell, but he couldn't be concerned with that at the moment. He was only concerned with Andia and her illness, and when he entered the chamber that his mother usually occupied, he could see the activity going on.

There was a fire in the hearth, keeping the chamber nice and cozy. It was an opulent room, given his mother's love of fine things, from the silks on the bed to the precious glass windows. He had specifically chosen this chamber for Andia because it was very comfortable, and as he looked about, he could see so many things that reminded him of his mother. She was a caring woman, and he knew for a fact that she would have wanted a distressed young woman to be comfortable and well tended.

Near the hearth, two women were slowly pouring water into a copper tub that was lined with muslin. The physic went straight to them and stuck his hand into the water to test the temperature. Deeming it appropriate, he went over to the table where his satchel was open and his medicaments were spread out over the tabletop. He selected an earthenware phial that turned out to be oil, and he poured it into the tub.

The heavy scent of peppermint and cloves filled the air.

Torran was still standing back by the door, waiting for the physic to give him some direction. His attention inevitably moved to the bed where Andia was lying on her side, curled up. He could only see her back. As he was looking at her, the only male servant at Lockwood entered the chamber with a bucket full of steaming water. The physic quickly waved him over and a little of it was splashed into the tub. Once that was done, he had the servant set the bucket down and leave the chamber. When the door closed, the physic motioned to Torran.

"Bring her over, my lord," he said. "Quickly, now. There is no time to waste."

Torran didn't hesitate. He went over to the bed and carefully rolled Andia onto her back. She was flushed and half awake, dressed in a sleeping shift. He hesitated.

"Should you not remove her from her clothing?" he asked.

The physic continued to motion to him. "Nay," he said. "Bring her over. Put her straight into the water."

Bending over, Torran scooped Andia into his arms, holding her against his broad chest. Had the situation not been so dire, he might have relished the feel of her against him. It was extremely rare that he was this close to a woman. But in this case, there was no romance involved. He could feel that Andia was hot even through his clothing. Taking her over to the tub, he carefully lowered her into the waiting water.

The moment she touched it, her eyes flew open.

"Nay!" she said, panic in her expression as the tepid water closed in over her body. "Nay, I do not have time. I must go."

She was clinging to Torran, trying to use him to pull herself out just as he was trying to settle her in. He ended up on his knees, forcing her to stay in the water.

"My lady," he said calmly, "there is nowhere to go. You are not needed anywhere."

She looked up at him, and he could see that she was a bit dazed. "You do not understand," she said. "Aeron has been naughty again and Papa will blame me."

He could see that this fever, which had come on quickly, was affecting her thinking. Rather than argue with her, or try to explain the way of things, he simply gave in.

"I will explain it to your father," he said, settling down next to the tub because she refused to let him go. "And I will keep watch of Aeron. He will not misbehave anymore, I swear it."

Andia gazed at him a moment, focused on him as the physic and a maid began to wipe her neck and arms down with the lukewarm water. "You are very nice," she said. "Who are you?"

"I am Sir Torran, my lady."

"Torran," she repeated as if she'd heard the name but couldn't quite place it. Then she blinked and began to look around the room. "Where am I?"

"You are at my family's home, my lady."

"Where is my brother?"

"He was helping with the horses the last I saw of him."

She was still looking at the walls of the chamber. "Is the battle over?"

"It is."

"Where am I?"

"At my family's home."

"Where is it?"

"Near London."

He was very calm as he spoke to her, so she seemed to relax as well. She settled back against the tub, sighing heavily as she was gently swabbed. The physic dragged a cold, wet cloth across her face, roughly, and she sputtered, sitting up and rubbing her eyes. When she stopped rubbing and focused on him again, her expression changed.

"Torran," she said. "You are taking me to Henry, aren't you?"

Suddenly, she was lucid again, but that had been happening on and off since they came to Lockwood. Torran was still holding on to her just as she was holding on to him, and for a moment, they simply stared at one another. She didn't let him go and he didn't let her go. After a brief hesitation, he nodded.

"I am, my lady," he said quietly.

She blinked and started looking around, orienting herself. "I remember now," she said, rubbing her eyes again. "I... I thought I was dreaming, I think. I felt as if I was dreaming. I was dreaming about Aeron lighting fire to the soldiers and—"

"He *burned* soldiers?" Torran interrupted her, aghast.

Andia leaned her head back against the tub. "It is not as it sounds," she said wearily. "He would find men sleeping on duty and put straw in the soles of their boots and light the straw on fire. No one was ever really burned, but Papa would swat Aeron for it."

Torran pushed her hair out of the way as the maid swabbed her neck and shoulder. It was an incredibly intimate gesture, and a gentle one, but he did it without thought. It needed to be done so he did it. But he was still holding on to her, his enormous hands on her upper arms as she gripped his forearms.

"I would imagine your father was right to do so," he said. "But I am surprised to hear it because your brother seems as if he's not known much discipline in his life."

She smiled faintly. "You knew that," she said. "You spanked him for it."

He snorted softly. "I did," he said, his smile fading. "He deserved it."

Torran's mind drifted back to Yancey and that terrible day. He'd been able to push it out of his mind for a while, but now it was difficult not to get caught up in the grief of it again. There was a building maelstrom of emotions swirling around in his chest because something was happening at this moment, something he couldn't quite describe, but he knew it had to do with the lady who was still clinging to him. She was causing the emotions. Her hands were hot, searing the flesh on his forearm, but he let her hold on to him because it seemed to him that she needed something to cling to at the moment.

This lady of lost dreams.

This lady who was increasing stirring something within him.

"He did deserve it," Andia said, breaking into his train of thought. "I told you that I was grateful for the mercy you showed toward him. He's fortunate a spanking was all he received. Do you have children, Sir Torran?"

One of the female servants poured a bucket of cold water into the tub and Andia gasped, digging her fingers into his arms. As the physic instructed the girl to bring more hot water and the swabbing continued, now wetting Andia's scalp, Torran shook his head.

"Nay," he said, trying to keep her distracted because she wasn't particularly happy with the cold water. "No children."

Andia's face was growing pale, the rosiness gone from her cheeks as the tepid bath did its job to help bring her temperature down. "Surely you must be married," Andia said, gasping uncomfortably when the physic wiped her face with cold water again. "God's Bones, does he have to do that?"

Torran eyed the physic as he answered. "Your fever is quite high," he said. "But he will refrain from wiping your face like that again."

He said it loud enough for the physic to hear it, and the man simply shrugged. But Andia was beginning to shiver because the water was growing colder.

"I am truly sorry to have been so much trouble," she said. "I'm certain you have far better things you could be doing that watching over me, but I am grateful for you kindness."

He simply nodded, studying her, thinking how different she seemed from the woman he had seen last night. That stubborn, almost spiteful, streak was perhaps something out of character for her, because she didn't seem like that the first time he'd met her. Truth be told, he did have far better things he could be doing and could have easily had one of the other Six watch out for her.

But like she were a guilty pleasure, he wanted to do it himself.

"You are no trouble," he said, looking to the physic. "Her mind seems clearer. Is she better?"

The physic put a leathery hand on Andia's forehead and then again on her neck. "She is cooler," he said. "But if we remove her from this bath, I fear the fever will rage again."

"You cannot keep her here forever."

The physic shook his head. "Nay," he said. "But I am brewing a potion made with willow bark. It will help and she will be able to sleep well."

"Good," Torran said, returning his attention to Andia. "Did you hear that? He is going to provide you with a potion to help your fever."

Andia nodded wearily. "And then to Henry?"

"When you are well."

"And then what will you do?"

"What do you mean?"

"Will you remain and watch over my brother and me?"

He shook his head. "I will return to my regular duties."

Another maid appeared and dumped a half of a bucket of hot water into the bath, causing Andia to yelp. She very nearly climbed out, and would have had Torran and the physic not pushed her down again. But Torran noticed something he'd not noticed before, and that was the fact that her sleeping shift was transparent because of the water. He looked up to find beautiful, full breasts in his face with dark, puckered nipples. He pushed her back into the tub but wasn't entirely sure he was going to recover from that sight. Therefore, he struggled to distract himself, holding her down in the water again as the physic put a cool cloth behind her neck.

"I will return to my regular duties, which include helping Henry plan his travel," he said. "Henry's private guard travels with him everywhere, so there are routes I must plot and destinations I must send word to on Henry's behalf."

Andia's gaze lingered on him. "Then I will not see you again," she said. "I am glad I had the chance to thank you for your kindness in a difficult situation. I cannot thank you enough."

"You have done so repeatedly," he said. "I know you are grateful."

"And now you have me in your very own home when you should have taken me to Henry already," she said. "It is a beautiful home."

He smiled weakly. "You have not even seen all of it."

"This room is beautiful," she said, looking off to her left, into the bulk of the chamber. "I have seen enough to know that. Whose is it?"

"My mother's."

She looked at him. "Your mother is still alive?"

"She is."

"Is she here?"

He shook his head. "Nay," he said. "My parents live at Bexhill Castle."

Andia pondered that. "Bexhill," she said. "I have heard of it before. It is near Hastings?"

He nodded. "You know of it?"

"I think I heard my father speak of it," she said. "He had to pass through Bexhill to get to Eastbourne, where merchant ships sometimes dock. Kennington has cattle that my father has been known to sell to the French. What becomes of my father's herds now?"

She seemed to be relaxing, so Torran loosened his grip on her. "Canterbury remained at Kennington to ensure everything is handled properly," he said. "He will ensure the herds are taken care of."

"You mean confiscated by Henry."

"I do not know, my lady. That is the truth."

Andia didn't push him. She was feeling weak but better as the bath did what it was supposed to do. Her fever wasn't getting any worse and she was surprisingly clearheaded now. Earlier, as she'd told Torran, she felt as if she were in a dream. She wasn't quite awake and she wasn't quite asleep. But she was fully awake now, and the physic left her long enough to collect the brew that was steaming over the fire. The willow bark had a bitter, tangy taste to it but she drank it down as instructed, making a face as she handed the cup back to the physic.

"Keep her in this tub a little while longer, my lord," the man said to Torran. "Let the potion do its work."

He returned to his medicaments as the female servants wandered away, gathering mops to soak up the water that had spilled out from the tub. Andia sat back against the tub, eyes closed, with her hands over her wet chest and her knees raised. Her hair was wet from the physic having poured water over her head in an attempt to control her fever, so she simply sat there and shivered.

All the while, Torran was watching her.

He'd done nothing but watch her since he came into the chamber, and the more he sat with her, the more curiosity he felt about this woman. Also, the more comfort. He wasn't comfortable with women by nature and, in fact, had known to be downright awkward with them. But at this moment, in this setting, he didn't feel awkward.

He felt entranced.

"If I can find a lute, will you play something for me?" he asked after a moment.

Her eyes opened. "Now?"

"When you are feeling better."

"Certainly, if you wish," she said. "Don't you sing? Some men do, you know."

He shook his head immediately. "Not me."

"Not at all?"

"I sound like a bull calling to its mate."

She grinned. "Surely you have some hidden talent," she said. "Knights are usually trained in things like that."

He averted his gaze, an embarrassed smile playing on his lips. "Trained, aye, but if one has no talent, then he is doomed to humiliation," he said. "I have no talent for such things, if you must know. My talent lay in military tactics and battles and mathematics."

She looked at him, interested. "Mathematics?" she said. "Truly?"

"Truly. Latin and biblical studies, also."

"Then you are a scholar."

He nodded as if she'd just hit the nail on the head. "Now you understand me," he said. "My mind is full of other things. There is no room for singing and dancing."

"Torran?"

Someone was knocking on the chamber door, calling his name, and Torran looked up to see Kent and Jareth standing in the doorway. Leaving the lady in her cooling bath, he stood up and went over to them.

"I thought you two were sleeping," he said. "It is still very early. Why are you awake?"

"Because the rain has stopped and we want to get back to London before it starts again," Kent said. Then he looked over Torran's shoulder at the lady in the tub near the hearth. "How is Lady Andia?"

Torran glanced back at her. "Her fever was high," he said. "That is a tepid bath you see, ordered by the physic. He has also given her a potion to bring the fever down, so time will tell. She is still quite ill."

"And that is why you should go to Henry personally," Jareth said in a low voice. "We have been speaking on this subject and the general consensus is that you should be the one to tell Henry about the lady. Stefan has volunteered to remain here until she is well and then he will bring her on to London, but there is really no reason for you to remain, Torran. Henry will want to hear about Kennington and Ashford from your lips."

Torran felt as if he'd been caught in something. He wasn't sure what, but his immediate reaction was to refuse to go. He didn't want to leave the lady. He wanted to stay here until she was well, but then, he was equally paranoid that Kent and Jareth might be able to read his refusal in his expression. He didn't want his men to know that there was something about the woman that intrigued him.

That would be a scandal worthy of the the very word.

The Guard of Six didn't get mixed up with women. It was a little-known fact that women were the entire reason they'd come into

Henry's fold—every single one of them had issues with women in the past, issues solved or brokered by Henry, that put them in his debt. Therefore, one of them having an interest toward any woman was simply not done.

And that included Torran.

This was a situation he never thought he'd find himself in.

"While I understand what you are saying, I am not leaving the lady," he said flatly. "Her health is a direct reflection on me and I will not leave it to the management of anyone else. Henry asked for hostages and I will give him hostages, but I need to make sure she is healthy before I deliver her to him. I'd be a poor knight, indeed, if I cared so little for Henry's directive that I would allow a valuable hostage to die under my care."

They had no reason not to believe that his desire to remain at Lockwood with the lady was purely duty oriented. Torran had a better sense of duty than most, but Jareth wasn't so certain this was something Henry would want.

"I do not know about this, Torran," he said, scratching his head. "Henry will want to talk to you."

Torran shook his head firmly. "Not until that woman is healthy enough to travel," he said, jabbing a finger in Andia's direction. "If she dies, Henry's faith in me will be diminished and I cannot stand for that. Is that clear?"

That sounded like the Torran they both knew—concerned with himself, concerned with Henry—so they both nodded the affirmative.

"Very well," Jareth said. "I will tell him everything. But what if he wants to come to Lockwood and see for himself?"

"Then I invite him to come," Torran said. "Henry is more than welcome to come to the lady. But it may be days before the lady can come to Henry."

Jareth acknowledged that statement and headed off, leaving Kent behind, his gaze lingering on the woman in the tub. "Do you really need to play nursemaid, Torran?" he asked. Out of the entire Guard of Six, Torran was the closest to Kent, so the man could speak freely. "Stefan has already volunteered to remain with her and, quite frankly, refuses to leave even when the rest of us do. I think his father has told him to stay with the lady and her brother until she is delivered to Henry."

Torran pursed his lips irritably. "You mean that Canterbury wants to ensure she is not mistreated."

"Exactly."

"Does the man honestly think I would do that?"

Kent simply shrugged. Torran didn't have a reputation for brutality with the weaker sex, but he was also known to carry out Henry's orders to the letter.

No matter what they were.

"Well," Torran said, still irritated with Daniel and his paranoia, "Stefan can remain here if he wants, but as soon as the lady is well, we are off to Westminster. I will see you there."

Kent nodded, following Jareth's retreat. When he vanished down the corridor, Torran returned his attention to the chamber. He could see that Andia was sleeping against the side of the tub, which probably wasn't the best thing for her should she slide down into the water and end up drowning herself, so he shut the door and went on the hunt for something to dry her off with. The servants had already brought an enormous drying towel, however, one that belonged to his mother, and it was the physic and the female servants who got Andia out of the tub, stripped her out of her wet sleeping shift, and then proceeded to swaddle her up in the towel and get her back to the bed.

All the while, Torran stood out of the way, watching the situation, turning his head away when the lady needed privacy, but returning to his vigilant stance when she was back in bed and covered up. He ended up sitting in a window seat, watching everything from afar, and thinking what a damn liar he was.

He was lying to everyone, and possibly even himself, about his true motives.

The sun was beginning to rise and the rain had moved away, leaving a soggy, cold world outside. In the great yard below, he could see the Guard of Six and about half of Henry's soldiers departing for London. Jareth, who was usually in command when Torran wasn't available, had left behind about twenty royal soldiers, the Penden carriage, and Stefan.

With a heavy sigh, Torran leaned back against the wall, feeling his fatigue. The physic had Andia back in bed, and down in the bailey there were a few servants moving about as the day began. Horses needed to be fed and other chores attended to. Torran's father didn't even keep soldiers here because the manse itself was so fortified that the servants didn't need any. Lockwood, the manse built by his great-grandfather with permission from Henry II. He was also the man who first held the title Earl of Bexhill, a title that now belonged to Torran's father and someday would belong to him, God willing. Lockwood was a place where the family had always felt comfortable, including Torran. But he wasn't feeling that now.

He was feeling uncertain.

And the young woman sleeping in the bed several feet away from him was the reason why.

What are you getting yourself into, you idiot?

Whatever it was, he knew instinctively that it wasn't good.

CHAPTER SEVEN

Etchingham Castle, Sussex
Seat of Lord Dudwell

"KENNINGTON FELL. IF ever Henry has provoked his enemies, this is the time."

The man speaking the words meant them intently. He was older, with hair that had mostly gone gray and skin that was nearly the same color as his hair. He had dark eyes with bags underneath them, as if he hadn't slept in days.

Which he hadn't.

Donnel de Meudon was a man in turmoil.

At the moment, he was in the great hall of Etchingham Castle, a long and narrow building with a high ceiling and a hearth that was taller than he was. Even now, servants were cleaning the ashes out after the night's feast as Donnel and a guest sat in the corner of the hall. The topic was the fall of Kennington Castle.

The man seated opposite him appeared uneasy.

"And you know this for certain?" he asked in a heavy French accent. "Who has told you?"

"Ashford men!" de Meudon exclaimed. "Soldiers escaping the carnage have come here because they know my sister was married to Ashford. It is true that Anselm and I have not spoken in years, but we are still family. The decision to cease communication was not mine, but his."

"Why?"

"Because he cheated me in a game of chance and would not admit it."

"I see," the Frenchman said. "Then he did not send to you for help when the castle was besieged?"

De Meudon shook his head firmly. "Nay," he said. "God curse the man for not sending for my help, because his stubbornness has led to his doom. I am told that Anselm is dead and Henry's men have taken my niece and nephew with them. Undoubtedly to London to face Henry's wrath."

The Frenchman grunted at the horror that thought provoked. "He would punish the children of his enemy?"

De Meudon threw up his hands in exasperation. "How am I to know?" he said. "Anselm sided with de Montfort. I told him not to do it, but he did. He was vocal about it. Do you know how I have kept my castle, Gaubert? By keeping my mouth shut. De Montfort had my money to raise armies, but I did not give him my men or anything more. That kept Henry away from me. I was smart. Anselm was not!"

Gaubert Chambery knew the situation. He was a relative of Henry's wife, Eleanor of Provence, and had been one of the Savoyard lords who received lands from Henry years ago, when he'd married Eleanor. Gaubert had been part of Eleanor's entourage. But like his neighbor, Donnel, Gaubert had kept a low profile as much as he was able. He hadn't angered any English warlords as far as he knew, so there were no complaints about a Savoyard with English lands. However, he had a connection to Simon de Montfort in that he and Simon had engaged in the Cathar Crusade together many years ago, when Gaubert had been a young squire and Simon a knight. Fate saw them become friends, but Gaubert had kept that relationship quiet because he wanted to keep his

English lands.

That didn't stop him from funneling money to de Montfort, just like Donnel.

Anything to undermine Henry, a man he very much disliked.

But that was another story. The situation, at this moment, was that Henry had taken out his vengeance on a vocal supporter of Simon de Montfort and evidently reduced the man's property to rubble. More than that, the children of Anselm St. Albans were going to pay for the sins of their father. At least, that was what it sounded like.

And such a move would be very bad for Henry, indeed.

"Henry will make more enemies if he punishes Ashford's children," Gaubert said after a moment, watching Donnel fidget with anger. "I hope he simply intends to hold them hostage and nothing more."

Donnel shook his head. "I do not know what he intends," he said. "All I know is that my sister's children are being taken to London, to be passed judgment upon."

"Possibly not."

"Why else would Henry want them?"

Gaubert sighed heavily and ran his fingers through his thick gray hair. "I do not know what can be done about it," he said. "Henry has been punishing those who supported de Montfort ever since Evesham. Simon's death meant his supporters became Henry's targets, only it took him three years to go after Ashford."

Donnel grunted. "It wasn't only Henry's army," he said. "Ashford soldiers said that Canterbury and Radnor were there, also. That is Daniel de Lohr and Davyss de Winter. Between those two armies, they could probably conquer half of England if they wanted to. The truth is that Kennington never stood a chance. It was murder. The murder of an entire family."

Gaubert looked at him. "Tragic, indeed," he said. "Mayhap you should petition the king to assume your dead brother-in-law's property.

You could also petition him to be the guardian of the children. You are not Henry's enemy, after all."

Donnel eyed him. "I have thought of that," he said. "But my nephew is still alive. At least, that is what the soldiers said. He is the Earl of Ashford now."

"Then petition the king to be his guardian."

Donnel snorted. "Not that lad," he said. "The last time I saw him was three or four years ago. He could do no wrong. No discipline, no manners. The boy would try a saint's patience."

Gaubert shrugged. "You would not tolerate him for control of Kennington?"

Donnel shook his head. "I would rather cut Henry's throat and be free of his rule than take on young Aeron."

Gaubert grunted. "You are looking at this all wrong," he said. "Teach the boy to hate the man who killed his father and convince him to cut Henry's throat. Our problem would be solved."

Donnel found some humor in that. "Sending a tiny assassin after Henry," he mused. "And Aeron *would* have a reason to kill him."

Gaubert nodded faintly. "It would certainly be just vengeance for Henry's attack on Kennington," he said. "It would also be justice for every man who has been wronged by the king."

Donnel liked that idea. He seemed to be calmer now, pondering a world in which Henry was not his king. "It does not need to be Aeron, truthfully," he said. "Henry would not suspect a child, but a skilled assassin would do just as well. Better, probably. One man could accomplish with de Montfort's army could not. I do not suppose you happen to know an assassin who could get close to Henry, do you?"

Gaubert shrugged. "I am Eleanor's cousin," he said thoughtfully. "Henry and I have always been friendly. I could get very close to him."

Donnel looked at him, his eyes widening when he realized what the man was inferring. "*You?*" he said, suddenly electrified again. "Would you be willing to do it?"

Gaubert was amused. "That seems to excite you a great deal."

"Because it is entirely plausible!" Donnel said enthusiastically. "Why have you not thought of this before?"

Gaubert shrugged. "Because I live quietly on my lands and I give no man a reason to oppose me," he said. "I am not a warrior any longer, Donnel. I raise my sheep, I gamble when I feel like it, and I even like my wife. Why would I want to put myself in a position of killing a king?"

Donnel's dark eyes were intense. "Because I know a dozen warlords who would all pay you handsomely for a job well done."

Gaubert grinned. "They would have to pay me quite a bit of money," he said. "More than they would be willing to pay, I am certain."

"How much?"

"Are you serious?"

"Verily."

Gaubert wasn't sure how serious he was because he was a man who didn't like to take chances with his own life. At least, not in his old age, but in his younger years, he had been a stellar warrior with a brutal reputation.

He had the chops for an assassination job.

But it would have to be worth it.

"A thousand pounds," he finally said. "If you and your warlords can pay me a thousand pounds, I will do it."

There was joy in Donnel's eyes. Astonishment, but also joy. He shook his head with awe. "What mighty armies could not accomplish, one man can," he muttered. "You. *You* can succeed where de Montfort failed."

"De Montfort did not have my greed."

"Is that what this is about? The money?"

"What else would it be for?" Gaubert said. "Oh... and you will also give me Kennington."

Donnel's delight faded. "That belongs to my nephew."

"Then what else can you give me?"

Donnel cocked his head in thought. "I am not certain," he said. "But there are many enemies of Henry who, I am certain, will be happy to reward you for a job well done."

"Then you will find them for me."

"Gaubert… are you truly serious about this?"

Gaubert shrugged. "I have nothing to lose and everything to gain," he said. "Once, I was a warrior beyond compare. I can do exactly what I say I can do, but if you do not pay me and ensure I am well rewarded, I will kill you, too. That is the bargain, Donnel."

Donnel was coming to think this deal was beginning to veer out of his control. "You'll have to give me some time to send word to men I know who would be willing to pay," he said. "I must have their pledge to pay you."

Gaubert lifted his eyebrows. "Ten men to pay one hundred pounds each," he said. "It is not so difficult."

Donnel knew it wasn't as easy as all that. In fact, he was starting to regret having this conversation altogether, and he certainly didn't like that Gaubert seemed to have the upper hand.

He wanted to change that.

"I will work on it," he said. "But until I can get their agreement, I will make you a counteroffer."

"What is that?"

"I worry for the safety of my niece and nephew," Donnel said. "I know my sister would be frantic with worry. Get them back for me and I will see that you are paid revenue from Kennington for years to come. I cannot give you the property, but I can ensure that you gain some wealth from it. With Anselm gone, the new earl will need my help in managing his estate. I am his uncle, after all. I will make sure the man who released him from Henry's clutches is well compensated."

Gaubert was interested. "Oh?" he said. "*How* well compensated?"

"A quarter of everything Kennington earns for the next ten years."

"And how much would that be?"

Donnel's eyebrows lifted as he thought on the question. "Kennington has cattle," he said. "Good cattle on good lands. It is possible that you would get your one thousand pounds and more quite easily."

Gaubert liked that estimate. "A pleasing prospect," he said. "In fact… if there is truly money to be had in this, it might be more efficient if I were to hire a skilled assassin and gain him entry to Henry's quarters."

"What good would that do? *You* are the one who can get close to him."

"True," Gaubert said. "But it would be easier if someone else were to do the job while I had an alibi. Think about it, Donnel—if I have access to Henry and Henry is killed, whom do you think they will suspect?"

That made sense to Donnel. "So you would facilitate his death, but not actually kill him?"

"That might be better for all of us, don't you think?" Gaubert said. "Especially if you want me to free your niece and nephew. I cannot do that if I have half the palace chasing after me because Henry is dead."

Donnel nodded as he understood the logic. What they were talking about was an enormous undertaking because the more the conversation progressed, the more things were coming to light.

The more devilment entered the scheme.

But to be rid of Henry, it would be well worth it.

"I think you and I have some planning to do," Donnel said quietly.

Gaubert's dark eyes glimmered. "Bring me your finest wine and we shall do precisely that."

Donnel did.

CHAPTER EIGHT

Five days later
Lockwood Tower

"**I** AM AN earl and you will bow to me," Aeron said imperiously. "Down on your knees!"

Six days after their arrival to Lockwood Tower, Aeron was making friends wherever he went. In this case, it was with the stable boy he'd been following around since his arrival, a tall and lanky lad who was twelve years of age and already knew more about horses and hard work than Aeron could comprehend. The first full day of his time at Lockwood had seen Aeron trailing after Emile, inspecting everything the young man did and, eventually, telling him what he was doing wrong.

Emile had simply laughed at him.

Torn between rage and curiosity, Aeron made it his life's work to follow Emile around and learn what he could from him, but, of course, he would not give Emile the satisfaction of knowing it. Aeron had to be the one to tell Emile what to do, in all things, and now it had come to a head. Aeron had revealed himself to be a titled lord and demanded respect, but Emile had laughed at him—again—and gone about his business.

That wasn't sitting well with Aeron.

"Do you hear me?" he said, following Emile into the stable. "I am the Earl of Ashford. If you do not want to feel my wrath, then you will bow down to me."

Emile grinned, picking up a bucket with the intention of filling it with a little water for a poultice he needed to make for one of the horses with a swollen fetlock.

"Is that so?" he said.

"Aye, it is so," Aeron said, scooting after Emile when he took the bucket out of the stable and over to the kitchen yard where the well was. "Where are you going? Don't you believe me?"

Emile was still grinning as he began to draw the water. "Certainly, little man," he said. "You are a great lord and I must bow down."

"Well?"

"I'm too busy to bow down."

Outraged, Aeron went after him, watching him put dirt into the water he'd drawn. "What is so important that you cannot show me proper respect?" he said, eventually helping Emile put dirt into the water. "If you do not show me respect, how am I do know that I will make a good lord and you will make a good subject?"

Emile was mixing the dirt and water with his hand as Aeron put more dirt into it. "You'll make a fine lord," he said. "You are already demanding and rude. I saw it from the first."

Instead of being insulted, Aeron was actually encouraged. "Do you think so?" he said. "You think I will make a good lord?"

Emile nodded. "You'll make a fine knight, like Sir Torran."

Aeron frowned. "But I am an earl."

"Sir Torran will be an earl when his father dies," Emile said. "His father is the Earl of Bexhill. Didn't you know that?"

Aeron hadn't, but he couldn't let Emile know. "Then we shall be peers together," he said. He eyed the young man. "Is... is his father a good lord?"

Emile had the mud to the desired consistency and he stood up, heading back to the stable. "A very good lord," he said. "If you truly want to be a good lord, then you should stop making demands and show more kindness. Nobody likes a nasty, demanding lord. They end up killed in battle because no one will help them."

That brought Aeron pause. "No one would dare kill me!"

"If you are not good to your vassals, they might."

More outrage from Aeron as he pondered that prospect. Lords weren't killed by their own men… were they? That wasn't something his father had ever told him. In fact, his father had always told him to be bold and fearless and make his wants known. That was what he'd been doing, only Emile didn't appreciate it. He was the first servant outside of Kennington that Aeron had ever had any contact with, and at Kennington, of course, everyone did what he said.

But not at Lockwood.

Was it possible his father had been wrong?

"Tell me about Lord Bexhill, then," he said. "Does he not give you orders? Does he not command respect?"

Emile glanced at him. "He commands respect by being a good man," he said. "Did that ever occur to you?"

It hadn't, but again, Aeron wasn't going to let on. "But he must be brave," he said. "His vassals will not respect him if he is not brave."

"Bravery has nothing to do with it," Emile said. "Men would rather serve a man who is strong and kind, not a man who is a cruel bully. Understand that, little man, and you'll have happy vassals."

"And Lord Bexhill has made you happy?"

Emile nodded. "He has," he said. "My mother works in the house, and when I was very young, Lord Bexhill brought me to work in the stable. He gave me a position and something to work hard at. I've been here ever since."

"And you like it?"

Emile reached the horse he wanted to work on. "I like it very much," he said, patting the horse's rump affectionately. "I get to work with these beautiful animals, and they like me. I earn a few shillings every month and my mother and I save our money. Someday we want to buy a home of our own."

"Where do you live now?"

"Here, at Lockwood," Emile said. Then he glanced at Aeron over his shoulder. "I heard your home was destroyed in a battle."

Aeron leaned against the end of the stall, watching Emile go to work on the horse's rear right leg. "Henry's army destroyed it."

"Why?"

Aeron shrugged. "My father served Simon de Montfort," he said, sounding rather glum. "Henry punished him for it."

Emile paused, looking up at him. "Was it a terrible battle?"

"Aye."

"Were you frightened?"

Aeron nodded. But then he realized that surely made him look weak, so he stiffened up. "But I killed a knight myself," he said, back to his bragging ways. "Henry and his army may have destroyed my castle, but I killed a man. I'd do it again if I had to!"

Emile could see that it was a frightened boy talking. That was never so obvious. He went back to the horse's leg and began applying the mud.

"I've never seen a battle," he said. "Is that what happened to your sister? The battle made her sick?"

"How do you know about my sister?"

Emile shrugged. "My mother told me," he said. "She's been helping your sister get well."

Aeron instinctively looked in the direction of the manse, as if he could see Andia through the walls. "She is much better now," he said. "Her fever is gone and she was up this morning. I saw her walking."

"Are you and your sister going to stay here now that your home is destroyed?"

Aeron shrugged. "Nay," he said. "Sir Torran is taking us to Henry."

"Why?"

"Because he is going to punish us."

"Who is going to punish us?"

The voice came from the stable entry, and Aeron and Emile turned to see Andia entering. She was clad in one of the garments Lady Penden had given her, sent along in a fine satchel that had once belonged to Desiderata. She wore a simple white shift with a deep neckline and long sleeves underneath a bright red surcoat that was fastened snugly around the torso, with sleeves that were long and draping. Sleeves like that were called angel's wings because they were rather dramatic, especially when the wearer moved her arms. Andia's hair, nearly the same golden-brown color as her eyes, was pulled away from her face with a red ribbon that went with the garment. Truthfully, Lady Penden had been most generous with her daughter's things, passing them to a young women who had lost everything, and Andia wore the items with gratitude.

"Well?" she said to her brother. "Who were you talking about? Who is going to punish us?"

Aeron shrugged. "Henry," he said. "We are going to London now that you are well, aren't we?"

Andia's warm expression faded. "Aye," she said honestly. "Torran has not yet said when, however."

"Shouldn't you ask?" Aeron said. "Don't you want to know?"

Andia turned to look at the manse behind her. Such a lovely manse with lovely furnishings, and she felt very much at home here in spite of the circumstances. Green ivy embrace the entire north side of the building and another flowering vine, with purple flowers, ran delicate fingers near the entry. She'd walked the entire length and breadth of the manor, peeking into chambers, catching a glimpse of the views from the upper windows. She'd been fully ambulatory for two days now, ever since the physic had deemed her fever abated and told her that she needed to regain her strength—but regaining strength, in Andia's mind, meant walking in the sunshine while the weather remained good and exploring this place she found herself in. She'd always been very curious about buildings and the way they'd been constructed. But Lockwood had an extra attraction.

Torran.

The man had hardly left her side for six days, but along with him, Stefan also lingered, though he tended to spend more time watching over Aeron than her. Still, the big, quiet knight was a shadow to Torran, who seemed irritated by the man's presence because he always spoke very loudly to him. Stefan didn't seem to mind, but Andia was certain, at some point, that Stefan was going to demonstrate just how much he didn't like being shouted at.

Truth be told, Andia was a little irritated by Stefan's presence, too.

Maybe she, too, wanted just a little alone time with her jailor.

But he wasn't so much a jailor over the past few days as a companion. Andia and Torran had had a few good conversations since her arrival at Lockwood, conversations that had avoided things like politics and Henry and even Kennington. Instead, they spoke of Lockwood itself, and of Torran's family, and of his father—who, Andia discovered, was the Earl of Bexhill. Torran had even spoken of his mother, Genevieve, and the fact that he had a younger brother and sister, Rhys and Aurelia. He hadn't said much about either of them, except for his brother, who was a knight serving their father. Andia got the impression that Torran wasn't close to his family.

An interesting situation, indeed.

"He will tell us when we are to go," she said, breaking from her train of thought. "Do you want to go walking with me? I was thinking about going down by the river."

Aeron nodded eagerly, jumping up and rushing out of the stable as Andia followed along behind him. She wasn't moving very swiftly these days but managed to follow him through the kitchen yard and to a big, heavily fortified postern gate that opened up onto a small bank with a wide moat beyond that had a small canal straight into the Thames.

Aeron came to a halt, and Andia right behind him.

"A moat?" she said, surprised at what she was seeing. "I did not realize there was a moat around Lockwood."

Aeron hadn't either, mostly because he hadn't ventured out of the manor grounds since his arrival. With Andia ill, he had wanted to stay close. Neither one of them had noticed it when they arrived in the driving rain, at night, and Andia's chamber faced the yard of the manse with no view of the river.

"What do we do?" he asked. "I don't want to swim!"

Andia put her hand on his shoulder and pulled him back in through the gate. "You do not have to swim," she said. "Let us go to the front gate. Surely no one will have any objection to our walking out over the bridge if we stay in sight of the manse."

Aeron shrugged and ran on ahead, but as he did so, he nearly clipped Stefan, who was entering the yard. Stefan had to step aside so the boy could run past him, watching him tear off across the ward as Andia came up behind him.

"Greetings, Sir Stefan," she said. "It is a lovely morning."

Stefan didn't move. He continued to watch Aeron before finally turning to see Andia standing next to him. He dipped his head politely.

"My lady," he said. "You are looking well today."

Andia smiled, but she was puzzled by his delayed response to her greeting. "I feel better, thank you," she said.

Stefan tilted his head slightly. "My lady?"

He acted as if he hadn't heard her correctly, so she said it again. "I said that I feel better, thank you for asking."

Stefan forced a smile before clearing his throat in a somewhat nervous gesture. "My apologies," he said. "I do not hear very well, so if I ask you to repeat yourself—or if I do not hear you at all—it is not because I am not interested. I simply cannot hear you."

That honest but surely humiliating sentence told Andia everything. No wonder Torran yelled at the man. And no wonder he hadn't heard her greeting. But more things about his seemingly uncaring behavior came back to her, like the night of the end of the battle at Kennington and how Stefan was guarding the landing but never heard her leave her chamber.

Aye… everything came clear at that moment.

"I did not know," Andia said, a little louder. "To be quite honest, I have seen Sir Torran practically shouting at you and thought he was being rude."

Stefan's smile turned genuine. "Nay, he was not being rude," he said. "He was speaking so I could hear him."

"Then I will, too," Andia said. "I will try not to shout."

He chuckled. "Actually, it is easier for me to hear women's voices for some reason," he said. "It is the lower voices I have trouble with."

"I see," Andia said loudly. "Have you always had this issue with your ears?"

He shook his head. "Nay," he said. "I was born with good hearing, but right after I was knighted, I noticed difficulty in hearing my father's commands. Even speaking in a normal tone was difficult to hear. The physics say I will eventually lose my hearing altogether. A condition I have evidently been born with."

Andia was greatly sympathetic. "I am so sorry," she said. "That must be difficult."

He shrugged. "It was, at first," he said. "I still think the physics might be wrong, but I suppose time will tell."

"I suppose," Andia said. "Is there nothing to be done?"

"I wish there was."

Andia smiled sadly. "I am sorry for you, truly," she said. Before she could continue, Aeron was running back in her direction, shouting about guards not allowing him through the main gate and the fact that he was going to punish them. She rolled her eyes. "I suppose if there is a bright moment in your situation, it is that you cannot hear my brother's idiocy. You can just ignore him."

Stefan laughed softly. "I have a younger brother just like him," he said. "But he grew up well enough. Your brother will outgrow his willfulness."

Andia cocked an eyebrow at him. "You think so, do you?" she said doubtfully. "If he does not, I shall make sure to find you wherever you may be and tell you that you were wrong. I will further curse you for giving me false hope."

Stefan continued chuckling. "Then let us hope I am right," he said. "But where was your brother going? What did he say about the gate?"

Andia pointed to the enormous fortified entry gate. "Aeron and I were going to go for a walk by the river," she said. "Would you like to accompany us?"

Stefan's eyebrows lifted. "I think I'd better," he said. "You never know what you might find outside these walls."

"Is it dangerous?"

He shrugged. "It could be," he said. "But more than that, I do not think Torran would like you outside of the walls without a guard."

Andia understood his meaning. "So we will not run away," she said, trying not to be offended. "Truly, my lord, where would we go? We do not know anyone in London. More than that, I could probably run just a few feet before I collapsed. I am not entirely strong yet."

"Then mayhap we should not walk," he said. "Mayhap it would be better if you were to rest for now. You have a big day ahead of you tomorrow."

"Why would you say that?"

"Because Torran is taking you to London."

Andia's heart sank. There was the answer for Aeron's question—they would be going to London tomorrow.

Tomorrow...

A day that would change her life forever. Tomorrow, she would become the prisoner of a king. A man who hated her father and who, most assuredly, had no love for her or her brother. They were to be at the mercy of a man who had no consideration for either of them. All she could see ahead of her was a future of mystery and misery. A future where there was to be no happiness, no hope.

No dreams.

Her dreams were gone.

"Indeed," she managed to say. "Sir Stefan, would you please do me a favor?"

He nodded. "If I can, my lady."

Andia pointed to the gate where Aeron was shouting at the guards. "Would you please take Aeron down to the river, if it is not too much trouble?" she said. "I find that I must lie down. I'm feeling rather tired."

Stefan was watching her closely. "Do you feel ill?" he asked. "Should I send for the physic again?"

Andia was already turning for the manse. "Nay," she said. "That is not necessary. All I need is some rest. But I would very much appreciate it if you would let Aeron run himself out. It may be his last chance before... before we reach London."

With that, she began to walk quickly toward the manse, struggling not to tear up. She felt like sobbing. As she came up the wide stone steps into the manse, the tears were already starting to come and she couldn't stop them. She began to wipe at her face, not wanting to be seen crying, but the moment she stepped inside the manse, she plowed into a very big, warm body. She hit it with such force that she heard a grunt.

Torran grabbed her to steady her.

"Lady Andia?" he said, concerned. "My deepest apologies. I should have been more careful. Did you hurt yourself?"

Andia couldn't look at him, though the truth was that she'd stubbed her toe ramming her slipper into his booted foot and it hurt a great deal. "Nay," she said. "But I am sorry for being so clumsy. I was not looking where I was going."

Torran still had hold of her, seeing that she was crying. "What is wrong?" he asked, straight to the point. "Why do you weep?"

Andia tried to brush him off. She was prepared to give him an answer and walk away, but she made the mistake of looking into his eyes. Those beautiful blue eyes. They were so full of concern that her composure left her.

If he was truly so concerned, why was he taking her to the king?

"Nothing is wrong," she said as she burst into tears. "I am quite well."

Torran's sense of concern grew. "I can see that," he said sarcastically. "Who has made you weep? Was it Aeron? Do I need to spank him again?"

She shook her head. "Nay," she squeaked.

Torran's brow furrowed. "Then who?" he demanded lightly. "Stefan? Must I beat down that big dolt? I'll make it hurt, too. Just tell me what he said."

He was being slightly comical, enough that Andia noticed. She'd had no idea the man even had a sense of humor.

"Nay, he's done nothing." She sniffled, wiping her cheeks. "No one has done anything except… you."

Torran's eyes widened. "Me?" he said. "What did I do? Do I need to thrash myself?"

She burst into a fresh around of tears and pulled away from him. "Leave me alone," she said. "You are taking us to London tomorrow and I want to be alone. Let me spend my last few hours of freedom in peace."

He was following her as she headed toward the stairs. "Lady Andia, wait," he said. "Come with me. Let us speak on this."

"Nay," she said firmly. "There is nothing left to say. Just… leave me in peace for now. I will be ready on the morrow when you want to leave."

"You are not going."

She had taken three stairs by the time she realized what he said. When his words registered, she came to a halt and turned to him.

"What did you say?" she asked, incredulous.

He came to the bottom of the stairs. "I said that you are not going to London," he said quietly. "I am, but you are not. Neither is your brother. You are going to remain here for now."

Tears forgotten, Andia looked at him in shock. "But… *why*?" she said. "Stefan said we were leaving for London tomorrow."

Torran didn't answer her right away. He simply looked at her. Then he sighed sharply and held out his hand to her, silently asking her to take it. She did, without hesitation, and he pulled her off the stairs, holding her hand as he took her over to the solar. Once they got to the solar, he continued to hold her hand even as he shut the door quietly.

Then he faced her.

"Because I think it is better if you remain here for now," he said softly. "You have been very ill. You do not need to go to London, to the dank halls of Westminster—or worse, to the Tower—and have your health threatened again. I am going tomorrow to explain it all to Henry."

Andia was still wiping tears off her cheek, but she couldn't help but notice he hadn't let her hand go. In fact, she looked at her hand, enveloped within his, and was starting to think that there was something more to Torran's decision.

Now she was curious.

"It is kind of you to be concerned for me," she said. "But won't Henry be angry?"

Torran shrugged. "Possibly," he said. "But a healthy hostage is better than a dead one."

He wouldn't look at her. He, too, was looking at her hand as he held it. When Andia realized that, she gave his a squeeze.

"Is that the truth?" she asked quietly. "That you want me to remain here because of my health? Or are you truly afraid that Henry is going to make an example out of me?"

He didn't say anything for a moment. He just looked at their hands, one in the other. Then, very slowly, he lifted her hand. Andia thought he was going to kiss it, and her heart began to thump madly. From the sheer expression on his face, her heart began to thump madly. But he didn't kiss her hand—he simply lifted it to his face, putting her palm on his left cheek as his big hand held it there. Then he closed his eyes as if to experience something he hadn't experienced before.

Or, at the very least, had been dreaming of experiencing again.

The soft, gentle touch of a woman's hand.

"My lady, may I ask you a question?" he said, eyes still closed.

Andia could hardly breathe. Everything in her body was quivering from his bold, yet very sweet, gesture.

"What is it?" she asked breathlessly.

He didn't say anything. He continued to hold her hand against his face, eyes closed, for what seemed like a small eternity. Andia was actually feeling lightheaded. But, suddenly, he lowered her hand and stepped away from her, heading for the solar door.

"Nothing," he said hoarsely. "Forgive me. I should not have done that, so please... forgive me. Forget it happened."

He had released her hand so swiftly that she'd nearly fallen over. She'd been anticipating what he would do next, so the sudden release was enough to throw her off balance. But that brief moment told her something—it told her that he felt the same attraction for her that she felt with him. They'd shared some pleasant moments of conversation, and in every one of them, she could feel a pull toward the man. A man who was essentially her jailor. But now, his actions told her that he'd been feeling the same pull toward a woman who was his prisoner.

Perhaps her dreams weren't so broken after all.

This one being most unexpected.

"Wait," she said, scurrying around him and blocking the door as he tried to exit. "You are not going anywhere. What were you going to ask me?"

He wouldn't look her in the eye. "My lady, please…"

"Andia," she said softly. "My name is Andia. My family calls me Andie, and I give you permission to use the name too. Call me whatever you wish, Torran. I will answer."

His eyes came up, and for a moment, they stared at one another. He started to say something, but she shook her head, not wanting to hear denials or lies from his mouth. Denials of what he was feeling, lies for why he'd put her hand against his face. She wanted truth and wasn't going to move away from the door unless he gave them to her.

The next thing she realized, his hands were on her face and his lips were slanted over hers.

It was a kiss of the greatest magnitude.

Andia had been kissed before, by the knights at Okehampton who wanted to court her. The older knight's kisses had been a little sloppy but always passionate, while the younger knight's kisses had been wildly inflaming. Truthfully, she'd only been kissed a handful of times, but she had never in her wildest dreams been kissed like this.

Scorching…

Powerful...

Lustful.

So much lust.

Andia's arms went around Torran's neck and she squeezed, holding the man so tightly that she was very nearly strangling him. He responded by wrapping those enormous arms around her, pulling her close as his lips feasted on hers. But that wasn't good enough for him. He had to taste her, so his tongue gently snaked inside her mouth, experiencing her honeyed orifice with the greatest of pleasure.

But it was more than that.

To Torran, there was much, much more.

There was the feel of her body against his, her soft and pliable body with those magnificent breasts against his chest. He remembered her naked body through the wet shift on the night her fever raged, the full breasts with nipples that had been shockingly taunting. He had to admit that he'd dreamed about those beautiful breasts, imagining his mouth upon them, his tongue on those nipples, savoring them like the finest fruits.

He was consumed.

Lifting Andia up, he carried her over to his father's table, sitting her down on the edge as his mouth ravaged her lips and face. She gasped in delight as he began to feast on her chin and neck, one big arm still around her as the other hand began to roam. She was wearing a garment that was laced up the front, a beautiful red surcoat, and his hand moved to those ties. He had to get to those breasts before they drove him out of his mind.

Andia was so overwhelmed with his kisses that she failed to realize when he'd loosened the ties. She only realized that when he began to pull the neckline of her shift off her shoulder, kissing every bit of flesh that it revealed, inch by inch. The left side was down to her elbow in a short amount of time, but Torran's mouth was everywhere—arm, shoulder, collarbone, cleavage, and then back to her neck. Andia had never been touched like this, not even by the knights at Okehampton, so this was all new territory for her, but she knew very quickly that she liked it. It was igniting a fire deep in her belly that made her entire body twitch. Her arms and legs tingled and the place between her legs, her woman's center, seemed to be twitching and tinging also. Then Torran loosened her surcoat enough to pull it, and the shift, off her left breast.

Andia was taken to a new level of passion when his mouth clamped down on a nipple.

She gasped loudly, shocked and overwhelmed as he suckled her fiercely. It was also the single most pleasurable thing she'd ever known. Her head tilted back and she found herself looking at the ceiling as her entire body went limp, surrendering to Torran's heated mouth. Even her arms went limp, and it was only by his great strength, supporting her as he devoured her breast, that she was even sitting upright. She'd turned to liquid fire long ago. Facing no resistance, Torran pulled down the shift on the right side. With both breasts exposed, he'd found his paradise.

Andia ended up lying back on the table, her chest naked, as Torran nursed on her, fondling both breasts with the greatest of pleasure. He was suckling her so hard, so forcefully, that the junction between her legs was twitching and contracting wildly. Something was happening down there, something she'd never experienced before, and it was only a few more minutes of Torran's attention before Andia experienced her first climax. She didn't even know what it was, but Torran did. When the throbbing started and she began to cry out in pleasure, he slanted his mouth over hers again to quiet her, toying with her nipples as the release washed over her, again and again.

It was a magical, and deeply intimate, moment between them.

And now, the situation had changed.

After that, his kisses became deep and passionate, and Andia's hands found their way into his hair, holding his mouth against hers. They couldn't seem to get enough of one another, and Andia's legs were instinctively parting for him, wrapping around his hips as he practically lay on top of her on his father's table. He moved away from her mouth, kissing a trail down to her breasts again, where he began to suckle her tenderly.

Until they heard the entry door to the manse slam back on its iron hinges.

"Torran?"

It was Stefan. Torran's head shot up and he practically yanked Andia off the table, quickly helping her pull up her shift. She was frantically trying to put herself together as Stefan called again and Torran knew he had to answer him. Silently, he gestured to a small alcove in the solar, one that contained his father's financial books and records, and she rushed into the alcove even as she was fixing her bodice and tightening up the lacings. When she was out of sight from anyone who might be standing in the solar doorway, Torran called to Stefan.

"In here," he said, moving for the door but immediately realizing he had a full-blown erection that he needed to deal with. He was wearing leather breeches and a tunic, which draped over it for the most part, but he adjusted himself quickly before opening the door. "Here, Stefan. What is it?"

Stefan was already at the door. "You'd better come," he said grimly. "A royal escort has been spotted down the road, coming this direction."

Torran's brow furrowed. "Royal es...?" He didn't even need to finish that statement. He already knew. "Henry is here."

Stefan nodded ominously.

Oh, God, Torran thought.

He braced himself.

CHAPTER NINE

ANDIA WAS IN a panic.

An hour since the king's arrival and she still hadn't seen Aeron, who had been outside the gates when Henry approached. Stefan had brought him inside the manse walls, but after that, no one seemed to know where he'd gone. At the moment, Torran and Stefan and a host of knights and advisors were down in the solar with Henry, but there was no sign of Aeron.

Andia was ready to burst.

Torran had told her to go to her chamber and lock the door, not to come out no matter what, so here she was, trying to look out every window in her chamber in the hope that she could see her brother down below in the ward.

But no Aeron.

And Henry was on their doorstep.

It was too bad, too. Andia would have loved nothing more than to have lingered on her encounter with Torran, to spend these moments reflecting on something that may never come again, but she couldn't. She was too terrified for her little brother to think of anything else, and that included herself, but after an hour of terror, her mind began to wander.

She couldn't help it.

It wandered to her time at Okehampton Castle when she'd let the captain of the army, an older knight who had been married before, kiss her chastely on the hand. He'd done that a couple of times until he graduated to kissing her on her cheek. Only once on the lips, and that had been a secretive and stolen kiss. The truth was that Andia wasn't like other young maidens. She wasn't shy and retiring, with a healthy fear of the male sex, and she had quickly discovered that she liked being kissed. That probably made her wicked, given that she had a propensity toward sins of the flesh, but she didn't much care. She liked being kissed and she liked what Torran had done to her earlier in the solar.

She liked it very much.

Settling down at the window seat and keeping an eye out for her brother in the bailey below, she couldn't help but think of Torran's touch. His kisses had been sweet but passionate, and his touch had left her boneless and weak with submission. She'd never thought much about her breasts one way or the other, but clearly, he had. She could still feel his mouth on her nipples, nursing on her like a starving child. She loved it when his big hands fondled her, squeezing and tugging at her.

And that was when the explosion had happened.

Whatever had occurred between her legs was something she'd never known before, but she certainly hoped she knew it again in the future. As many times as opportunity would allow. As she sat there and gazed out of the window, her hand moved to her breast and she slid it inside the shift, timidly touching a naked nipple. Instantly, her body seemed to jolt at the mere touch, and it was both exciting and naughty. She giggled, feeling positively wicked that she'd touched herself, but Torran had managed to make her feel as no one else ever had, and she was eager to relive his touch. That brief encounter with him had introduced her to another level of pleasure, and she was intrigued.

But darker thoughts plagued her as well.

The truth was that she didn't know him well. A sullen, quiet, dutiful knight who had come alive once he'd touched her. She could only hope he wasn't taking advantage of their situation, as her jailor and as a man who held power over her. Somehow, she didn't think so, but she had surrendered to him quite easily. Frankly, she didn't much care. He had made her happy, even for just a brief few moments, and she wasn't sorry in the least, but she would be sorry if that was the end of it now that Henry was here.

Her future was, once again, uncertain.

Torran had told her that she wasn't going to London, because a healthy hostage was better than a dead one, or words to that effect. But that had been before Henry arrived. She knew that Torran was dedicated to Henry, and if the king demanded that she and Aeron be sent to London, she was fairly certain Torran would have to obey. Not that she blamed him, because she understood that he served the king. He was obligated to obey the man's commands.

Therefore, she braced herself for the inevitable.

And she knew that, at some point, it would come.

⅓

"I RECEIVED A missive from Daniel de Lohr that told me everything you just told me, but I wanted to hear about the hostages from you. Is the lady still ill?"

Henry III of England had asked the question. The man had been king since nine years of age, so he'd ruled England almost all of his life. He was surprisingly unaffected as kings went, a man of compassion and kindness when the mood struck him, but he also had fierce bursts of temper. He was approaching an age that was termed "elderly" and didn't travel much these days, but a journey from Westminster to Lockwood wasn't really travel. It had taken all of two hours in good weather.

But he'd come for a reason.

That reason had just been brought up.

"The lady's fever has abated, your grace, but she is still weak," Torran said. "I am certain that Jareth told you this, but I truly thought that it was best, given her condition at the time, to stop at Lockwood and seek help for her condition."

"And you found a physic?"

"I did, your grace," Torran said, nodding. "The physic tended her quite ably and has only just allowed her to get out of bed and walk a little, just to help her regain her strength."

Henry listened intently. "Good," he said. "Do you think she will be able to make the journey to Westminster soon?"

Torran had expected that question. He knew that was why Henry had come. Jareth, Kent, Britt, Aidric, and Dirk had accompanied Henry from Westminster after informing him of the battle of Kennington, and they'd told the tale of a lovely young woman and her spoiled brother who were currently guests at Lockwood because of the lady's illness. That was all that Henry knew, and, being impatient, he'd had to come see for himself. But given what had happened with Andia in the solar not two hours earlier, Torran found himself in a bind. He didn't want her to go to Westminster but couldn't make it seem as if was for personal reasons.

This was a game he had to play very carefully.

There was too much at stake not to.

"I would say in a couple of days she should be well enough, your grace," he said after a moment. "My entire reason for stopping here so she could convalesce is because I am assuming you want a healthy hostage and not one on her deathbed. To bring her to Westminster in her condition would have been reckless."

Henry nodded. "I understand that and I appreciate your caution," he said. "In fact, I am grateful for it. It sounds as if you and the Six have been careful with the lady and her brother the entire time."

Torran nodded. "There was no reason to be anything less, your grace," he said. "I was told that she is your distant cousin and I will always, of course, be most respectful of anyone in your family."

Henry waved him off. "Pah," he said. "She is such a distant cousin that I forgot to tell you myself, but I am glad you were told. Who told you?"

"Riggs Penden, your grace."

Henry smiled. "Rochester?" he said. "I knew the man's father and grandfather. Good men, both of them. Did you stop at Rochester on your travels from Kennington?"

"For one night, your grace."

Henry continued to smile. "I hope Riggs is well, because I've not seen him in some time," he said. "But that is a conversation for another time. Let us focus on facts, and the fact remains that Anselm St. Albans betrayed me and now his children are my prisoners. There must be consequences for such a betrayal."

Torran struggled to remain neutral in the face of that declaration. "Seeing Kennington razed and Anselm St. Albans killed were indeed serious consequences, your grace," he said. "I will say that I have come to know the young boy a little, and the sister, and they do not have political inclinations. They do not seem particularly worldly, to be honest, so keep that in mind. I doubt either of them would be any threat. The boy is young and malleable, and the daughter is old enough to marry to a husband loyal to you."

"How old is she?"

"I would say at least eighteen or twenty years of age."

"Is she beautiful?"

"Quite."

That seemed to whet Henry's interest. "Is that so?" he said thoughtfully. "Mayhap a marriage would indeed be the solution. She can marry a man of my choosing, a loyal man, and I will breed the rebellion out of her bloodlines. Punishment enough for Anselm, wouldn't you say?"

Wars were won in such a way. To the victor went the spoils. Torran knew that all too well. He'd seen Henry operate in that manner for years. Although he was the one who had suggested a marriage for Andia, the truth was that he didn't like the idea of her marrying someone. Someone who could gaze at her beauty every day and touch that silken skin the way Torran had touched it. Someone who could treat her in a manner that his whims dictated, which could be good or it could be bad.

Nay… Torran didn't like that idea at all.

"Indeed, your grace," he said after a moment. "Punishment can come in many forms, including a marriage."

Henry was interrupted from replying as one of his courtiers handed him a cup of wine, which he took gratefully. After a long swallow, he smacked his lips and set the cup down.

"I should like to meet her," he said. "Do you think she is feeling well enough?"

Torran nodded. "I think so, your grace," he said. "Shall I fetch her?"

"Please."

Torran headed off without hesitation, which was his intention. He didn't want anyone, especially Henry and most especially his fellow Six, to see anything strange in his behavior when it came to Andia St. Albans. The truth was that he was trying to think of a way to keep her at Lockwood indefinitely, and he thought he had a good plan, but it would have to involve a bit of a deception. And only if she was willing, which he suspected she was. That was why he'd volunteered to fetch her.

He had to speak to her first.

"Bah!"

Torran was on the stairs, nearly to the top, when someone jumped out at him from the shadows. It was a small body, and it took him no time at all to realize that it was Aeron. He grabbed the boy before the child could knock him off balance and ended up throwing the lad over his shoulder as he took the last few stairs. Once he came to the landing, he put the child on his feet.

"What was that about?" he demanded.

He was holding Aeron by the arm, and the boy was quite unhappy. "I thought you were Henry," he said. "I was hiding. I was going to knock him down the stairs!"

Rolling his eyes in disbelief, Torran dragged the boy over to Andia's chamber door. He knocked, frowning at Aeron as the child tried to break his hold, but when the door opened, he practically tossed the boy inside.

"Why did you let him out of the chamber?" he asked Andia.

She looked between Torran and Aeron in confusion. "He was never *in* the chamber with me," she said. "You told me not to leave the chamber, so I have been in here, looking from the windows and searching for him. Why? What has he done?"

"He was hiding on the stairs, trying to kill the king," he said. Then he pointed a finger at the boy. "I was unable to prevent you from killing the knight at Kennington, but I will prevent you from killing Henry if I have to toss you in the vault and lose the key."

Andia had been relieved to see her brother, but only until Torran told her what Aeron had been up to. At that point, she rushed at Aeron, grabbed him by the arm, and began swatting his bottom angrily.

"What is the matter with you?" she said as Aeron yelped. "You are going to get us both killed, you foolish whelp!"

Torran put himself between the pair, pulling them apart as Aeron tried to punch and kick his sister now that he was free of her grasp. But Torran stopped the thrashing hands and feet in Andia's direction, pointing to the bench seat under the window, and Aeron took the hint. He marched over to the seat and climbed on it, hanging out of the window and looking at the bailey below. Torran and Andia watched him for a moment, and when they were convinced he wasn't going to jump out, they turned to one another.

"Henry is in the solar," Torran said, lowering his voice. "I've been sent to fetch you."

Andia visibly paled. "Why does he want to see me?"

"Simply to talk to you."

"Did you tell him I have been ill?"

"I did."

"I do not feel very well at the moment, Torran. I cannot meet him."

He could see that she was starting to panic, so he reached out and took her hands, pulling her over to the bed. Forcing her to sit, he continued to hold one of her hands as he took a knee in front of her.

"Listen to me," he said quietly. "You are going to meet him, but we must have a plan."

She was eyeing him warily. "What do you mean? What plan?"

Torran cocked his head. "I think you should remain here, at Lock-wood," he said. "I think it would be better for you and certainly better for that bully of a brother you have. It would be peaceful and safer than in London. Do you want to remain here?"

Her expression was becoming one of curiosity. "Rather than go to Westminster?" she said. "Of course I would rather stay here, but I cannot."

"Why not?"

She thought that was an odd question. "Because this is your family's home," she said as if the answer were obvious. "You took me from Kennington with the intention of taking me to the king, so why should I remain here? I am well enough to travel now. Or, at least, I will be."

"Then you *do* want to go to Westminster."

She shook her head. "Nay," she said. "I would rather go home. Sir Torran, why are you asking me these questions?"

He snorted softly, grinning. "When we are alone like this, please call me Torran," he said. "You need not be formal."

Andia was flattered by the request, thrilled even, but she still wasn't sure what he was driving at. "As you wish," she said. "But why are you asking me these questions?"

His smile faded. Then he shook his head and averted his gaze. "Because I am stupid," he said. "Stupid and reckless. I am taking a terrible chance."

"A terrible chance for what?"

He sighed heavily. "Because I do not think you should go to London," he said. "I think you should stay here."

Andia watched him, his body language, the tone of his voice, because she was trying to figure out what he wanted. "But... but Henry wants me as a hostage," she said. "You told me that yourself."

He sighed again, this time sharply. "I know what I told you," he said. "Andia, you must swear something to me."

"If you wish it, I will."

"Swear to me that what I say to you will never be repeated."

She nodded. "I would not repeat anything you tell me," she said. "But I do not understand..."

He put up a hand to silence her. "I am trying to tell you, but I am not doing a very good job," he said. "I want you to stay here, at Lockwood. I think it would be safer for you, and I... I would feel better if you did. I will not say more than that right now, but if you wish to remain here, then please tell me so. If not... if not, then I will take you to London on the morrow without further delay."

Andia studied him for a moment. "I would rather stay here, of course."

He seemed relieved. "Then you are going to have to tell Henry that you are still recovering from your illness," he said. "If Henry sees that your health has been restored, then there is nothing I can do. I must take you to Westminster as ordered. But if he thinks you are still ill… Do you understand?"

Andia nodded. "Aye," she said. "A deception?"

"A reprieve."

A smile spread across her lips. "I will agree under one condition."

"What?"

"That you tell me why you would feel better if I stayed."

He couldn't look at her. "I told you why," he said. "I feel it would be safer."

"Is that the only reason?"

"What other reason should there be?"

She raised an eyebrow. "Honestly, Torran," she scolded softly. "Are you going to make me pry it out of you? You kissed me quite passionately a short while ago and… and other things… but if you think to keep me here to toy with, I'll not stay. I'm not to be trifled with."

He bit off a smile, lifting his gaze to hers. "Nay," he said after a moment. "I do not believe you are. And you would be the last person I would toy with."

"Then tell me why you want me to stay."

"Because you need protecting, and I wish to protect you."

That wasn't the answer she had expected. "Protect me against Henry?" she said, suddenly serious. "Torran, you led the army that razed my family's home. You were commanded to bring my father to London to face the king, but in his absence, you took me and my brother. And now you want to *protect* me?"

He nodded weakly. "Aye, I do," he said. "Look me in the eye and tell me you do not hold to your father's politics and that you had nothing to do with de Montfort."

She waved him off irritably. "I care not for false kings, arrogant earls, or men who think they know better than anyone," she said. "All I know is that I want to live in a peaceful country. I want to play my music and sing for those who appreciate it. War… I do not understand it. I do not understand why men fight, and to be perfectly honest, the battle at Kennington frightened me to death. It was the worst thing I have ever experienced because I felt as if we were battling for our lives, every second. I've never had to do that before. And when your men finally broke into the inner ward…"

She stook her head, unable to continue, and averted her gaze. He gave her hand a gentle squeeze. "You thought you were going to die?"

She nodded, looking at him. "I heard what you said to Aeron," she said. "About the knight we killed with the iron pot. You knew it was us?"

Torran nodded faintly. "I knew," he said. "Aeron told me the night that the battle ended, when I spanked him. That was partially why I did it."

"His confession?"

"His *gleeful* confession."

She cocked her head curiously. "Did you know the knight?"

"He was a very good friend."

Andia sighed with deep regret. "Forgive me for taking part in his death," she murmured. "I am sorry to have taken your friend away, but as I said, I thought we were going to be killed. We thought we were protecting ourselves."

Torran didn't want to get back onto the subject of Yancey. It was something he'd been trying to forget. He remembered well his sense of vengeance to punish those responsible, but now that time had passed and he'd come to understand the circumstances, that vengeance inside of him was at rest. Looking at Andia, he knew she had taken no pleasure in it.

Perhaps that was what cooled his vengeance the most.

He couldn't fathom punishing her now.

"I know you were," he said after a moment, stroking his thumb across the hand he was still holding. "But it is over and done with, so let us not speak of it again. At the moment, there is Henry to deal with, so simply tell him that you are feeling ill. I can delay your journey to Westminster if you are convincing enough."

His gentle caresses weren't lost on Andia. "But what good will that do?" she said. "I must go at some point."

"Or Henry will realize he is satisfied with the destruction of Kennington and forget about you," Torran said. "He has been known to do that. Out of sight, out of mind, as it were."

Andia understood that, sort of, but her gaze moved to Aeron, who was still hanging his head from the window, watching the activity in the bailey. "But what about my brother?" she asked. "He is the Earl of Ashford. Henry isn't simply going to forget about him."

Torran shook his head. "Probably not," he said. "But for now, he is safe. I will ask that he remain here with you, but I also think he needs to be sent away to foster. He's old enough, Andia. He must learn to be a man."

Andia was aware of that fact. "My father had already made arrangements to send him to Okehampton," she said. "They are expecting him at some point."

But Torran shook his head again. "Henry will want him sent to a very loyal ally," he said. "De Courtenay has been known to weaken his support from time to time. My guess is that he will send Aeron to Canterbury or Norwich Castle with de Winter."

Andia watched Aeron ball his fist and shake it at someone down in the bailey. "I suppose it would be good for him," she said. "Father spoiled him so, as you can tell. He needs discipline badly."

"You don't say?" Torran quipped, watching her grin. Then he stood up and pulled Andia off the bed. "Do we have a plan, then? You know what to do?"

Andia nodded confidently. "I know what to do."

"Good," Torran said, bringing her hand up for a tender kiss. "Then do it. And let us hope that Henry complies."

The kiss sent bolts through her again, the same bolts his touch had caused earlier in the solar. It was difficult not to focus on them. But she knew she had work ahead of her, and she struggled to focus on that which she needed to accomplish. Releasing his hand, she went over to the satchel Lady Penden had given her to find the hairbrush. As she tidied herself up in the polished mirror that belonged to Torran's mother, Torran went over to the window and pulled Aeron inside. Andia could see him speaking to Aeron in the reflection of the mirror but couldn't hear what was being said. All she knew was that when Torran was finished speaking, Aeron plopped down on the window seat and simply sat there glumly.

He didn't move.

Torran headed back in her direction.

"Ready?" he asked.

Andia put the brush down and smoothed at her braid, straightening up her dress. "Aye," she said. "I am ready."

Torran took her by the arm and led her to the door. As they stepped through and he shut it behind them, she looked at him.

"What did you say to Aeron?" she said. "I was positive we were going to have a battle on our hands when we left to see Henry and he was not invited."

Torran grunted. "Simple," he said. "I told him that if he caused a fuss, I would spank him like I did before."

Andia giggled. "You have the power to soothe wild beasts, my lord."

Torran fought off a grin as they headed down the stairs. "The last thing I want is for Henry to talk to him," he said. "Aeron would try to kick him and the boy would end up in the vault, chained to the wall. I think that is something we would all like to avoid."

Andia couldn't disagree. "But Henry will want to meet him at some point, won't he?"

Torran nodded. "At some point," he said. "But not now. We still have time to condition Aeron to behave when it comes to Henry. We'll simply tell the king that Aeron has contracted your fever and it would be best not to expose anyone to it."

They were moving down the stairs at that point, and Andia grasped Torran's arm to steady herself. "You would lie to Henry?"

Torran shrugged. "We do not know for sure he has *not* contracted what you had," he said. "Mayhap it simply has not shown itself yet. It is enough of a reason to keep Aeron away from Henry… for now."

They reached the bottom of the steps and Andia could see the solar ahead. She wasn't hard pressed to admit that she was feeling her nerves.

"For now," she repeated softly. "Shall we go in?"

She dipped her head in the direction of the solar and he grasped her by the elbow. "Indeed, my lady," he said quietly. "The king awaits."

Andia swore that she had never heard more terrible words.

☙

HENRY HAD KICKED him out.

In fact, he'd kicked everyone out of the chamber when Andia arrived in her bright red surcoat. She'd looked like an angel, and when Henry saw how pretty she was, he ordered everyone to leave.

Now, people were lingering in the entry of Lockwood, including the Six. The courtiers, advisors, and servants mostly had taken to wandering around, looking in chambers, as Torran, Jareth, Dirk, Aidric, Kent, and Britt remained near the solar door should Henry have need of them.

Now it was a waiting game.

Torran thanked God that he'd had the chance to speak with Andia before she had an audience with Henry. He was confident she would play the part of a lady still recovering from her illness, but the truth was that he didn't know what she would do. He didn't really know her at all. He didn't know if everything he'd seen over the past week had been an act on her part, pretending to be a woman of honor when she was more like her father—dishonorable, disloyal. In a sense, this would be their first test of trust. If she passed it, then she would remain here. But for how long, and to what purpose, was still a mystery to him.

Maybe not so much a mystery as it was the fact that he didn't want to acknowledge his intentions.

Deep down, Torran knew he was no good for her.

"I heard the lady became quite ill after we left," Jareth said, breaking into his thoughts. "Stefan said she was down for a few days."

Torran rubbed his eyes wearily. "It was the right decision to keep her here at Lockwood," he said. "There is no knowing if she would have even survived the next two hours to London. She was quite ill."

Jareth leaned against the wall, next to Torran, as the others began to gather around them. Aidric, Dirk, Britt, and Kent, all of them collecting in a group for the conversation.

"I heard she was ill," Kent said. "She looks much better than she did the last time I saw her."

Torran nodded. "She is healing," he said. "But she's not completely well. She's still quite weak."

"And the brother?" Aidric asked. "Did he come down with it, too?"

Torran shook his head. "Nay, though I wish he had," he said. "That boy is a tyrant to say the least. A strong fever would do him good. It might tame that wild streak."

Aidric gave him a half-grin. "The spanking you gave him did not ease him?"

Torran shrugged. "It did," he said. "But Ashford spoiled that lad so badly that he thinks the entire world should submit to him. Worse still, it seems that he subscribes to the idea that his father could do no wrong, meaning he views Henry as the enemy. I am going to suggest to

Henry that he send the boy away to foster with either de Lohr or de Winter, someone who is loyal to the Crown. Whoever he fosters with is going to have a task ahead of him to change the child's way of thinking."

"Canterbury is still at Kennington," Jareth said. "At least, he was. He sent Henry a detailed missive with one of his knights, who gave Henry a full report of the battle, and Henry is giving Kennington to de Lohr. It will be his property."

Torran looked at Jareth in surprise. "What about the Ashford earldom?"

"He's stripping it from the family," Jareth said quietly. "The boy is no longer the Earl of Ashford and he has no property to speak of. That is Henry's decision."

Torran didn't appear overly concerned. "He is not the first earl to lose his lands, especially in this de Montfort mess," he said. "But Henry was allowing some warlords to keep their lands by paying enormous fines. Not Ashford?"

"Do they have anything to pay with?"

"I would not know."

Jareth shrugged. "In any case, Ashford's titles belong to Henry and the lands belong to de Lohr," he said. "I'm sure the boy will be trained as a knight, and if he is smart, he'll serve in Henry's ranks and show his loyalty. Henry might be persuaded to return his title and lands in that case."

Torran didn't have much to say to that. Given how spoiled and ill-mannered Aeron was, the loss of the title might teach him some humility.

"Well," he said, yawning to convey the fact that the subject bored him so no one would suspect the opposite. "I would say the situation is none of our affair. I am eager to return to my regular duties. What is the latest from London?"

Aidric spoke up. "Henry is convening a conclave of some of his most loyal followers," he said. "They should be gathering at Westminster in the next few days."

"Why?"

"It seems that Prince Edward is going on crusade," Aidric said with some irony. "He is expecting knights and armies and money from his father, who has none to give because of the wars with de Montfort."

Torran shook his head with disapproval. "Edward knows that," he muttered. "Henry's finances are not very strong. More than that, *Henry* is not very strong. Edward has been assuming much of his father's duties because of it. And now he wants to leave on crusade and return the burden of England's rule to his elderly father?"

"Henry isn't happy about it," Jareth said. "He is speaking of raising taxes, and you know that will go badly for him."

Torran understood the situation. "So he is convening his warlords and begging for money and men from them," he said with disgust. "He should not have to be doing that. It should be Edward's responsibility to raise the money."

"They will both be looking for revenue by any source," Jareth said. Ever the shrewd politician, he understood how these things worked. "In fact, it is possible that Henry sees Ashford's daughter as revenue. He could sell her to a rich lord. The highest bidder, mayhap. Enough to add to Edward's war chest."

Torran tried not to look too shocked by that suggestion. "I cannot imagine she'll bring a significant amount," he said. "She's a beauty, but she has no dowry. Her only source of income was killed several days ago."

"Then she'll be at the mercy of whomever Henry solicits for her hand," Jareth said. "Not an ideal future for a young woman, but in her situation, the best she can do. In any case, we have a conclave to prepare for. I hear the de Shera brothers have been invited."

Torran couldn't help his surprise then. "The Lords of Thunder?" he said. "God's Bones, is it possible?"

Jareth smirked. "Not only possible, but probable," he said. "Alas, the lads who sided with de Montfort, the lads with more noble and royal blood in them than almost anyone in England, have been invited, but I believe there is a self-serving motive for Henry."

Torran frowned. "Of course there is," he said wryly. "But what is it?"

Jareth tapped his head to indicate the smart move on Henry's part. "Gallus de Shera, Earl of Coventry, has married into the Welsh royal house," he said. "The man married the heiress to the Earldom of Anglesey and his young son is the hereditary king of Anglesey, through his mother's father. Henry needs allies like that."

"Then it is about money and control."

"When is it ever about anything else?"

That was the truth. Torran knew Gallus, Maximus, and Tiberius de Shera. Every fighting man in England did. They were honorable, honest, and powerful warlords in their own right, and they'd all married well over the years. Gallus and Tiberius in particular. But they'd sided with de Montfort in the conflict with Henry because they believed in some of the man's ideals of a government ruled by the people, for the people. However, with their connections, not the least of which was the House of de Lohr, Henry was willing to forgive them and bring them back into his fold. Torran had heard a couple of years ago that the price for that forgiveness was half of the de Shera wealth. Whatever the case, the coming conclave would be interesting with the de Shera brothers in attendance.

Torran was almost looking forward to it.

"Well," he finally said, "it seems there is a good deal to do in my future, and part of that means leaving Lockwood empty once again. Stefan can return to his father at Kennington. Where is Stefan, by the way? Has anyone seen him?"

Britt was the one to answer. "He's outside, Torran," he said with some hesitation. "He had a conversation with Henry when the king arrived and couldn't quite hear what was being asked of him, so Henry got angry and walked away."

Torran rolled his eyes, putting his head down and rubbing at his forehead as if to rub away the callousness of the king's behavior. "Why?" he demanded quietly. "Henry knows the man cannot hear well. Why become angry?"

"Because Stefan didn't hear him initially and Henry thought he was being ignored."

"Christ," Torran muttered. "That had better not get back to Daniel. He will not like that in the least."

"I was thinking," Aidric said. "Stefan's performance at Kennington was exceptional and he worked well with us in battle. I know that Stefan does not usually follow the pattern of those of us who serve Henry as his personal guard, but he is an astonishingly good knight. He is also a bit of a misfit, like the rest of us, so in that case, he is exactly what we are—he is different. He is a man with flaws. What if we were to invite him to be part of us?"

Everyone looked at him. "I would welcome him," Torran said. "But it is not up to us. Not only would Canterbury have to approve, but so would Henry."

"You would subject Stefan to Henry's behavior on a daily basis?" Jareth said, frowning. "That is a cruel thing to do, Aidric."

But Aidric shook his head. "Think on it," he said. "Stefan deserves a prestigious post but, because of his hearing, Daniel keeps him close. To invite Stefan to be part of the Six is a prestigious invitation, one that would flatter Daniel, and Henry would have a de Lohr as a personal guard. That would please him. Even if Stefan couldn't hear Henry's commands, we would be around him and be able to communicate with him. I think it's something to consider."

Torran pondered that for a moment. "As I said, I would welcome him," he said. "I think he would make an excellent addition to our group. But at this moment, I feel as if I should make sure he is not too terribly upset by a callous old man."

"I'll go with you," Aidric said.

Torran pushed himself off the wall, glancing at Jareth as he did so. "Send for me if Henry is finished with the lady before I return," he said. "And under no circumstances bring the boy to him before I've had a chance to speak with the lad. The child has a tongue that will get him into trouble if he is not careful."

Jareth smirked, conveying his thoughts on the mouthy young boy who was in more trouble than he knew. As Torran started to move toward the entry with Aidric in tow, the door to the solar flew open and Henry appeared.

"Quickly," he said, waving his hands at the solar frantically. "Help the lady. She has fainted."

Torran rushed into the solar to find Andia lying on the floor, out cold. He dropped to his knees beside her, running his hands gently on the back of her head to see if she'd hurt herself when she fell.

"What happened, your grace?" he asked.

Henry was still at the door, unwilling to enter in case the lady's terrible fever had not entirely abated. He didn't want to catch it.

"I do not know," he said. "We were speaking of her accompanying me to London and, suddenly, she fainted. Do something!"

Torran leaned over Andia, lifting up an eyelid only to see her squint at him. He released the lid quickly and she opened the eye again, looking at him, before closing it.

That told him all he needed to know.

Carefully, he picked the faking fainter off the floor and turned to the king. "I told you she was weak, your grace," he said. "Mayhap the discussion was too much for her."

Henry was looking at her fearfully as Torran carried her out of the chamber. "Then put her to bed and do not let her get out until she is well," he called after the man. "I do not want her, or her brother, in London until she is completely well because if this fever is contagious, he might have it as well. I do not need either of them starting an epidemic in London. Do you hear me?"

Torran was nearly to the stairs. "Aye, your grace."

"We are leaving for London within the hour, Torran, and you are going with me."

"With pleasure, your grace."

Torran carried Andia up the stairs, trying not to hit her head on the walls as he went. In fact, he wasn't even upset that he'd be leaving Lockwood before the day was out. He had what he wanted. Andia and her brother were remaining.

He considered Henry's visit a victory.

But what he didn't realize was that the truly difficult days were yet to come.

CHAPTER TEN

Westminster Palace
London
The Painted Chamber

I T SOUNDED LIKE a shouting match.

Not that these gatherings didn't *usually* sound like a shouting match, but this one was different. It was a gathering of men loyal to Henry, but men who also had known Anselm St. Albans. It was a conclave of some of the most powerful warlords in England and did, in fact, include men who had fought for Simon De Montfort. These were men who had paid their fines and had their lands returned to them, but the stipulation with their forgiveness was their staunch and undying loyalty to Henry.

One wrong move and they would find themselves much as Anselm had.

The gathering had been going on for two days. The first day had been about Edward's crusade and the fact that the man needed money and men for his cause. Edward himself, who was quite a persuasive speaker, had taken charge of the first day and implored his father's vassals to do their duty and contribute to his quest. Henry had been at the meeting, but he had been seated silently on a comfortable chair while his son badgered his warlords. It had been an exhausting day, one that it had ended very late. As a reward, and perhaps even as entice-ment, there had been a lavish feast late into the night and early morning hours to pacify the weary.

Now, the second day was in full swing and it was already well into the afternoon. It seemed that Edward mostly got what he wanted, commitments for donations for his crusade, and now they were on to other business that pertained to the kingdom. One of those issues was some trouble in Ireland, but then someone brought up the destruction of Kennington Castle and that seemed to be all anyone wanted to talk about.

The Earl of Canterbury had been summoned from his reconstruc-tion of Kennington to talk about the siege and the death of the Earl of Ashford. Some of the warlords hadn't heard about Ashford's death, so an entire hour was taken up with men disappointed over the death and grieving the loss of a man who had been a friend of many.

During this meeting, the Six were patrolling the painted hall be-cause Henry was there. It was business as usual. Whenever there were meetings like this, two of them stuck by the king's side while the other four prowled the room, looking for any threats. Not that they really expected them in a crowd like this, but stranger things had been known to happen. Vigilance was always the order of the day when it came to the protection of Henry.

Torran was one of those guarding the king, along with Kent, while the others moved around the room discreetly. That meant Torran was at the forefront when they began to discuss Kennington and the fall of Ashford. Edward was out of the conversation at this point since he had nothing to do with it, so Henry was forced to get involved. It had been at Henry's order that the castle was sacked, and he found himself having to justify his actions to a room full of warlords who thought, after three years, Henry's punishment of those who had supported De Montfort might have been over.

As they discovered, that wasn't the case.

Henry was still bitter.

The men in attendance were some of the finest in England—along with the Earl of Canterbury, Daniel de Lohr, Davyss de Winter was also present. All three de Shera men were present, though far away from Henry, and mostly standing with Daniel, who was their mother's nephew. There were a few other de Lohrs about, Daniel's eldest son, Chad, included. The Earl of Selbourne, Becket de Nerra, was in attendance, along with Sir George Edlington, Lord of Corfe Castle.

The list went on, but these were some of the more important men in the hall, men, as Henry was aware, who were devoted to one another probably more than they were devoted to Henry. Some of them, anyway. They'd fought with Henry and some had even died for Henry, and for the sake of keeping their lands and titles, they were loyal to the king. But even Henry knew not to make a misstep with this group. He wanted their fealty, not their animosity. Therefore, when the subject of Ashford came up, he was prepared to defend his decision.

"Before this turns into a debate, I will tell you now that what happened to Anselm St. Albans was inevitable," Henry said firmly. "He was given ample opportunity to make amends to me after Evesham, yet he chose not to. He chose to continue this path of destruction, and in the end, he was killed by his own ambition."

George Edlington, an old vassal of Henry's, spoke first. "I cannot speak for everyone in the chamber, but I will say that I believe fair justice was dispensed upon Ashford," he said. "If a man chooses to defy his king, what else can he expect?"

"Understanding," Daniel said, watching most of the faces in the hall turn to him. "He can expect understanding, acceptance, and forgiveness."

Edlington frowned. "Henry is not the pope," he said. "Forgiveness is not his responsibility."

"I disagree."

"If he forgives every warlord who has turned against him, how effective will he be at ruling a country?" Edlington's voice was raised. "He would have chaos. Anarchy and chaos. Nay, my lord, the king's justice must be swift. It must be decisive."

Daniel wasn't thrilled with Edlington's contradiction. He knew the man and had for years. Edlington was an excellent administrator and very proud to serve Henry, belligerently so. However, he was not a warlord, but a garrison commander. He didn't have as much to lose as some of them should he fall out of favor.

He could afford to run his mouth off a little.

"Justice *was* dispensed," Daniel said evenly. "Ashford is dead and his castle has been sacked. Ashford's children are hostages of Henry. What more justice do you think there should be, Edlington? The man's legacy has ended."

There was some sarcasm there, and Edlington's hackles went up. "If there are children, there is still a legacy," he said. "The children should be made examples of."

Men began to speak up loudly, disagreeing with the idea that children should be put in peril. They'd begun arguing about it when a deep, loud voice lifted above the rest.

"A king who makes examples of children is a king who will sorely test the approval of his warlords." Maximus de Shera, the big and rough middle brother, spoke up. "For a man to make an example of a child shows weakness of character, for a child cannot defend himself."

Those were provocative words, aimed at the king but said in a way that made it seem like a blanket statement. Daniel, who had been standing with his cousin, put his hand on Maximus's shoulder.

"I will agree that any man who puts a child in danger is a man without honor," he said pointedly to anyone who would challenge Maximus. "The children should be left alone. They should not pay for the sins of their father."

Edward wasn't happy with what he considered a slight against his father. Henry was a veteran of battle, but Edward was the warrior in the family far more than his father. He was also tall and imposing, and he focused on Maximus, who was himself quite tall and quite muscular. All of the de Shera brothers were. Born and bred for war, they were beyond compare.

But Edward didn't fear them.

"I would be careful when accusing men of weakness of character for utilizing a necessary tactic," he said. "Men who have opposed the king in the past can be considered men without character. You cast stones, Maximus de Shera, when you should not."

Maximus wasn't one to take insults from any man. His elder brother, Gallus, was the statesman, while younger brother, Tiberius, was simply a likable man. He wanted everyone to get along. But Maximus called a situation as he saw it.

And he didn't like what he saw.

Or heard.

"True, your grace," Maximus said. "But, then again, I never opposed my father, so mayhap you should consider *your* past actions as a poor son when casting stones as well."

That was a direct insult at Edward, who had sided against his father more than once in his lifetime. Furious, Edward moved toward Maximus, and both Gallus and Tiberius had to pull their brother away from the charging prince as Daniel and even Davyss de Winter, who had been over by Torran, jumped into what could be a nasty confrontation. Henry was on his feet, shouting at his son to back away from Maximus. The truth was that Maximus was a knight's knight and had fists the size of ham hocks. He could take a man down in one blow, and Henry didn't want to see Edward, as skilled as he was, flattened.

He also didn't want to see Maximus fall victim to Edward's sword.

When the groups were separated and Maximus was far away from Edward, who had been pushed back by Davyss and Becket de Nerra, Henry stood in the middle of the hall and looked at the two sides.

"It seems that we have some dispute on how hostages are to be treated," he said. "The truth is that families are often punished for the sins of their fathers. We are all aware of that. Anselm St. Albans provided a good deal of money and support to my enemy, an enemy I finally defeated, and the sting of Anselm's betrayal has not left me. But whether I do anything with his children is my decision alone. I will not discuss it at this conclave."

"Your grace, if I may speak," Davyss said as he dared to leave Edward's side. "I do not think anyone is here to challenge your decisions, but I believe you understand that Anselm St. Albans was a friend to many in this room. I know that Daniel had a close friendship with him for years, so by nature, these men are concerned for his children. I think that is a natural reaction."

The king looked at Davyss, head of the de Winter war machine. Henry could hardly have won the battles against Simon de Montfort that he had without Davyss and his sword. *Lespada*, it was called, the sword held by every de Winter firstborn male for nearly two hundred years. *Lespada* was a legend in and of itself. But Henry also knew that Davyss hated politics, even though both of his parents, most especially his mother, had been adept political figures. Davyss was simply a knight, a fighting man, and that was all he really wanted to be. Henry was fairly certain he hated being in this room at this moment, so for him to speak on the Ashford children meant he felt strongly about the subject.

Henry took that into consideration.

"I am aware, Davyss," he said. "And if it will reassure anyone, I do not intend to harm the children. But something will be done with them, and I will make that decision alone."

Davyss knew that was probably the best answer they were going to get, and he glanced at Daniel, who simply nodded once. They both knew that Henry wasn't apt to say more than that, so it was the end of the subject. As Davyss headed over to Maximus to make sure the man was calm, as Davyss had been the best friend to the de Shera brothers for years, another warlord entered the hall.

Roi de Lohr, Earl of Cheltenham and Henry's chief justiciar, had made an appearance, followed by his two eldest sons, Rex and Beau. Roi came up behind Daniel, his cousin, and affectionately patted the man on the arm as both Rex and Beau hugged him. Roi was the third son of the great Christopher de Lohr, the man who had helped shape England as a nation. Having served three kings, he was a legend. Roi, as the man who oversaw the laws of the land, wielded a tremendous amount of power, and Henry relied on him a good deal. When Henry saw his favorite advisor, he waved him over.

"Roi," he said, sounding relieved that a man who would defend him had just entered the hall. "It has been weeks since I last saw you. And I see you brought your older sons with you, hopefully to leave them to me? I need a de Lohr sword at my disposal, you know. My father and grandfather and uncle all had de Lohrs at their disposal."

Roi, a handsome man in his sixty-sixth year, smiled faintly as he glanced over his shoulder at his sons, who were still working their way through the crowd.

"Rex will be ready soon, your grace," he said. "He just turned twenty years and two and already he reminds me a good deal of my father."

Henry pointed to the pair. "But what of Beau?" he asked. "He's of age."

"He has just seen twenty years, your grace. He has more growing to do."

Henry frowned. "Growing?" he said in disbelief. "He is already the biggest man in the room. He is to grow more?"

Roi chuckled softly. "I meant mature," he said. "He is hotheaded like my Uncle David, Daniel's father, and he needs to learn how to control his temper of we shall have a monster on our hands."

"Time and experience will teach him that."

"I hope so," Roi said, but his attention kept moving to Torran, standing several feet behind Henry. "If I may greet a few familiar faces, your grace?"

Henry waved him on. "Go," he said. "I must speak with my son as it is. Speaking of hotheads, he and Maximus almost came to blows."

"Oh?" Roi said with interest, looking between Maximus and Edward on the far ends of the hall. "I would have liked to have wagered on that fight."

Henry looked at him, a twinkle of mirth in his eyes. "And who would you have wagered on?"

"Edward, of course."

"Liar."

Henry walked away as Roi snorted, his smile fading as he discreetly caught Rex's attention. Motioning his son with him, he headed straight Torran, who dipped his head respectfully when Roi came near.

"Lord Cheltenham," Torran greeted him. "I am glad you have arrived. Mayhap you can mediate the arguing that has been going on."

Roi cocked an eyebrow. "Mayhap later," he said. "I must speak with you. Now."

"Or course, my lord," Torran said. "Alone?"

"Bring Jareth and Kent."

Torran nodded, immediately catching Jareth's attention and then pointing to Kent. Jareth took the hint and gathered Kent, and the three of them followed Roi and Rex into a small, enclosed entryway with a door that lead to another chamber.

Roi came to a halt and faced the men.

"As you are aware, my eldest brother and his sons are in charge of the Executioner Knights," he said in a quiet voice. "I've come with news from the world of spies of something pertaining to Henry."

The Executioner Knights were a longstanding guild of the most elite knights in England, all of them spies, assassins, and warriors who helped keep England solvent and safe. The guild had been formed by William Marshal, Earl of Pembroke, about sixty years earlier, and the de Lohrs had taken on the mantle to continue the work. It was a secret organization, only known to those who also operated in the shadows, as the Guard of Six sometimes did. Torran had to admit that the expression on Roi's face had him concerned.

"We are listening, my lord," he said. "What is amiss?"

Roi looked at Rex, who often acted as an agent for the Executioner Knights. Tall and blond, like most of the de Lohr men, Rex had his father's build and his mother's good looks. He was one of the more sought-after marriage prospects in England, given his father's wealth and connections, but he was quite pragmatic and wise beyond his years. Marriage wasn't of interest to him, or so Torran had heard.

Rex had great things to accomplish first.

"My connections over at The Pox tell me that a Frenchman was in there the other day seeking an assassin," Rex said. "He was discreet about it, of course, but one of our agents engaged him, pretending to be a man for hire. They spent the afternoon drinking and talking, enough to loosen the Frenchman's tongue. Evidently, he is seeking to get close to Henry."

The Pox was the most notorious tavern in London. Every criminal from the western shores of Ireland to the wilds of Rome and beyond had been there at one time or another, but great knights and warlords also populated the place because it had the finest food in London. It was a paradox of an establishment, but if one wanted to know anything about the seedy underbelly of the criminal world, The Pox was the place to be. Therefore, Torran wasn't surprised to hear the latest news.

If it was dark, dirty, or deadly, it could be found at The Pox.

"Who is this man?" he said. "Did he identify himself?"

Rex shook his head. "That is the one thing the agent could not get out of him," he said. "No one knows who he was, although he did mention a companion or fellow conspirator in Lord Dudwell. It was a brief mention, and he would not repeat it, but the agent was sure of the name."

"Dudwell?" Torran repeated, trying to place the man. "I do not recognize the name. Who is that?"

"Etchingham Castle," Roi said. "Donnel de Meudon."

Torran shook his head. "I do not know him," he said. "Who is he to Henry?"

Roi shook his head. "No one," he said. "At least, not that we know of. The man isn't political and has never given Henry any trouble, so the fact that he was mentioned by a man seeking an assassin to kill the king is puzzling."

Puzzling, indeed. Torran frowned in confusion. "Does he have any family connections?" he asked. "Is he related to anyone close to Henry?"

Roi didn't have an answer for him. "I do not know," he said. "We are trying to find out, but until we can, you must be on your guard if Lord Dudwell makes an unexpected appearance or otherwise tries to engage with Henry. Be cautious."

Torran nodded. "Understood," he said. "What happened with the Frenchman? Was he able to hire an assassin?"

Roi waggled his eyebrows. "He hired our agent," he said. "I think we've managed to curb the plot for now, but you must be vigilant. We are not sure if the Frenchmen was only one man in a larger scheme."

"Where *is* the Frenchman?" Jareth asked. "Is he being watched?"

Roi nodded. "He is," he said. "Our agent has made himself a friend of the Frenchman, whether the man wants him or not. He will not let him out of his sight."

Jareth nodded, but Torran wasn't so satisfied. "Then we must be on heightened alert," he said. "Do we tell Henry?"

"I would not," Roi said. "This may come to nothing, so I would not concern the man until, or unless, we have more information."

Torran nodded in agreement. "Then we shall be alert," he said. "Thank you for the information, my lord. If there is anything else, send word to me as quickly as possible."

"I will," Roi said. Then he turned for the hall again. "We'd better break up our gathering before Henry gets suspicious," he said. "I think I shall see to Maximus. We do not want the man driving his fist into Edward's face."

Torran fought off a grin as they began to head back toward the gathering. "You heard, did you?"

"Henry told me. I told him I would have wagered on such a fight."

"It would have been an explosive one, to be sure."

Roi chuckled as he and Rex headed over to where Maximus was standing with the de Lohr men gathering around him. Torran watched him go, coming to a halt as Jareth and Kent stopped beside him.

"A potential assassination attempt is not something I am looking forward to," he told them. "But thank God de Lohr has his eyes and ears in London. At least we will be prepared."

"As prepared as we can be, anyway," Jareth said. "Do we go to heightened protocol?"

Torran nodded. "Aye," he said. "There will always be one of us by Henry's side, no matter where he is. In bed, in the bath, on his daily walk… I do not care where he goes, but one of us will always go with him. You had better tell Aidric and Britt and Dirk."

Jareth nodded, heading off to find the other three members of their group, leaving Torran and Kent watching the room.

"What are you thinking, Torran?" Kent asked quietly. "You look like a man with much on his mind."

Torran glanced at him. "Not really," he said. "Just the usual. But I would like to return to Lockwood to see how Stefan is faring with the Ashford siblings."

"Why?"

"Because the lady was still unwell when we left her four days ago," he said. "Henry wants her in London when she is recovered, so I suppose I should assess her health."

"Stefan can do that."

"It is not Stefan's responsibility to do that," Torran said, looking at him in full. "Besides, it was suggested bringing Stefan into the Six, and we did not have the opportunity to ask him. This will give me a chance."

Kent understood. "When will you leave?"

"Not tonight," Torran said, turning his attention back to Henry. "Let this meeting be settled and let us get through the night, and I will probably go on the morrow. You can assume command until I return."

"As you wish."

There was no more fighting after that, at least none that Torran witnessed, but Gallus and Tiberius took Maximus away from Westminster and away from Edward. It was probably for the best, because Maximus wasn't one to cool down easily. The assembly went on into the evening, when more food and music awaited the warlords who were growing weary of days of turbulent meetings and a prince who only wanted to talk to them for the money they could provide.

Edward was starting to wear out his welcome.

Usually, gatherings like this didn't bore or bother Torran, but in this case, he found himself subjected to both reactions because there was something alluring at Lockwood that had his attention. All he could think of was Andia, so it was a struggle to keep his mind on his work.

A struggle he'd never had to deal with.

Mercifully, toward the early morning hours, Henry retired and Daniel and Roi departed. They cleared out, leaving the younger men to drink and converse. With Henry in his chamber, Torran and the Six were officially off duty, so they headed to bed. However, Torran had just entered his small, dark apartment when one of Henry's servants summoned him. Thinking he was going back on duty, Torran found himself in Henry's private audience chamber, a small room that was part of the king's bedchamber suite, and prepared himself for whatever Henry wanted of him.

The chamber was dimly lit by tapers, flickering phantoms on the walls. Henry was seated in a chair with many cushions as Roi sat across from him, on a carved oak bench, and Daniel seemed to be busying himself with some wine. It seemed that neither Roi nor Daniel had left Westminster, but ended up in Henry's chambers instead. Torran stood by the door, more than curious as to why he'd been summoned. When Henry caught sight of him, he waved him over.

"I am sorry if we took you from your bed, Torran," Henry said. "But we have been discussing Ashford's children since earlier today, and I would like to speak to you about them without an entire room full of men interjecting their opinions. Since you have been involved with both Lady Andia and her brother from the start, you should be part of this conversation. Will you sit?"

It was a most unexpected topic, and Torran found himself on edge as he lowered himself into the nearest chair. Daniel passed by him with two cups of wine in his hand, extending one to Torran, who thought perhaps it was an omen. Perhaps he was going to *need* the wine and Daniel was simply giving him a head start on it. He took it, but he didn't drink.

He wanted his wits about him.

"How may I be of service, your grace?" he asked.

Henry rubbed his eyes wearily. "You led my armies at Kennington," he said. "You and Canterbury and de Winter. I am told you performed remarkably well."

Torran looked at Daniel, seated near Roi, to see the man's reaction to that statement, but Daniel merely smiled.

"Thank you, your grace," Torran said after a moment. "I did my best."

"You helped sack a castle with a minimum of casualties. You are to be commended."

"Thank you, your grace."

Silence fell as Henry sat back in his chair and propped his feet up. "How long have you served me now, Torran?" he asked. "At least ten or twelve years, is it?"

"Twelve, your grace."

Henry smiled wryly, wagging a finger at Torran. "When your father first asked if I would accept your fealty and told me why, you know I had some misgivings," he said. "After all, you had been caught in a bit of a scandal. You were a priest, caught seducing the Earl of Norbury's wife, and the only way Norbury would not kill you was if you came into my service, far from Norbury and far from his wife. Your father was at his wits' end with you, Torran. I felt, in the beginning, that he was making you my burden."

Torran didn't like to reminded of what happened those years ago. He didn't like it spoken of in front of men he admired like Roi and Daniel. But he'd learned years ago, when he became part of the Guard of Six, to speak his mind to Henry because the king liked to know his opinion. The whole business about the seduction and being thrown out of the priesthood was old news. Ancient news.

Torran didn't want to hear it.

"Your grace, I have explained that Lady Norbury seduced *me*," he said. "I did not seduce her. She was a patroness of Worth Abbey and she'd spent a year trying to gain my attention, but when all else failed, she summoned me to her home under a false pretense and tried to seduce me. Lord Norbury discovered us and branded me the villain."

"I know," Henry said quickly. "I was simply thinking about how you came into my service. Norbury swears you tried to seduce his wife, but I have met Lady Norbury and have heard salacious things about her. I could well see that what I'd heard about her was true. There is evidently not a soldier or a knight in Norbury's ranks that she has not lured into her bed."

Torran knew that. "Yet I received the worst of it," he said quietly. "My own father did not believe me."

Henry grew oddly serious. "He does not know you," he said. "He may be your father, but Luc de Serreaux does not know you. If he did, he would not have believed Norbury. I wonder if he does, still."

Torran shrugged. "I do not know, your grace," he said. "To be honest, my father and I have very little contact. He dotes on my younger brother and, I am certain, wishes Rhys was his heir while he pretends I do not exist."

Henry glanced at Roi, at Daniel, before continuing. "Do you know why?"

"Because he is ashamed of me, of course."

"Nay," Henry said. "I've heard… differently."

That was an unexpected comment. Torran's brow furrowed. "What have you heard, your grace?"

Henry sighed as if he were hesitant to continue, looking at Roi for assistance. Roi took the hint.

"Torran, his grace is not trying to embarrass you," he said. "I want to be clear. But my father, and Daniel's father, had been involved in politics for a very long time. Decades of knowing even the slightest details of allies and enemies alike. The upper class of England is awash with rumors and innuendos."

Torran was listening. "What does that have to do with me?"

"There is a point to this, I promise," Roi said. "There was a longstanding rumor, many years ago, that you were your father's bastard. The result of an illicit love affair. That is probably why your father was so ashamed with the scandal with Lady Norbury. Your father had tried to bury his own scandal many years ago and he probably feared it would rise again with you. In any case, if you've not heard that about your birth, I am sorry to be the one to tell you."

For a moment, Torran stared at Roi. He'd never been particularly close to his mother, either, and in fact felt as if she'd always been relatively uninterested in him. If what Roi said was true, then her behavior all of these years made some sense.

He was shocked.

"Strange that in a country full of men who are fond of gossip that I have never heard that," he muttered.

"Not once?"

"Never."

"That is surprising, considering."

"Was this rumor ever confirmed?"

Roi shook his head. "Nay," he said. "Your mother always swore you were her son, but the sequence of your parents' marriage and your birth was rumored to have been altered by your grandfather. You do not remember, but some say that you did not come to live at Bexhill until you were about a year old. Your parents were married for far less than a year and, suddenly, there was a baby. *You.* Mayhap you will never know the truth, but in any case, what happened to you was unfair. Greatly unfair."

"Exactly," Henry said. "Torran, you have been a loyal knight and the scandals from the past will remain in the past. You have more than proven your dedication and character to me, over and over again. The latest example is with Kennington and Ashford's children. You carried out your orders flawlessly, and when it came to the health and safety of the children, your decisions were sound. That is what I wish to speak to you about."

Torran was still reeling from the revelation of his past and it was a struggle to move with the change in subject. "Your grace?"

Henry sat forward, reaching across a small table for the wine that sat in front of Roi. He took it from the man before answering.

"You have been loyal to me from the beginning in spite of the circumstances of your coming into my service and I expect you will be loyal to me until the end," he said. "I have been discussing the situation about Anselm's children with Roi and Daniel. When I first discovered that Anselm had perished in battle and that his young son was the new Earl of Ashford, I immediately stripped the boy of his titles and lands. I was going to give everything over to Daniel, including the guardianship of the children, but I believe we've come up with another solution. It was Daniel's suggestion, actually."

Torran looked at Daniel, who simply nodded but did not speak because that was Henry's privilege. Torran had to admit that he was growing more puzzled, and probably more concerned, by the moment.

"And how may I be of service, your grace?" he said, realizing he was afraid to even ask.

But Henry took a drink of wine before replying, perhaps drawing out the anticipation. "First, I must ask you a question."

"Of course."

"Do you have any intention of returning to the priesthood?"

Torran shook his head without hesitation. "Nay, your grace," he said. "I once thought my path was service to God, but I believe that God does not want me to be a priest. He has other plans for me and I believe those plans are what I am doing now. He needs me here, with you."

"To do as I bid?"

"Absolutely, your grace. And to protect you."

"Good," Henry said. "Then hear me well—I am granting you the title of Earl of Ashford, Torran. It is my privilege to do with the title as I wish and I am granting it to you. I am also giving you Lady Andia, Anselm's daughter, in marriage. She needs a husband, a husband loyal to me, and you are the perfect candidate. As for the boy, I will send him to Canterbury to foster and Daniel can beat the ideals of the father out of the son, but you will be the boy's guardian until he comes of age. Do you understand me so far?"

Torran was sitting like a stone, his focus on Henry in completely astonishment. "You… you want me to assume Ashford, your grace?" he managed to say. "And marry…?"

Henry nodded. "I know this is a great deal to accept, and I further know that you will inherit the earldom of Bexhill when your father dies, but Ashford is an important title with important lands," he said. "Roi and Daniel and I agree. You are the perfect political marriage for Ashford's daughter, to bring back the reputation of an old earldom that has greatly suffered thanks to Anselm. I could not place it in better hands."

Torran was so astonished that he sat back in his chair, his hand going to his face. It took him a few moments to realize that his mouth was hanging open, so he quickly closed it, lowering his hand and looking to Daniel and Roi.

"*Me?*" he said. It was all he could manage at the moment. "The Earl of Ashford?"

Daniel grinned. "We will be close allies, you and I," he said. "Our properties are not so terribly far from one another. And I have men rebuilding Kennington as we speak. That is why I remained behind even after you departed for London. Your castle is being repaired."

Torran had no idea what to say. Astonishment didn't cover what he was feeling. But before he could reply, Henry spoke up.

"Of course, you do not have to accept this honor," the king said before finishing off the wine in his cup. "You can refuse. You would still remain with me, with the Guard of Six, and nothing more will be said. But I hope you will consider it."

Torran found his tongue. "I do not have to consider it, your grace," he said. "I accept with all my heart. To have something granted to me as a reward for service means far more to me than inheriting Bexhill. But I shall serve both earldoms flawlessly, and my sword, and my life, will always be yours. My gratitude could not be deeper."

Daniel banged his hand softly on the table, a gesture that was in support and in agreement with Torran's declaration, as Henry smiled with satisfaction.

"And that is why Ashford must belong to you, Torran," he said. "I must have a loyal lord there. You will marry Anselm's daughter and breed the rebellion out of her. All of her sons, all of Anselm's grandsons, will be loyal to me. *That* is how I wipe the memory of de Montfort from this land. As if he, and his loyalists, had never existed."

Torran couldn't argue with him. To the victor went the spoils, and in this case, Henry was the victor. But so was Torran.

He could still hardly believe it.

"I will do my best, your grace," he said. "I will raise my sons to be loyal to the Crown, I swear it."

"I know you will," Henry said. "And with that, I am certain you would like to return to Lockwood and tell Lady Andia of her fate? She's a lovely woman, Torran. Congratulations on your beautiful wife. I hope your marriage is a pleasant one."

Torran tried not to grin but couldn't help it. What was it Andia had said once? She'd lamented that she had a dream that would never come to fruition now that her father had been defeated, and Torran told her not to give up on it just yet. Even so, he could have hardly imagined that he had been right.

As it turned out, he seemed to have a dream also.

Andia.

"Thank you, your grace," he said after a moment, raking a nervous hand through his hair. "I must say that I'm rather overwhelmed with all of this, but I will return to Lockwood as soon as possible and inform the lady of our betrothal."

"Go tomorrow," Henry said. "I can spare you."

Torran nodded, but now that his shock had worn off, his mind was racing with what was to come. "What is your pleasure for the wedding?" he said. "Shall we marry as soon as possible or would you prefer a festive occasion?"

Henry waved him off. "Marry her immediately," he said. "The sooner you beget her with child, the sooner Anselm's legacy fades."

Torran understood, but to be honest, he was finding the king's reference to breeding rebellion out of Andia a little off-putting. Andia wasn't like her father, but Henry didn't know that. She was a gentle woman, to be treated gently and sweetly. She wasn't the rebel her father was.

But he knew someone who was.

"And the boy, your grace?" he said. "I will admit that Aeron has been… difficult. Too much of his father in him. Should I send him directly to Canterbury?"

Daniel answered. "Send Stefan back to Canterbury with him," he said. "He is at Lockwood still, is he not?"

Torran nodded. "He is, my lord," he said. "He has been guarding the lady and her brother in my absence. And that brings me to another point, if I may, my lord. It is about Stefan."

"What about him?" Daniel asked.

Torran looked between Henry and Daniel as he spoke. "Forgive me for changing the subject, but this seems like the time to do it," he said. "It was brought to my attention recently that Stefan is a stellar knight, honorable and brave and skilled. It was suggested that he would make a fine addition to the Guard of Six if neither you nor his grace have any objections. Henry would have a de Lohr by his side and Stefan could enjoy the prestige of a royal position that he is quite worthy of. May I ask that you at least think about it?"

Daniel was clearly surprised, but Henry was the first to speak. "Stefan is a de Lohr and a knight beyond compare," he said. "I heard he did very well in battle at Kennington. But the truth is that the man cannot hear very well and his own father says he will be completely deaf someday. Is it entirely wise to have a knight like that in my personal guard?"

Daniel sighed heavily, hating to hear that kind of talk about his son, as Torran answered. "Stefan is very good at watching a man's body language and he is a master at hand signals, your grace," he said. "Moreover, you will find no finer sword in all of England. He is a de Lohr, after all. If the man cannot hear, then there are six fellow knights who will make sure he knows what needs to be done. I believe he deserves this opportunity or I would not suggest it."

Henry rubbed his eyes again, pondering the request. "I will think on it," he said. "Daniel and I will discuss it."

"Thank you, your grace."

Henry motioned toward the door. "Seek your bed, Torran," he said. "And congratulations on your future."

"Thank you, your grace."

As he headed for the door, Torran heard his name and turned to see Daniel behind him. He opened the door and stepped out into the corridor with Daniel on his heels. As the door shut softly, Daniel turned to him.

"About Stefan," he said quietly. "He is an excellent knight, one of the finest I've ever seen even if he is my son. He is very worried for his future, Torran. Surely you know that."

Torran nodded. "I know," he said. "I can only imagine the torture he is going through, knowing he may wake up one morning and his hearing will be completely gone. But I swear to you, my lord, that we will take care of him. The Guard of Six is a brotherhood like no other. If Stefan cannot hear, then we will be his ears. And he will serve flawlessly."

Daniel had tears in his eyes with the realization that someone saw Stefan beyond his handicap. Stefan was an amazing knight, highly trained and educated, but the hearing issue had limited the life he could make for himself. He always had a place with Daniel, but that wasn't what he deserved.

He deserved more.

Torran was willing to give it to him.

"Are you sure?" Daniel said hoarsely.

"Very sure, my lord."

"I worry so for Stefan, but this... I will not worry for him any longer."

Torran smiled faintly and put his hand on the man's arm, giving him a squeeze. "He has earned this," he said. "If Henry seems uncertain, I will work on him. He will agree eventually."

Daniel simply nodded, slapping Torran on the shoulder as he turned toward the door, sniffling away his tears. Torran watched the man return to the chamber, the door shutting softly, leaving Torran standing in a darkened corridor, still reeling from the course his life had taken this night.

The Earl of Ashford.

Marriage to Andia.

He couldn't wait to get to Lockwood and tell her.

CHAPTER ELEVEN

Lockwood Tower

"**A**ERON, IF YOU are not going to help, then I am going to lock you in a room and throw away the key."

Andia had just delivered an ultimatum.

She was busily sweeping the entry of Lockwood while the two female servants, including the cook, were scrubbing the floor with hot water, vinegar, and ash from the hearth. It was a solution that had proven quite effective in cleaning, which Andia had undertaken after Torran and the king departed Lockwood. Truthfully, she wasn't sick any longer, and at the risk of becoming bored while she waited for Torran to return, she put herself to work. Lockwood hadn't been properly maintained in years because Torran's family remained south at Bexhill Castle, so she took it upon herself to clean the manse to repay Torran for his kindness in letting her and Aeron remain.

The trouble was that Aeron wasn't thrilled about being forced to work.

"I've done what you wanted me to do," he said stubbornly, standing near the entry with an empty bucket. "I want to go to the stables. Emile is going to teach me how to tend a horse's injured hoof."

Andia's eyes narrowed at her brother. "But I need you to bring us more hot water from the kitchen," she said. "You will do that, please."

Aeron was starting to pout. "But when can I go to the stable?"

"When we are finished with our work."

With a growl of frustration, Aeron stomped out of the entryway and headed for the kitchen. Andia shook her head at his behavior, but when she turned around, she could see that the servants were grinning.

That made her chuckle.

"Are all boys like that?" she said. "He is the only one I have ever had any experience with, honestly. I do not seem to recall the pages at Okehampton Castle being so disagreeable."

The cook, a big woman with big arms, went back to scrubbing the floor with a vengeance. "Boys need direction, m'lady," she said. "Even my Emile needed a purpose and focus. They need discipline and they need to know the value of hard work. He's young, your little brother. He'll learn."

Andia brushed hair out of her face with the back of her hand. "I hope so," she said. "Or I really will lock him in a chamber and throw away the key."

"What's this about a chamber and a key?"

The question came from the entry, and Andia turned to see Stefan standing just outside the door, unwilling to walk on the wet, scrubbed floor.

"Ah," Andia said with some volume to her tone. "Sir Stefan. How are you with a scrub brush?"

Stefan grinned, that toothy de Lohr grin that made him look so much like his grandfather. "Terrible," he said. "You would be so frustrated with me that you would beat me with a broom. I would make a terrible servant."

She laughed. "I do not believe it," she said, trying to coax him into helping her. "Why not show me first and let me decide how bad you are?"

Stefan eyed her suspiciously. "That will not work," he said. "I will not fall for your clever invitation."

"Nay?" she said, shrugging. "Very well. I will try something else to get you to do it."

"There is nothing you can say that will see me on my knees with a scrub brush in my hand."

"Not even if I promise the cook will make you something special for supper?"

That had his interest. But, then again, over the past few days, everything about Andia had Stefan's interest. "That depends," he said. "What did you have in mind?"

"What will it take?"

"I asked you first."

She broke down into soft laughter, shaking a finger at him. "Stop being so evasive," she said. "I do not like it."

"My apologies, my lady."

"Then prove it by picking up a scrub brush."

He clapped a hand over his forehead. "That again?" he said. "I will not do it. Not even if you beg and scream. I am immune to your pleas, so you may as well stop."

She made an unhappy face at him. "We'll see," she said. "I will ply you with food and drink, and when you are too weak to fight me off, I shall demand your surrender."

That had more than one meaning to Stefan. As he watched her smirk, a smile crossed his lips. "I would surrender to you in any case, my lady," he said quietly. "You need not beg."

Andia caught on to his tone almost too late. She was preparing to make a witty quip, but that deep, almost seductive tone had her looking at him again. He was smiling at her, and although he was a very handsome man, and charming if she were to admit it, the truth was that her heart belonged to someone else.

Someone she missed very much.

"Well," she said, trying to keep the conversation light, "that is not true, but I will not call you a liar. I've asked you to help me with the floor but you have denied me. I suppose it is beneath your dignity, so I will capitulate. We are at an impasse, I'm afraid."

If Stefan was disappointed by her refusal to engage in a conversation that had a romantic flavor to it, he didn't let on. He simply nodded his head.

"As long as we remain friends, I am satisfied."

"We remain friends. But I may challenge this impasse at some point."

He grinned. "That is your privilege, my lady."

She chuckled, waving him off irritably, as she gathered her broom once again. "Did you come here just to harass me?" she said. "Or did you have a purpose?"

Stefan nodded. "I did, in fact, have a purpose," he said. "You may want to dry these floors because I received a missive from Torran this morning. He is on his way here and should arrive soon."

Andia's heart leapt at the news. "Thank you for telling me," she said. "I hope he is not too angry that I wanted to clean the manor. It was in desperate need of it."

Stefan shook his head. "I am sure he will be most appreciative," he said. "You make a fine chatelaine."

Andia's smile was genuine. "That is kind," she said. "I've worked hard enough at it, so I am glad I was able to contribute what knowledge I have."

He returned her smile, nodding, before heading back out into the yard, as Andia watched him go. She knew that he was probably disappointed she wasn't responding to his gentle flirting, but that couldn't be helped. It seemed that Stefan had enough to be disappointed over in his life, most predominantly the loss of his hearing, and now he was trying to show his interest in a woman who had none in return.

Truthfully, she felt sorry for him.

But she couldn't dwell on it. Swiftly, she turned to the women who had paused in the floor scrubbing at the mention of Torran's return and clapped her hands.

"Quickly, ladies," she said, rushing to grab an empty bucket on the floor. "We must dry what we can of the floor. We do not want Sir Torran slipping and breaking an arm."

The servants were on their feet, rushing for rags that they'd been using along the edge of the room. Briskly, they began to rub the wet wood, drying it as best they could.

Meanwhile, Andia slipped away.

It was truly remarkable how her thoughts and feelings on life in general had changed over the past several days. She didn't even know Torran before the siege at Kennington Castle, but now she couldn't remember when she hadn't known him. When he hadn't been a fixture in her life. When her thoughts hadn't revolved around him all day. She'd never met anybody who had shown her more consideration or interest, and, of course, attention that made her heart race every time she thought about it.

It was that attention that gave her a reason to get up in the morning.

She knew that he was fond of her. She knew that she was fond of him. But what concerned her was the fact that he'd been gone for almost a week, and that was time enough for him to realize that he'd been hasty in his actions. She was afraid that maybe he had changed his mind, although she knew Torran was a man of honor. She would never believe that what happened between them had been on impulse, an opportunity and nothing more. She had to believe that it was because he wanted to kiss her and because it meant something to him.

She only hoped that it was really true.

In the beginning of their association, her concerns had been about

Henry and what he was going to do with her and Aeron. How he intended to punish them for Anselm's crimes. She and her brother were being taken to London to answer for their father's sins. Those were still her concerns, of course, but now she had other concerns nagging at her.

Concerns about a knight who would one day be an earl.

There was some doubt there. If Andia was being honest, then she had to admit that even though she was the daughter of an earl, she was the daughter of a *disgraced* earl. That was worse than if she were nothing at all. Her home, the rich and prestigious Kennington Castle, was now rubble. Everything considered assets of the Ashford earldom was now in ruin. But there was still the matter of the coin she had hidden when the battle started, and she was confident it would never be found. It was money that belonged to her brother, but it was also possible to use it for a dowry. A man as important as Torran de Serreaux would require a bride who could bring something to the marriage. All Andia could bring was the vestiges of a bereft house that had once been important and established.

She, too, had been reduced to rubble.

Was there any point in hoping Torran would be able to see a bride in her?

Perhaps that was part of the reason she'd decided to clean and organize the manor. Perhaps she wanted Torran to see that she was useful. She wanted him to know that there was some value to her even if she didn't come with a dowry or the backing of a father with a big army. But it was equally possible that she was just fooling herself.

Time would tell.

In any case, Andia wanted to look presentable to him. She was wearing a simple broadcloth dress that had been included in Lady Penden's stash, but there was another dress as part of that collection that was equal to the stunning red surcoat she'd worn. Lady Penden had included five garments in all, including one the color of sapphires.

It had gold embroidery around the square neck and long, drapey sleeves. After Andia stripped off the broadcloth and quickly washed with water and a bar of soap that smelled of rosemary, she donned the blue dress, braided her hair, and took a look at herself in the Genevieve's bronze mirror.

Then she went downstairs to wait.

There was nothing more to do.

CHAPTER TWELVE

H E'D MADE A shepherd's sling and Emile had helped him.

The real reason Aeron had wanted to go to the stable where Emile was working wasn't because Emile was going to show him something about hooves. He didn't care about hooves.

Emile was helping him fashion a simple, but painful, weapon.

It was easy, really. Two strips of leather and a cloth cup in between them for the rock, or dung, or anything else one wanted to shoot across the yard. Put a stone in it, whirl it above your head to gain momentum, and then release one side of it and the projectile went sailing. Emile had helped Aeron perfect it with the caveat that he not use it on the horses, and Aeron promised he wouldn't. But he never promised he wouldn't use it on people, birds, goats, and anything else that moved.

Some of the male servants around the manse were the first to feel the sting of a pebble slung by Aeron as he practiced. There was one old man in particular who wasn't very nice that Aeron took special aim at. The old servant felt stings to his cheek, neck, back, and the back of his head, finally realizing that Aeron was shooting things at him when he saw the boy duck behind a pile of straw in the yard. Then he went on the hunt, but Aeron was too fast.

He found other people to shoot at.

Stefan was one of them. He was at the gatehouse, waiting for Torran, when he felt something hit him in the right buttock. He thought he might have been stung by a bee until he felt another sting to his left shoulder and saw the pebble fall to the ground. Realizing he was under attack, he turned around and spied Aeron where he shouldn't be—on the wall walk of the manor—and his eyes narrowed. He fully intended to find the lad and discover what was going on when one of the servants, who had been out on the road, told him that a rider was approaching. That had Stefan heading out of the manor, going to the edge of the road as Torran came cantering down the avenue.

Beneath the sun and scattered clouds, with a light breeze blowing from the south, Torran rode in on a big black and white warhorse, which was difficult to miss, and Stefan waited until the man slowed down before lifting his hand in greeting.

"Welcome back," he said. "You made it before the rains came."

He turned to look at the dark clouds coming in from the south, pushed along by the wind, and Torran came to a halt, dismounting his sweaty steed.

"Indeed, I have," he said loudly for Stefan's benefit. "How have things been here in my absence? Peaceful, I hope."

Stefan nodded as they began to head toward the entry gate. "Peaceful enough," he said. "But I should warn you that the moment you go through that gate, you will probably be under attack."

Torran looked at him in puzzlement. "Attack?" he said. "From whom?"

Stefan fought off a grin. "From a boy who has learned how to throw rocks," he said. "I, myself, have been a victim today, and I know he is hiding near the gate, so I would be prepared if I were you."

Torran found himself looking at the gate, imagining Aeron lying in wait for him. "Is that so?" he muttered. "I cannot say that I am surprised, but as we know, an enemy must be subdued. I will enter first to distract him. You will come in after me and discover his position.

Capture him and I promise that you will get the first opportunity to spank him."

Stefan's grin broke through. "You cannot know how I have wanted to do that over the past few days."

Torran started to laugh. "Aye, I think I do," he said. They'd reached the gate at that point, and Torran held out a hand to keep him Stefan going any further. "Do not let my sacrifice be in vain, please."

Stefan chuckled, watching Torran go through the gate and continue toward the stable as if quite oblivious to the world around him. At that point, Stefan crept up to the edge of the gate and peered through, waiting for the pebbles to come flying. It wasn't a long wait—Aeron stood up from behind the ladder he'd been crouched behind and Stefan watched him hurl a pebble at Torran with a slingshot.

Stefan was on the move.

As Torran had predicted, Aeron was focused on him as he entered the grounds and moved for the stable. As Stefan pursued Aeron, the boy got off two pebbles that crashed into Torran's arm. The third one hit the horse, who started at the sting. But Torran kept walking. He didn't look to see where the projectiles were coming from. He pretended he didn't even feel them. It was enough of a puzzlement to Aeron that he grew sloppy. He came away from his hiding place and started to pursue.

And that was when Stefan grabbed him.

Torran grinned when he heard a yell go up, echoing off the walls of the manor. He'd reached the stable yard at that point, turning around to see Stefan entering the yard with a squirming child under his arm. Torran handed his horse off to Emile, who looked quite puzzled at Aeron being hauled around sideways under Stefan's arm. Torran, however, faced Stefan and Aeron as they closed in on him.

"I see some things never change," he said, looking at Aeron. "We meet again under less than pleasant circumstances, lad."

Aeron could see another spanking in his future. "It was an accident," he said quickly. "I was aiming for birds and then Stefan grabbed me. I did not mean to hit you!"

"How do you know you hit me?" Torran said. "I never said anything about your hitting me."

Aeron knew he'd been caught in a lie. He could tell by Torran's voice that the man knew exactly what he'd been up to. He struggled to free himself from Stefan's grip.

"It was an accident," he repeated. "Let me go!"

Torran looked at Stefan, a smile playing on his lips, and nodded his head. Stefan immediately put down the child, who promptly turned around and tried to kick him. Stefan shoved him back by the head and Aeron ended up on his bottom.

"You pushed me!" he accused.

Torran snapped his fingers at the boy, catching his attention. "Enough," he said quietly. "*You* know that you were throwing rocks at me and *I* know you were throwing rocks at me. We all know. The responsible thing to do would be to admit it and accept your punishment."

Stefan held up the shepherd's sling he'd taken off Aeron, who made a face as he stood up and brushed himself off.

"I wanted to try it out," Aeron said, weakly defending himself. "I will become very good with practice."

"Possibly, but not with that one," Torran said. "That one now belongs to Stefan, and if I see you with another shepherd's sling anytime soon, my hand will become acquainted with your backside again. Is this clear?"

Aeron's face was in a permanent frown. "Can I buy it back, at least?"

"With what?"

"I'll earn money and buy it back."

Torran wasn't going to argue with the child. He was more than eager to see the boy's sister and the delay was making him irritable, so he pointed at Stefan.

"You will have to negotiate this with him," he said. "I must speak to your sister."

That kept Aeron with Stefan, and even as Torran headed for the manse, he could hear Aeron's high-pitched pleas and Stefan's low replies. He had to grin, however. Aeron was, if nothing else, persistent and clever. That would serve him well as a knight someday.

If he lived that long.

Entering the manse from the kitchen, Torran passed through the darkened corridor that opened into the dining hall and then the entry beyond. He could smell vinegar as he passed through. He was about to take the stairs when he heard a voice from the solar.

"Welcome home, my lord."

He paused, foot on the bottom step, as Andia emerged from the solar. She was dressed in a lovely blue gown, a smile on her lips in greeting. Torran couldn't help but smile in return as he beheld her, that beautiful woman who now belonged to him. He could still hardly believe it. He could only hope she felt the same way. Switching direction, he headed for her, but the closer he drew, the more tongue-tied he became. That lovely face was smiling up at him, and as he came near, he did the first thing that came to mind.

He threw his arms around her and kissed her.

Instead of being shocked by his behavior, Andia seemed to welcome it. She wrapped her arms around his neck and responded feverishly as he picked her up, carrying her into the solar before finally setting her down somewhere near his father's table. All the while, his mouth was fused to hers and his heart was beating wildly. Heat flowed through his veins, setting him on fire. The more he kissed her, the more he wanted.

It was a hell of a greeting.

"Would it be too forward of me to tell you that I have missed you these past days?" he murmured against her mouth.

"Nay," she breathed as he kissed a fiery path down her neck. "It would not be too forward. I have missed you too."

He stopped kissing her and looked at her. "Have you truly?"

She nodded. "Of course I have," she said. "In case you've not yet realized, I'm rather fond of you."

He stared at her a moment before a smile creased his face. "I have never had anyone tell me that."

"I will tell you it often if you will let me."

Grinning, he kissed her once more before taking her hand and pulling her over to a bench that was in front of three arched windows that faced over the yard. He sat her down before planting himself next to her, holding her hand and smiling like a fool. She giggled at his expression, and then he laughed, and they ended up laughing together and having no idea why, only that they were happy to be together again.

He kissed her hand before speaking.

"I come with news from Henry," he said. "I pray that it good news to you, because it was to me."

She cocked her head curiously. "What news?"

There was a lot to tell her, so he tried to figure out where to start. He'd planned it all out in his mind on the ride from Westminster, but once he looked in her eyes, all of his planning flew out the window.

Therefore, he started at the beginning.

"As you know, the very reason you're at Lockwood is because I was taking you and Aeron to Henry," he said. "But there have been some changes. You will not be going to Westminster."

"I won't?"

"Nay. You will staying here."

Andia's eyes widened in relief. "Truly?" she gasped. "Praise God, Torran. I cannot tell you how happy I am to hear that. But why did he make that decision? What changed his mind about Aeron and I going to Westminster?"

"He discussed the situation with men he trusts," Torran said. "Canterbury was one of them. I think he was your biggest advocate. He convinced Henry to be merciful when others wanted to see you made an example of. Truly, the past few days in London have been… intense. There are several warlords in London right now and everyone has an opinion about how punishment should be dispensed."

She seemed to lose some of her joy. "Then he has decided to punish us?"

Torran shook his head. "Nay," he said. "But you are to be married to a man loyal to Henry. This man is also to be given the Earldom of Ashford and will become your brother's guardian. Henry feels that it is the best way to ensure you and your brother remain loyal to the Crown."

Her joyful expression vanished completely. "Aeron will not be Earl of Ashford?"

"Nay," he said quietly, seeing her distress. "That is in punishment for your father's actions. It could have been much worse, Andie. Stripping Aeron of the title is harsh, but it is not painful. He will not suffer. And Henry has ordered him to Canterbury to foster, where he will learn to become a knight. He will have a good life, I promise."

Andia had to absorb all of that. It was a lot to take. "But he will be safe, won't he?" she asked.

"Very safe," Torran said. "Canterbury will watch out for him and ensure he receives a good education and good training. This is an excellent solution, Andie. At least he will not spend years in captivity, wasting away. Please trust me on this."

She nodded, though she clearly wasn't happy about it. "I do," she said. "I promise, I do. You have always been honest and kind. But… you said I am to be married?"

"Aye."

"To whom?"

"To me."

A look of pure astonishment washed over her features and her mouth flew open. "*You?*" she gasped.

He grinned. "Aye," he said. "Me. Are you pleased?"

Her answer was to burst into tears, and, suddenly, he was concerned. Was she not happy? Did she not want to marry him? Doubts filled him until she lifted her head and he could see that she was smiling. With tears coursing down her cheeks, she was smiling.

"You told me not to give up on my dreams," she sobbed. "You told me I must have faith. I did not have faith, Torran, I will admit it. I felt like I was a feather in the wind, at the mercy of Henry, but now... I am to marry *you*? Truly?"

"Truly."

More tears, but also some laughter. She put her hands on his face, holding it gently. "You are a dream I never knew I had," she said, sniffling. "I cannot believe... He truly said that? We are to be married?"

Torran laughed softly, realizing she was happy about the situation because she kept asking if it was the truth. "Aye, dearest," he said sweetly. "We are to be married."

"When?"

"As soon as you wish."

Andia erupted out of her chair, throwing herself at Torran and nearly knocking him off his seat. But she was laughing and crying at the same time, kissing his face and then leaping to her feet to spin in circles as she giggled. Torran watched her, feeling her joy because it matched his own.

"Tell me I am not dreaming," Andia begged softly. "Tell me this is real."

"It is real, love."

She stopped spinning and looked at him. "But how do you feel about it?" she said. "I should have asked you from the first, and I am sorry that I did not. Are you happy?"

"Never happier in my life."

She was smiling at him, tears still in her eyes, but she scooted over to him and sat down, looking at him rather eagerly.

"Then I must tell you something," she said. "I... I have had suitors before, men who have asked my father for my hand. But I did not love them. I only found them pleasant and companionable. I did not feel for them as I feel for you. I have not felt for anyone the way I feel for you."

He smiled at her rather tame confession. "You are a beautiful young woman," he said. "I did not think that would go unnoticed by men of marriageable age."

"You are not troubled by it?"

"Of course not. But if they come around you from this point forward, I will kill them."

She smiled. "They will not," she said. "There were only two of them, knights at Okehampton."

"Clearly, your father denied them."

She nodded, her smile fading. "He did not want me to marry," she said. "He wanted me to be devoted to Aeron, always. He wanted my entire life to revolve around my brother, only to serve him."

Torran grunted. "That is an unhappy prospect," he said. "And a fate you do not deserve."

Her smile returned. "But it must have been God's will," she said. "My father denied those men because God knew you were in my future. All I had to do was wait."

The warmth in Torran's eyes waned. Since she was confessing her past, as mild as it was, he knew he should do the same. A woman deserved to know whom she was marrying, but he had to admit that he was apprehensive to tell her, hoping it wouldn't douse her excitement.

Truth be told, he wasn't looking forward to it but it had to be done. If she was to be his wife, inevitably, she would hear things about him, and he wanted anything sordid to come from his lips.

"Speaking of God," he muttered, "there are a few things you should know about me, also."

Andia reached out, taking his hands in hers. "Of course," she said. "What is it?"

Torran found himself looking at her hands in his. He had very big, very rough hands. Hands that killed men, hands that fought in battle. Her soft, pale hands were such a tremendous contrast, perhaps reflecting the two of them and the lives they had lived. Hers had been relatively uneventful.

His had been full of battles.

"I am older than you," he said. "More than likely fairly significantly."

"I have seen twenty and one summers."

He smiled ironically. "I have seen thirty and six."

She smiled. "That is not too terribly old."

He chuckled. "It feels like it sometimes," he said. "The point is that I have lived longer than you have and, therefore, have done more with my life. You should know that I never intended to wed."

"Why not?"

"Because I used to be a priest."

Andia's eyes widened. "You *were*?" she said in shock. "But... but you aren't any longer?"

He shook his head. "Nay," he said. "It is not as scandalous as it seems. Many priests are former knights and many knights are former priests because the knighthood is built around the worship of God. We are expected to be pious. For some men, however, the priesthood does not remain their path."

She was listening seriously. "And you chose to change your path?"

He lifted her hand, kissing it gently. "It was not exactly my choice," he said. "I will be honest with you—I was not entirely certain I wanted to be a priest. When I told my father I was considering it, he raged at me. As you know, I am his heir, so he saw it as a waste and a tragedy should I make that decision. Quite honestly, my father drove me into it with his attitude. Had he been supportive to make the choice best for me, who knows if I would have done it. But because he told me how stupid I was being for even considering such a thing, I joined the priesthood out of spite."

Andia's initial shock was fading as she listened to his explanation. "But what happened that took you out of the cloister?"

He sighed faintly, leaning back against the stone window frame. "One of the patrons of Worth Abbey, where I was serving, was the Earl of Norbury," he said. "He had a wife—a very young and frisky wife—who wanted to take me to her bed. She tried everything to catch my attention and I ignored her as much as I was able. It is difficult as a priest when you are supposed to be helping mankind find its way to God. You are supposed to be kind and understanding with your parishioners."

"Even a woman like that?"

He nodded. "Unfortunately, even a woman like that," he said. "Her husband is very rich, and when the bishop caught on to what she was doing, he told me to use my influence with her to get more money. It was truly a nightmare situation. Finally, she summoned me to her home when her husband was away, only I did not know he was away. I arrived thinking she needed my priestly services, but the truth was that she tried to seduce me. Here I am, in her bedchamber, and the woman is naked and trying to throw herself at me. Her husband must have suspected that something was afoot because he returned from his journey unannounced and found us together—her being naked and me trying to fight her off, only he thought I was attacking her."

Andia's eyes were wide with horror. "My God," she gasped. "What happened?"

Torran shrugged. "He tried to kill me but I returned to the abbey unscathed," he said. "Barely, I might add. I did not carry a weapon in those days. But Norbury complained to the bishop, and also to my father, and I was exiled from the abbey in disgrace. My father, thinking that I was, indeed, stupid and incorrigible, called upon Henry, who is an old friend, to take me into the royal fold as a knight. I certainly could no longer be a priest. And that is how I ended up in Henry's service, working my way up the knightly ranks to the position I am in today."

Andia shook her head in disbelief. "God's Bones," she exclaimed softly. "What a terrible situation you had to endure. And your own father did not believe you?"

"Nay," he said. "You should know that my father and I do not get along. Never a kind word out of his mouth for me."

"What about your mother and siblings?"

He found himself looking out of the window, thinking of the rest of his family and the revelation Henry had dropped on him about him being his father's bastard. Frankly, he didn't care if it was true or not because it didn't change his world in any fashion. The only thing that revelation did for him was clear up a lot of mystery surrounding his relationship with his father. Perhaps it even caused him some bitterness toward the man, because if it was true, then his father should have been more understanding of the situation, given his own clouded past.

"My mother is a distant woman," he said after a moment. "My brother, Rhys, is a good man. He and I are friendly. Not very close, but friendly. And my sister, Aurelia, is an angel. She's the one I miss the most."

Andia smiled faintly. "That's very sweet," she said. "I hope I am able to meet her someday. I hope I am able to meet all of your family someday."

He looked at her. "You are the daughter of an earl, which my father will approve of," he said. "But your father was also stripped of his titles, which he will *not* approve of."

Andia was thoughtful for a moment. "Then you can tell him that my paternal grandmother was a Baldwin, a descendant of the House of Flanders," she said. "Queen Matilda, wife of the Duke of Normandy, is my ancestor, which makes me a cousin to Henry. Did the king tell you that?"

Torran nodded. "I knew because Lord Penden told me," he said. "Henry has not mentioned it."

"I have royal blood in me. Shouldn't that make your father happy?"

"Possibly." Torran shrugged. "But I do not much care, to be honest. I have the only woman in the world I have ever wanted and I do not care if you are a queen or a pauper. You belong to me and that is all that matters."

Andia smiled. "I will do my best to make you proud, Torran," she said softly. "Truly, I will. But this is all so unbelievable. I am having trouble comprehending that this is the future. *Our* future together."

He lifted a hand, cupping her face gently as his thumb stroked her soft cheek. "For today, for tomorrow, and for always," he said. "It begins now."

She nodded, the glow of hope in her eyes never so bright. He pinched her on the chin gently and she giggled, finally throwing her arms around his neck and squeezing him so tightly that she nearly choked him. He hugged her in return, finally smacking her affectionately on the bottom as he pulled away.

"Now," he said. "We have a few things to attend to."

She stood up next to him. "What would you have me do?"

He grasped her hand and began to walk her toward the solar door. "I would say that all you need do is select the dress you wish to be married in," he said. "I will send Stefan for a priest, but meanwhile, I must tell your brother of his impending future. I do not suppose he is going to be happy going to Canterbury, but he will simply have to accept it."

Andia shrugged. "He may be naughty at times, and demanding, but he can be obedient," she said. "He seems to obey you well enough."

Torran thought on that spanking he gave the lad the first day he'd met him. "There is a reason for that," he said, his eyes twinkling. "He does not like to be spanked."

"No one does."

He eyed her. "Don't tell me that you have been naughty enough to be spanked."

She batted her eyelashes coyly. "That is something you'll have to discover for yourself," she said. "I can, indeed, be far worse than Aeron."

His eyebrows flew up in feigned apprehension. "Is that so?" he said. "God help me, then."

She burst into soft laughter and he grinned, pausing in the doorway of the solar and pulling her into a snug embrace. She was warm and soft in his arms as he captured her lips, kissing her deeply, loving the feel of this joy in his heart. How this had happened, so quickly yet without fanfare or effort, made it seem as if it had been planned since the beginning of time and was meant to occur at this very moment. Looking back on his life, Torran could see that everything he had endured, every road he took, led him to this moment.

It led him to Kennington.

And to Andia.

"I must send Stefan for a priest," he murmured, tearing his lips away from hers. "And if I do not separate myself from you at this very moment, I fear that I will never do it, and there is much to do."

Andia grinned as he released her and stepped away. But he blew her a kiss as he headed for the door, which she thought was very sweet, but she suddenly remembered where he was going. And whom he would be speaking to.

She called out to him.

"Wait," she said. "Before you find Stefan, I feel that I should mention something. I'm not entirely certain, of course, but I would be remiss if I did not tell you my suspicions."

He paused at the door. "Suspicions of what?"

She closed the gap between them. "Of Stefan," she said quietly. "When you tell him to summon a priest, you should know that… Let me be clear that he never said or did anything even remotely inappropriate… but I think he may be a little fond of me."

Torran's brow furrowed. "Fond?" he said. "Explain."

She shook her head. "I could be wrong," she said. "I hope I am. But I felt as if over the past few days, when you were away, that he was verging on flirting with me from time to time. I never responded, of course, but it's entirely possible that given the fact that he was charged to watch over an eligible young woman, with whom he shared several pleasant conversations, he might have felt… fondness. I am not sure I can explain it any more than that."

Torran took the hint. "So you want me to be considerate when I tell him we are to be married."

She shrugged, but she also nodded her head, and he understood. Perhaps it was a delicate situation, perhaps not. He didn't blame Stefan for finding Andia lovely and sweet, because she was. The man had good taste. But nothing could come of it and Stefan had to be clear on that.

Torran had staked his claim.

"Not to worry," he said. "I will take care of it."

With that, he headed out the door, toward the yard in search of Stefan. Andia stood in the doorway a moment, watching him go and hoping Stefan wouldn't be too crushed to find out the lady he might have had an eye for was marrying someone else. Stefan was a nice man and she didn't want to hurt him.

But her heart belonged to Torran.

Today, always, and forever.

CHAPTER THIRTEEN

S TEFAN WAS IN one of the small corner tower rooms, scanning the inventory of old and dusty weapons as Aeron gingerly pulled them out, setting them aside and brushing his hands off on his tunic as if he'd just touched something horrible.

"What do you want me to do with these?" he whined. "They're all rusty!"

"I know."

"And there are spiders on them!"

Stefan shrugged. "You wanted to earn money to buy back your shepherd's sling," he said. "This is a good opportunity for you to earn money by cleaning these up."

Aeron wanted money, but he didn't exactly want to earn it. He would rather steal it, or beg it off someone, but earning it? The lad was close to another tantrum as Stefan tried very hard not to laugh at him.

"I do not know how to clean these," he said as a spear fell down next to him and he jumped, startled. "Look at them—they're old and dirty!"

Stefan bent down to pick it up. Because Aeron's voice was high-pitched, he could hear the lad with relative ease, so conversations with him weren't difficult.

Even if they were tiresome.

"And that is why they need tending," he said, handing it back to Aeron. "Clean these and you shall be paid."

Aeron took the spear as if it had leprosy. "How much?"

"A shilling for each spear."

"How many shillings to buy my shepherd's sling?"

"Twenty."

Aeron's mouth popped open in outrage. "Twenty?" he said. "It will take me a long time to clean twenty of these spears!"

"Not if you try hard."

"I do not even know how to clean them!"

"I will give you a pumice stone," Stefan said. "You can use that on the rust. The shafts may need to be replaced, but you won't know that until you scrub them down with something coarse to see what is dirt and what is rot."

Aeron frowned. Then he let the spear fall back to the ground and crossed his arms angrily. "You are being unfair," he said. "These weapons are old and dirty. They will never be used, so why must they be cleaned?"

Stefan cocked an eyebrow. "There is a lesson to be learned here, lad," he said. "Life is full of lessons, each one teaching us something specific, and I suspect your father didn't teach you nearly enough of them."

Aeron wasn't sure, but he thought he might have been insulted. "My father taught me many things."

"Like what?"

Aeron cocked his head in thought. "Like… like how to command men."

"And how do you do that?"

"You yell at them."

Stefan shook his head. "There is a little more to it than that," he said wryly. "If your men respect you, they will do your bidding without your yelling at them."

That seemed to confuse Aeron. He found himself looking at the spears again, kicking the one that was closest to him. "He never told me to clean old weapons," he muttered. "It's useless."

Stefan watched the boy fidget. He'd caught most of that mumbled statement, enough to get the gist. "Cleaning old weapons is not useless," he said. "You wanted to earn money? I am giving you that chance. You can clean these weapons and take pride in a job well done. There are very few truly worthless tasks, lad. A task is as worthless as you make it. It is also as important as you make it. Be proud of everything you do and do it the best way you can, because if you do not, the only worthless thing is you."

Aeron eyed him. He was about to say something more when Torran appeared at the armory door, motioning to Stefan when the man looked at him.

"Stefan," he said. "A word, please."

Leaving Aeron to fume over the amount of weapons he was going to have to clean, Stefan came out of the armory, glancing up at the sky as he did so.

"Eh," he said. "It is not raining yet, but I smell it. It is coming."

Torran looked up at as well. "Probably," he said. Then he looked at the man. "What are you and the young lord doing in the armory?"

Stefan fought off a grin. "He wants to earn money to buy his shepherd's sling back," he said. "I told him he could clean the old weapons and I'll pay him a shilling apiece. He does not think that is a worthy task."

Torran snorted. "He wouldn't," he said. Then he motioned to him again. "Walk with me. I must speak with you and I do not want curious little ears hearing what I say."

Stefan knew what he meant because he had to raise his voice when speaking to him, so he started to walk with Torran, heading toward the main gate.

"I take it that your visit to London had results?" he said. "The fate of the lady and the boy, I would imagine."

Torran nodded. "Aye," he said. "And it was most unexpected."

"What has been decided?"

This was the moment Torran had been waiting for.

He knew that he had to couch the situation with some tact because if what Andia said was true, this would not be welcome news for Stefan. He genuinely liked the man and didn't want to hurt him needlessly, so he ventured forth as carefully as he could.

"The most important thing that has been decided is that the young Earl of Ashford is being stripped of his title and property," he said. "Now that spoiled lad in the armory is nothing more than a noble-born child with nothing to his name. Your father has decided that Aeron will go to Canterbury and foster there. Both he and Henry believe they can undo the damage that St. Albans did to him by turning him against the king. Your father is certain he can bring him back into Henry's fold because he's young and impressionable."

Stefan came to a halt, his eyebrows lifted. "My father decided that?" he said. Then he shook his head and let out a low whistle. "That is quite a task he has chosen for himself."

Torran cast him a expression that suggested that was a ridiculous statement. "Face the fact that it will be you and your father's knights who will beat the rebellion out of the boy," he said. "Your father wants you to take the child to Canterbury on the morrow."

Stefan nodded. "Very well," he said. "And the lady, too?"

Torran shook his head. "That is where the most unexpected thing happened," he said. "Stefan, I do not know how much you know about my background, but I used to be a priest, long ago."

Stefan folded his big arms across his chest, turning his head to the left because his hearing was better in his right ear. "Nay, I did not know that," he said with interest. "You left the priesthood?"

Torran grunted. "Not exactly," he said. "A noblewoman tried to seduce me, and when I refused her advances, she told her husband that I had seduced her instead. It was enough of an accusation to have me exiled as a priest, and my father asked Henry to take me on as a royal knight. That is how I ended up in royal service. But it is also something I do not speak of, so if you could keep it to yourself, I would be grateful."

Stefan nodded sincerely. "Of course, Torran," he said. "I will not tell anyone. But why tell me?"

"Because I have a point," Torran said. "My father is the Earl of Bexhill. I am his heir, so that path is already laid out for me. But Henry has decided that, as a reward for my service, he is not only stripping the Ashford title from young Aeron, but he is giving it to me. He is giving me all of Ashford's property. He is even giving me Ashford's daughter in marriage, something I had never anticipated. As a former priest, I have lived a celibate life, so I do not mind telling you that Henry's decision caught me off guard. It was… unexpected, as I said."

Stefan stared at him a moment as he digested what he'd heard. Processed it was more likely. The words were rolling around in his head, and clearly he thought he hadn't heard correctly because his brow furrowed and he leaned toward Torran.

"You are betrothed to Lady Andia?" he asked.

Torran nodded. "By Henry's decree."

There it was. There was no mistake now. Stefan averted his gaze, scratched his head, and pondered what he'd just been told. As the moments ticked away, he finally cleared his throat.

"Well," he finally said. "That is disappointing."

"Why?"

He shrugged. "She's a beautiful woman," he said. "I have enjoyed speaking with her. I was hoping… Well, I suppose it's ridiculous to hope for such a thing. Why on earth would the daughter of an earl marry someone like me? I have nothing to offer her. I will not even inherit. And in a few years, I won't even be able to hear her voice, so why should she… Forgive me, Torran. Forget what I said. I am glad for you, my friend. Glad you have been given such great rewards. You have earned them."

Torran could see that he was upset, or at the very least, trying not to seem like he wasn't. "If it is helpful to you, know that I will treat her very well," he said seriously. "I promise I will make certain that she is always warm and happy and safe. I will take good care of her, Stefan."

"I know you will."

Stefan was still looking at the ground, and Torran wasn't unsympathetic. In fact, he thought the man had handled the news very well. Probably better than Torran would have had the situation been reversed.

But he had something more to say to him.

Perhaps something to ease the sting.

"Stefan, I want you to think about something," he said. "This is off the subject, but now seems like a good time. I want you to know that the Six and I feel that you have much to offer. We were honored to serve with you at Kennington. You are talented and we feel that we work well with you. So well, in fact, that I want to know if you would consider joining the Guard of Six."

Stefan hadn't been expecting that offer. "Me?" he said. "Join the Six?"

Torran nodded. "Both Henry and your father are agreeable if you are," he said, stretching the truth a little where Henry was concerned. "In fact, your father was particularly agreeable, so take your time to think about it. I do not need an answer right away."

Stefan was looking at him, his brow creased with distress. "Torran, I am honored," he said sincerely. "Very deeply honored. But you know that I have an… issue."

"I know."

"It is difficult for me to hear commands."

"We told your father that we would be your ears."

Stefan sucked in his breath as if he'd been struck in the belly. "You… you told him that?" he said.

Torran nodded. "Stefan, you must understand something," he said. "The Guard of Six is not comprised of the most perfect knights in England. It is comprised of the most *im*perfect knights in England. We are all flawed, so if you join us, you will fit right in. You'll be part of our strength, perhaps the most talented swordsman we have, and we'll be your ears. It's as simple as that."

Stefan's eyes grew moist. Torran could see it. The man lowered his head and walked a few feet away, head down as he pondered the proposal. Torran watched him, waiting for some indication as to which way he would lean, but Stefan was stone-faced for the most part.

He was mulling over something that could conceivably change his life.

"My older brother, Chad, was always the center of attention," he finally said. "You are well acquainted with Chad."

Torran smiled faintly. "He is a friend."

Stefan nodded. "A friend, an ally, an annoying bastard when he wants to be," he said. "But one thing Chad has that I do not is the fact that he'll inherit the Canterbury title. My youngest brother, Perry, has married quite well. An heiress from Lincolnshire, you know. He was rich the moment he married her. But me… Honestly, Torran, what do I have? And I said it before—who wants to marry a man who will not even be able to hear them in a few years? And who wants a knight for the same reason? So this offer… I never dared to hope for such a thing."

Torran's smile grew. "Does that mean you will join us?"

Stefan drew in a long, thoughtful breath. "All of you have swords with names," he said, turning to Torran. "Not just any names, however. Names that define you. Your sword is Absolution."

"It is."

"Kent is Insurrection, Jareth is Obliteration, and Aidric is Retribution, I think."

Torran nodded. "He is," he said. "Dirk is Destruction and Britt is Annihilation."

"Did you choose the name for your sword?"

"Nay," Torran said. "That was left up to the group. How we see each other, as it were. Names meant to give us strength and truth. Nothing is more powerful than the truth."

"I do not have a name for my sword."

Torran chuckled softly. "I can remedy that."

"What name would you give it?"

"Given what we saw at Kennington?" Torran said. "That is simple. Domination."

A smile spread across Stefan's face. "I like that," he said. "I can, and do, dominate."

"I know."

That brought a toothy grin from Stefan. "You have had an unexpected offer," he said. "So have I. This is a day for the unexpected. And I think that I should like to join the Six, Torran. I could not be more grateful that you see something in me that is worthy of the brotherhood."

Torran went to him, clapping him on the shoulder. "Thank Jareth," he said. "It was his idea."

"I shall, indeed."

"Good," Torran said. "Now, as the first order of business as a new member of the Guard of Six, which is now the Guard of Seven but we will not change it from its original form, you are to find a priest and bring him to Lockwood."

Stefan's brow furrowed. "A priest?" he said. "Why?"

"To bless my marriage to Lady Andia."

That took some of the joy out of Stefan's face. "Of course," he said. "Where shall I find one?"

Torran gestured toward the west. "St. Mary Magdalene is about a mile in that direction," he said. "Tell the priest it is for the de Serreaux family and they will come. My parents are patrons of that church."

Stefan nodded. "I shall go right away."

Torran watched him turn for the stables, but he stopped him. "Stefan?"

The knight turned to him. "Was there something else?"

Torran couldn't help but feel sorry for the man. They were back on that sensitive subject, and he hoped it was something Stefan wouldn't hold against him.

"I really will take good care of her," he said. "And I am certain there is a lady out there who would be thrilled to marry a big, strapping son of de Lohr. You simply haven't found her yet."

Stefan forced a smile. He didn't seem too eager to hear it, but at least he was polite about it. Torran watched the man head to the stable before turning and following his own path back to the manse.

There was a certain young woman in there that he very much wanted to see.

CHAPTER FOURTEEN

THE PLAN HAD been simple, but it had taken time to get there.

On that dark night when Gaubert and Donnel first discussed the removal of a king, there were many facets to what they wanted to do, but the goal remained the same—Henry's death and the recovery of Donnel's niece and nephew. Plans and discussions, counter-plans and more discussions, that had gone on all night.

It was, therefore, decided that Gaubert should seek the proper man to carry out Henry's death while Donnel went to the king to plead for the return of his niece and nephew. Neither one of them wanted to be seen together, or associated with one another, even though their plans intertwined. Donnel at least wanted to speak to his niece and nephew, so he was determined to know their location, to ensure they were being treated properly. Given that he was a titled lord who had never given the king any trouble, he hoped Henry would take that into consideration. Once he found the children of his sister, he would decide how best to help them escape their captivity. Would Henry suspect him? Of course he would if Andia and Aeron escaped, but he intended to send them to Gaubert's home, where they would be safely hidden.

If Henry searched, he would never find them.

Gaubert, of course, had the more difficult task—slipping an assassin into Henry's chambers. Ambitious? Absolutely. But he was certain that he could because he knew Westminster well. He'd spent many a banquet or gathering there with his cousin, Eleanor, so he was confident in his goals. He was also confident enough in where he could find an assassin, and that was at the most infamous tavern in all of London, an establishment with the unsavory name of The Pox.

But that had been the problem.

The Pox was a gambling hell, and given Gaubert's love of gambling, he'd spent three solid days there eating, drinking, and spreading the word that he had a man to kill and was looking for a hire. On the second day, a beastly man the size of a horse answered the call and Gaubert was relieved to have found himself a man who could do the job. He knew that because he'd forced the man to prove himself, and he had, swiftly and quietly, on one of the seedy patrons who had been half drunk in the rear of the tavern. The man was alive one moment, dead in the alley the next.

Gaubert knew he had his man.

But his assassin didn't seem to like to be alone. Oddly enough, he ended up sticking to Gaubert like the moisture that rose from the river and clung to one's skin. No matter what Gaubert did, he could not get rid of the man, who had even taken up residence in Gaubert and Donnel's rented room. Gaubert resigned himself to his new companion, and as they discussed an appropriate plan when it came to Henry, Donnel spent days trying to obtain an audience with the king.

Unfortunately, he was flatly denied—he couldn't even get his request through the gatehouse—so he'd switched tactics and sent word to the king's chief justiciar. Perhaps if he were to speak to the man who enforced the laws in England, and based his request for audience on judicial grounds, he might make headway in seeing Henry. The fact of the matter was that the king had his family members—unlawfully, as Donnel claimed—and Donnel wanted them back.

Because the siege of Kennington was so recent, Donnel made a good show of acting the irate uncle when he showed up at Westminster. He'd spoken to the guards who, in turn, referred him to one of the chief justiciar's clerics, who listened to Donnel's demands. The cleric, a young man who was a scholar and a clerk, could only write down the complaint and pass it on to another man higher in the chain of command. That didn't gain him an audience with the king as he'd hoped, but it did gain him an audience with Henry's chief justiciar, the Earl of Cheltenham.

That was the audience Donnel was prepared for today.

Dressed in his best, he and Gaubert and Gaubert's assassin, a man who called himself Styx, made their way from the river district to Westminster. It was the first time Donnel had spent any time around Styx, who was quiet and brooding and seemed uninterested in what they were doing. While Donnel went to meet with the chief justiciar, Gaubert and Styx were to find their way into Westminster to reinforce their plan. Because Gaubert knew the layout of the palace well, he was confident they could get in and get out without much notice, but one of Donnel's goals of the day was to see if he could find out where Henry was located. Possibly the chief justiciar would tell him, and that information would be relayed to Gaubert.

A plan with many facets, indeed.

Westminster was not only a palace, but an administrative center. The same cleric that Donnel had spoken to the day before was there to meet him once he entered the main gatehouse. He entered alone, as Gaubert and Styx were off on their own fact-finding mission, so Donnel followed the man into Westminster and through a series of rooms. Big, well-appointed rooms, connected, until they reached a chamber with a vaulted ceiling and walls lined with books.

It smelled of smoke and leather. There was something cold about it with its dark walls and dusty hearth. There were a few people in the enormous chamber and the cleric went over to a large table, strewn with tapers, where a man with a full head of white hair was sitting. There were a couple of other men lingering nearby, both of them with vellum in their hands, and the cleric waved Donnel over.

Quickly, he went.

"Lord Dudwell, this is the Earl of Cheltenham, Roi de Lohr," the cleric said by way of introduction. "He is willing to hear your petition."

As the cleric scampered away, the earl extended a hand to the nearest chair. "Sit, Lord Dudwell," he said. "Know that under usual circumstances, I would not be hearing your case, but you mentioned Kennington Castle."

"Aye, my lord?"

"You heard that it was recently sacked."

"That is why I am here, my lord."

"Then speak."

Donnel sat down in a hard oak chair. "Indeed, my lord," he said. "Kennington Castle is the home of my sister, her husband, and their children."

Cheltenham's gaze lingered on him for a moment. "Your sister was the Countess of Ashford?" he finally said.

Donnel nodded. "My dear sister, Edeline, passed away after the birth of my nephew," he said. "Anselm raised the children. He never remarried. But Henry has sacked the castle, and I understand Anselm was killed in the battle. Where are my niece and nephew?"

Cheltenham sat back in his chair, regarding Donnel to the point where the man was feeling scrutinized. He knew that Roi de Lohr was part of the enormous and powerful House of de Lohr, son of the greatest knight of his generation, Christopher de Lohr, but Donnel had never met the man until this moment. He was Henry's highest-ranking law advisor, a man who wielded a great deal of power in his own right. But the man had eyes that could see through him, unnerving Donnel until he felt almost naked and vulnerable.

"I was not at the battle," Cheltenham finally said. "Your brother-in-law was punished for his support of Simon de Montfort. It is as simple as that."

Donnel was trying to keep his frustration at bay. "I realize that," he said. "But why was he not allowed to pay a fine as some warlords did?"

"That was Henry's decision."

"*Where* are my niece and nephew?"

"They are unharmed if that is the answer you seek," Cheltenham said. "In fact, they are being well taken care of. I would not worry."

Donnel frowned. "But I do worry," he said. "Those children are all that is left of my sister. I demand they be returned to me. They should be with their family, my lord. Can you not understand that? Think of the tragedy they have suffered through because of Henry's rage."

Cheltenham seemed unmoved. "I assure you, they are in good hands," he said. "Truly, you needn't worry."

Donnel's frustration was growing. "May I at least speak with them?" he said. "If you say that they are being well cared for, I will trust you, but may I at least speak with them? May I ask if they require anything?"

"They will be provided with anything they require."

"But I am their only family," Donnel insisted. "Would you truly deny them the chance to speak with their only living uncle?"

Cheltenham hesitated a moment before finally shrugging. "I do not see the harm in your speaking to them," he said. "I understand that the situation at Kennington has been a shock to your family, and I am not unsympathetic."

"Then you can return them to me?"

Cheltenham shook his head. "I will *not* return them to you," he said. "They are the king's hostages and it is his pleasure that they shall remain that way."

Donnel sighed sharply, averting his gaze for a moment because the justiciar seemed resolute. Begging wasn't going to see Andia and Aeron given over to him.

Perhaps sympathy would.

"I promised my sister that I would watch over her children should anything happen to her," he muttered. "Her husband tended the children when she died, but that did not mean I was not interested in their welfare. Now that their father is gone, I have a pledge to fulfill. I swear to you that I will take them back to my home and keep them there. I shall ensure they are loyal to Henry, as I am. I do not understand why they cannot be remanded to me."

Fortunately, Cheltenham wasn't heartless. Donnel made a good show of being truly heartbroken about the situation, and he hoped it would have the desired effect.

"As I said, I do not see the harm in your speaking to them," Cheltenham said. "Although I cannot divulge where they are, I will send word to their guardian and have them bring them to Westminster, where you can speak with them. Will that suffice?"

Donnel sighed heavily. "I suppose it will have to, for now," he said. "Are they near London, then?"

"They are in London."

Donnel perked up. "Then may I go to them? Please?"

Cheltenham shook his head. "Nay," he said. "It would be better if you saw them here. But I will send word immediately. Return in a couple of days and you can speak to them."

Donnel knew that was the best he was going to get, at least at the moment. If he could speak to Andia and Aeron, then perhaps he could get their agreement to escape wherever they were being held. Or, at the very least, let Donnel know where they were, and possibly he could pay a servant to turn the other way as he spirited them out. In any case, he would have to be satisfied with an audience.

For now.

"Thank you, my lord," he said, standing up. "I am grateful for your mercy."

Cheltenham nodded vaguely. "You are welcome."

"And you'll send the missive right away?"

"I'll send for a clerk now."

Donnel began to back away, heading for the door. "Thank you, my lord," he said again. "I will be back in two days."

"Where are you staying in case I need to send word to you?"

"Near the riverfront," Donnel said. "The Black Swan."

"If there is a change in the situation, I will send word."

Donnel nodded his thanks and backed out of the chamber, met at the door by the cleric, who pointed down the corridor as the direction to exit. Donnel pretended to leave, but he came to a halt about halfway down the corridor when the cleric went back into the chamber. Silently, Donnel made his way back to the chamber and peered around the door to see that Cheltenham was, indeed, sending for a messenger. But he ducked into the shadows when he heard someone in the corridor, who turned out to be a royal guard, and when the guard went away, he quickly made his way out of the building.

But he didn't leave the grounds.

Westminster was fairly open because of the business that was conducted on the grounds. People came and went and the security, at least at the gatehouse, was fairly lax. The entire palace of Westminster was a complex of buildings, and Donnel found a corner of a building to hide in, tucked back in the shadows, watching the building he'd just come from.

And he waited.

Nearly an hour later, the very cleric who had been his guide appeared and headed in the direction of the stables, which were off to the west. Cheltenham had said he was going to send for a messenger, and that was clearly what was happening because the cleric had something clutched in his hand.

A missive.

Donnel went in pursuit.

The area where the stables of Westminster were located was only heavily traveled if one was in the stables, or departing from the western gate, but it wasn't particularly crowded between the hall and the stable. There were trees, and to the south sat old buildings that were part of the armory. He found a corner of the stables to hide against, peering into the stable yard to see the cleric talking to a man with a horse.

A messenger!

There was another man standing there, a man with a leather apron, and he was speaking to the cleric, gesturing off to the east, as the missive was put into the messenger's hands. When the conversation ended, the messenger mounted his leggy steed and trotted out of the western gate.

The man with the leather apron wandered away.

Donnel was so caught up in watching which direction the messenger might take that he was nearly seen by the cleric, who was heading back to the administrative complex. But he managed to duck back in time, watching the cleric as the man moved out of sight.

That brought Donnel out of his hiding place.

He had an idea.

Hurrying into the stable yard, he gave the appearance of a frantic man. There were people milling around, horses being watered and brushed, and he scurried up to the man wearing a leather apron as he spoke to a servant with a blanket in his hands.

"You!" Donnel said, catching the man's attention. "You, there! Did that messenger just leave with Cheltenham's missive?"

The man, with dark hair that was poorly cut, eyed Donnel curiously. "Aye," he said. "What about it?"

Donnel made a good show of being upset. "Because Cheltenham has something else for him," he said. "Where is he going? I'll send someone to catch up with him."

The man in the leather apron gestured toward the east. "He's taking it across the river," he said. "East of Southwark."

"To a home?"

"Aye," the man said. "Lockwood."

"Thank you."

With that, Donnel rushed out from the western gate, silently congratulating himself on being so very clever. The missive was headed to the very place his niece and nephew were being held.

Lockwood.

He had to find Gaubert.

CHAPTER FIFTEEN

"REMEMBER LORD DUDWELL from our conversation last night?"

"Aye."

"He was here this afternoon."

Jareth and Kent's eyes widened as Roi delivered the news of a man who had come up in a conversation regarding an assassination plot against Henry. Standing in Roi's lavish series of chambers, as befitting the chief justiciar, Jareth and Kent were shocked at the news.

"God's Bones," Jareth muttered in disbelief. "Was he alone?"

"He was."

"No Frenchman?"

"None in sight."

"What did he want, then?"

Roi had the look of someone who suspected that something very strange was going on. "There is a connection between Dudwell and Ashford that even I didn't know about," he said. "The man is the brother of Anselm's wife. He is the uncle to Anselm's children and came here demanding they be given over to him for guardianship."

That made a great deal of the situation clear, but it also confused the situation greatly.

"So... the man is the uncle who now wants guardianship of the children," Jareth said, trying work out the connection. "Yet he's mentioned in an assassination plot against Henry?"

Roi nodded. "What better reason for him to want Henry dead?" he said. "Henry just sacked his sister's home and took her children hostage. Wouldn't *you* want him dead?"

Jareth had to admit that all made sense. "I would," he said. "So he sends an ally to The Pox to hire an assassin?"

"It would seem so."

"Then the audience Dudwell had with you was a ruse?" Jareth said. "Possibly only to get inside the palace to discover the king's movements or simply to get a layout of the grounds?"

"And then provide it to the Frenchman," Kent finished. "He had to be here gathering information."

"An advance scout," Jareth said.

"Exactly."

Both men looked at Roi to see how he was processing this information, but the man didn't seem too concerned. At least, not on the inside.

"What now?" Jareth asked. "How would you have us handle this latest threat, my lord?"

Roi was rubbing his chin. "He may or may not be genuinely interested in finding his niece and nephew," he said. "I suspect that he does, indeed, want them back because if he were he given guardianship of the former Earl of Ashford, he would be in control of Ashford's earldom."

"And finances," Jareth said. "The land, the cattle, the castle... the money."

"Precisely," Roi replied. "However, he does not know that the young earl has been stripped of his title."

"Then the news will a rude awakening when he is told," Jareth said. "But something tells me that we should warn Stefan about this."

"Why Stefan?"

"Because he is at Lockwood, watching over the St. Albans children," Jareth said. "What if Dudwell is able to locate them?"

Roi shrugged. "He does not know where they are," he muttered. "But that does mean he will not go looking for them. More to your point, however, Torran is at Lockwood. He departed this morning. I've already sent a missive informing him of Dudwell's visit and his desire to meet with his niece and nephew. But mayhap one of you should ride to Lockwood and tell Torran of this discussion as well. The missive was brief and did not go into the detail we've just discussed."

Jareth's eyebrows lifted. "Torran went back to Lockwood?" he said. "Why did he go?"

Roi nodded. "He had to."

"I do not understand."

Roi looked between the two men. "When was the last time either of you saw him?"

Jareth and Kent looked at one another because they'd both last seen him at the same time. "Last night, at the conclusion of the gathering," Jareth said. "He went to bed. We all did."

Kent was nodding as Roi looked between the two of them. "Then neither of you have spoken to him since?"

"Nay," Jareth said. "Why?"

Roi sighed and leaned back in his chair. "Because Henry and Canterbury and I met after the gathering," he said. "We made some decisions regarding Ashford's children and summoned Torran, since he has been responsible for them since the beginning. Henry feels strongly enough that he wants Anselm St. Albans' children to be given over to an appropriate guardian, but in the case of the young woman, she should be married to someone loyal to Henry. As Henry put it, he wants the rebellion of de Montfort and their father bred out of the family lines, so although he has stripped the St. Albans boy of his title, he has given it over—and pledged the sister in marriage—to Torran.

That is why he is at Lockwood—to marry St. Albans' daughter."

Jareth and Kent couldn't have been more stunned. They looked at Roi, then at each other, and then back to Roi again.

"Torran is to be the Earl of Ashford?" Jareth finally asked.

Roi nodded. "He is," he said. "The boy will be heading to Canterbury to foster with Daniel, who will most assuredly beat the rebellion out of him. Lord Dudwell may want his niece and nephew returned to him, but it is out of his hands."

That may have been the case, but neither Jareth nor Kent cared about that at the moment. They were still dwelling on the fact that Torran was the next Earl of Ashford, but more than that, he was getting married.

Married!

"How does Torran feel about this marriage, my lord?" Jareth asked with some hesitation. "You know he is a former priest. I've never heard him mention interest in marriage the entire time I have known him."

"How he feels is irrelevant," Roi said. "He is doing as his king has ordered."

"And his king has ordered him to marry?"

Roi simply nodded. Jareth could see that there was nothing more to say on the subject matter but, frankly, he was astonished. Torran de Serreaux was a dedicated knight, a consummate warrior, and a man devoted to his service to the king. He was not a man who ever spoke of marriage or even expressed much interest in women. The priesthood had seen to that. Jareth always thought Torran might return to the priesthood at some point, but not anymore.

Priests didn't have wives.

"I am not sure if I should offer Torran my congratulations or my condolences," Jareth said honestly. "But we will tell him about this conversation regarding Lord Dudwell so he is prepared."

"I agree," Roi said. "While you are there, find out when he is planning to marry the lady. Henry told him to do it immediately, so you may want to encourage him."

"I will, my lord."

"Return by tonight, because not all of the warlords are gone and I have a feeling the feasting in the hall may be come lively again."

That drew grins from Jareth and Kent. "Maximus is still here," Kent said. "I saw him this morning, surrounded by his brothers."

Roi chuckled. "And I have *not* seen Edward," he said. "Not to say that he is a coward, because he is certainly not, but if Maximus de Shera was angry at me, I cannot say that I would not find better things to do inside my locked rooms."

Kent and Jareth chuckled too. "We will return, my lord," Kent assured him. "I wouldn't want to miss the battle tonight. I mean, the conversation tonight."

Roi smirked. "You had it right the first time," he said. "Go, now. Let Torran know what I have told you and make sure he returns tonight as well."

Kent and Jareth begged their leave, heading out of the administrative office. They passed courtiers and servants, remaining silent until they left the building and headed toward the stables.

"Married?" Kent finally said. "Torran?"

Jareth kept his focus straight ahead, in the direction of the stables. "I cannot imagine he was pleased with this," he said. "After all, he is Henry's *seigneur protecteur*. That has been his entire life for years. There *is* nothing else."

"I know."

"If nothing else, we must go and comfort him. The man is going to be extremely unhappy."

Kent rolled his eyes in sympathy. "I am certain that is an understatement," he said. "But all that aside, he does need to know what was discussed about Dudwell. That man's visit, my friend, was not a coincidence."

Jareth shook his head. "Nay, it was not," he said. Then he abruptly came to a halt. "Mayhap you should ride ahead to Lockwood and speak with him. I will find the rest of the Six and tell them of this latest development. We'll wait for you and Torran to return tonight."

Kent nodded. "Understood," he said. Then he hesitated. "Will you tell them about his marriage?"

Jareth shook his head. "Not me," he said. "That is Torran's privilege to tell them. But you... make sure the man isn't going to throw himself on Absolution because Henry forced him into matrimony."

Kent waggled his eyebrows ominously. "I'll do my best."

With that, they separated, each man moving with a purpose.

The situation, it seemed, was changing rapidly.

CHAPTER SIXTEEN

H E WASN'T SURE he was doing it right.

God help him, he'd never done this before, as he'd been forced to admit to Andia, and every time he thrust into her body, she groaned. Twice, she'd even cried out, as if he was causing her great pain, and that had brought him to an instant halt. He'd apologized profusely, but she had assured him they were cries of pleasure, so he struggled to resume what he needed to do.

It was the most awkward, yet the most pleasurable, thing he'd ever done.

It was also messy and hot and lusty. It was their wedding night, after the priest from St. Mary Magdalene that Stefan had procured prayed over them and announced they were married. Stefan hadn't wanted to attend, understandably so, but they'd needed a witness along with the two female servants of Lockwood and Emile, so he had to suffer through a marriage ceremony that had been completely disheartening. The whole situation had been made worse when Torran told everyone to leave the manse because he wanted to be alone with his wife. Stefan knew why.

To consummate the marriage with the woman Stefan had hoped to woo.

Of course, Torran really didn't know all of this for certain, but he suspected. He could read it on Stefan's face. But that didn't prevent him from taking Andia up to his mother's bedchamber and, for lack of any real knowledge of sexual intercourse other than what he'd been told or what he'd seen on occasion, he stripped Andia of her clothing, stripped himself, got her into bed, and then resumed where they'd left off that day in his father's solar.

This time, he was going to let nature take its course.

He suckled, he kissed, he touched. That much, he knew. It was inherent. The actual penetration of his manhood into her body had been uncertain, and awkward, but they'd managed to join. Somehow, he made headway, but slipped out a couple of times, and then tried again before he was fully seated. After that, instinct took over and he started thrusting, but he'd climaxed so quickly that neither one of them really knew if that was how it was supposed to be, so they simply started kissing again.

The second time was better.

Much, much better.

Torran went slower the second time, drawing out the experience and learning from it. Andia's eyes were closed as he nuzzled her neck, the hand on her belly moving gently to her ribcage. His seeking lips found her mouth and he kissed her with the greatest of passion. The hand on her ribs moved to her breasts, feeling the silken texture, experiencing the feel of her. He squeezed gently, fondling her, and Andia groaned softly because it felt so good.

Torran heard her groan and resumed his kisses with force. He couldn't seem to kiss her enough, taste her enough, and the hand on her breast grew bolder. A pink nipple, soft and taunting, rubbed against his hand and, with a growl, his hot mouth descended upon it, suckling furiously.

Again.

He very much liked her breasts.

Andia cried out softly as his hot, wet mouth pulled her nipple into a hard little pellet. He wedged himself in between her legs again, his big body overwhelming her, and Andia welcomed him. In fact, she seemed more confident about this than he did, and when she put her hands down between them, timidly touching his erection, he had about all he could take.

It took a huge effort not to spill himself again.

In truth, Torran was in a haze of passion and desire. Her flesh was sweet and delicious and he nursed hungrily at her breasts, first one and then the other, but there were other fruits to be sampled. He knew how a man should pleasure a woman, in theory, though he'd never done it before, so there was no time like the present to give it a try. He slid down her body and grasped her buttocks with both hands, envisioning her beautiful pink woman's center, like a flower unfurling. His mouth descended on the sweet pink folds and he feasted.

But that was when things grew painful.

Startled by his action, Andia jumped and slammed her knee into the side of his head. Torran saw stars, trying to shake them off and keep going. If he hadn't been so inflamed by her, he might have just walked away. But he didn't, and when his fingers probed her, she jumped again, but at least she didn't kick him in the head. That was progress.

In fact, they were both making progress.

Overwhelmed with it all, Andia panted softly as she became ac-quainted with Torran's touch on a level she could have never imagined. She could feel heat building in her loins, something that promised pleasure should she only surrender, and she remembered the same heat in the solar when Torran had had his way with her. A heat that had built to an explosion of sparks. Torran was making her feel something she'd never felt before, and although, by his own admission, he'd never done this, he was certainly doing a good job at it.

As long as she didn't kick him again.

When Torran couldn't take any more of her sweet musk, he lifted himself up and, with less awkwardness this time, guided himself into her tender walls. Thrusting gently with his hips, he seated himself halfway on the first thrust and then completely on the second. Beneath him, Andia groaned with pleasure at the sensation of his enormous member inside her body, her hands making their way down his back, timidly grasping his buttocks as he thrust into her. It seemed like the most natural of things, his body buried deep within hers as it was always meant to be. The more he thrust, the more she found herself pulling him toward her, forcing him deep.

Andia was so highly aroused that by the third or fourth thrust, she cried out at the delight of a powerful climax. Torran could feel her wet heat throbbing around him, pulling at him, and he understood his second release when he hadn't really understood his first. A release where a man would plant his seed, creating children, but most of all, display his feelings for a woman that was very quickly coming to mean a good deal to him. Someone who was the future he never thought he'd have.

At this moment, he simply wanted to savor the event of their first coupling.

His thrusts were measured and deep even as he climaxed, his fingers in the crack of her buttocks feeling the moisture from their bodies running onto her flesh, dampening the linens beneath them. Messy, hot, and sloppy... but as it turned out, he rather liked it this way. He liked feeling the moisture from their bodies as it mingled. He continued making love to her, feeling another climax wash over her in short order, less powerful than the first.

Finally, it was over, and as he lay on top of her, still joined to her body, he knew without a doubt that it had been the most miraculous experience of his entire life. Nothing he had ever sampled had come close, not ever. The priesthood may have had its merits, but after this, he would never look at the secular life the same away again.

There was something to be said for making love to a woman.

"How is your head?" Andia mumbled.

He started to laugh. "I am still seeing stars."

She grinned as she felt him laugh against her. "I am truly sorry," she said. "I guess I'm not very good at this yet."

His head came up and he looked at her, his handsome face alight with mirth and wonder. "You must be jesting," he said, sounding as if he were verging on scolding her. "You were wonderful. This entire thing… It was wonderful. Do you not feel that way?"

She nodded quickly. "I do," she said. "Truly, I do. I suppose we'll get better with practice."

He grinned wolfishly, lowering his head to kiss her tenderly on the lips. "I have never looked forward to practice more in my life," he said. "And you? Are you well? I did not hurt you, did I?"

Andia shook her head, reaching up to run her fingers through his dark hair. "Not at all," she said. "At least you didn't kick me."

He chuckled. "True," he said. "I did… other things."

She snorted. "You certainly did," she said. "You did quite well for a former priest."

"How would you know I did well?"

"How much should I know in order to know I liked it?"

He cocked his head. "You have a point," he said. Then he eyed her. "Did you really like it?"

"Couldn't you tell?"

"I want to hear it from your lips."

"Aye, I very much liked it."

With a smile, he shifted his body weight off her and lay beside her, taking her in his arms. Her warm, soft, naked body pressed against his was like something out of a dream. He never knew anything could feel so breathtaking.

"I must say, this was one of the more pleasurable orders I've carried out for the king," he said, his lips against her forehead. "I will have to thank the man."

Andia snuggled up against him. "I'm glad you feel this was a pleasurable order," she said. "I suppose it could have been worse."

"True," he said. "Every knight has had to carry out unhappy orders in his lifetime, but this wasn't one of them."

"Not even when he first told you about it?"

He sighed faintly, thinking back to that very moment. "I suppose that I was more shocked than anything," he said. "But once I thought about it, I wasn't shocked. I was actually quite happy. Surely you knew that I was already fond of you."

"Fond enough to marry me?"

"That would have come with time, even if the king hadn't ordered me to it."

She lifted her head, suddenly serious. "Do you mean that?"

He looked at her, pushing a piece of stray hair out of her eyes. "I do," he said. "I've met many people in my life, Andie, both men and women. Sometimes, you meet a man and you know you are going to get on with him. You simply know you are going to be friends. But I've never met a woman who struck me the way you did. From the start, I knew there was something special about you."

"Even when you were transporting me to London in the back of a provisions wagon?"

A smile tugged at his lips. "I would have made anyone else walk."

She grinned. "Then I should be grateful."

"You should."

She giggled softly. "So you felt kindly toward me from the start," she said. "But you also mentioned knowing the same thing about men. Who did you mean?"

"The personal guard I serve with come to mind."

"Did you know you were going to get on with them from the start?"

He nodded. "I did," he said. "Right from the very moment we met. Each man is unique and brings something different to our group. We have similar manners and characteristics. As Henry's personal guard, we all have exceptional value."

"You did mention once that you were part of his personal guard once," she said. "How many of them are there?"

"Six," he said. "That is why we are called the Guard of Six."

She cocked her head curiously. "That does not seem like enough men to guard the king."

He smirked at the insult she didn't realize she'd dealt him, running his fingers through her hair, more focused on how beautiful she was and not particularly on the conversation. He didn't particularly want to speak of his cohorts on his wedding night, but she was asking.

"We are an army of six," he said. "Trust me when I tell you that we are enough. We guard the king personally to ensure his protection, in all things. Prince Edward appointed us from the king's ranks before the Battle of Lewes when the king's life was threatened by de Montfort, and we were instrumental in his defeat at Evesham. It is a position of great trust and great reward. But also of great responsibility."

"Fascinating," she said. "And each of you are a perfect knight. You must be if Prince Edward personally selected you."

Torran thought on how he would explain the men who comprised the group. "We are *not* perfect," he said. "Far from it. But we all have similar backgrounds, similar upbringings, and each of us has a unique path that brought us to this moment."

"Like being a former priest?"

"Exactly," he said. "My unique path is memorialized in the sword I carry."

"Is it?" she said. "I've only seen your sword in its sheath, I think. I've never really looked at it."

He pulled her back to him again, holding her snugly. "It is not in the sword's appearance," he said. "It is in the name. Our swords all have names to reflect something in our background, something that has made us who we are and something that has brought us to this point in our lives and in our careers. My sword is called Absolution."

She tilted her head up, looking at him curiously. "A holy name?"

"I can kill a man and give him Absolution at the same time."

"So... your sword delivers last rites?"

"The very last rights my enemy will ever receive."

She wasn't sure if he was serious or not. "I am not a warrior, so I do not know what to say of such a thing," she said. "But... Torran, are you proud of your past as a priest? I mean, is it something you look back upon as time well spent, even if you did commit yourself to the cloister out of spite?"

He shrugged. "Everything in my life has shaped me in one way or another," he said. "I am not ashamed of anything if that is what you are asking."

"Nay, that wasn't what I was asking," she said quickly. "I am not exactly sure what I am asking, only I want to know if speaking of your past as a priest is upsetting to you. You are the man I have married. I want to know everything about you and I want to know what pleases, and displeases, you."

He kissed the top of her head. "There will be plenty of time for that," he said. "But to answer your question, nay, speaking of my past as a priest does not upset me, but it is not something I really speak of much. The entire situation with Lady Norbury and her husband is wearisome to explain, so I would rather not do it."

"I understand," Andia said. "Thank you for telling me."

"You are welcome."

"Since we are speaking of the past, may I ask you something?"

"Of course."

"When do you plan to sing for me?"

She laughed softly. "Someday soon, I promise."

The conversation faded after that, but it wasn't uncomfortable. In fact, it was very enlightening because Torran was able to hold a nude woman against him for the first time in his life and could easily see what all of the fuss was about. In fact, the entire evening had been enlightening as his eyes were opened in many different ways, not the least of which was the joy and pleasure between a man and a woman.

That part was a revelation.

In Andia's case, it was much the same. For the first time in her life, she was feeling true peace and contentment. She had a sense of belonging, which was very strange. She wasn't really sure if she'd ever felt as if she'd belonged, anywhere. Not in Okehampton, not even her own home. But Torran made her feel... wanted. She was so warm and comfortable in his arms that she drifted off to sleep almost immediately. Her deep, even breathing made Torran smile when he realized that exhaustion had finally claimed her.

And damn... how he loved this moment.

He, too, was just drifting off to sleep when a knock on the door caught his attention. Andia, however, did not wake up even when he tried to rouse her. She simply rolled over and began to snore. Grinning, he got out of bed, found his breeches, and pulled them on as he went to the door. Finishing the last tie, he cracked the door open to see who it was.

It was a recognizable face standing in the darkness.

And he did not look pleased.

CHAPTER SEVENTEEN

S TEFAN WAS TRYING not to think about it.

Standing on the narrow wall walk of Lockwood, he was trying not to think about what was going on in the manse at the moment. He'd been trying not to think of it for an hour, but he couldn't quite seem to manage it. He was trying to think about other things, like his invitation to join the Guard of Six and the name Torran had given his sword... Domination.

He liked it.

What he didn't like, however, was knowing what was happening in the chamber high in the manse. Oh, he knew he'd get over it at some point, but the problem was that it was rare when he felt a connection with a woman, and Lady Andia had been a rarity. A woman who knew about his flaw but was still kind to him. She was lovely, too. But the more he thought about it, the more he realized that he should have known something was going on between the lady and Torran, because they'd spent a good deal of time together. Torran said that Henry had ordered the marriage, but from what Stefan had seen when the priest blessed their union, there was more to it than Torran let on. The man had an expression on his face when he looked at Lady Andia that suggested he was happy enough about Henry's order.

There was no crime in that.

But Stefan felt stupid for not realizing that from the beginning.

As he'd predicted, a storm had rolled in and it was starting to rain. The sun had set about an hour or so earlier, just about the time the priest blessed Torran and Andia's union, so Stefan stood next to the main gate, just inside the wall, watching the rain fall and thinking about the course his future was about to take. He had an offer from the Six, and the more he thought on that, the more pleased he felt. It was something to focus on. Because of his handicap, he'd gotten the impression over the years that he'd somehow disappointed his father even though Daniel had never expressed such a thing, but he hoped that his position in Henry's inner guard circle might actually make the man proud of him. A post like that was something not even his brothers had achieved.

Stefan was up to the challenge.

The rain began to come down more heavily and he looked over at the old troop house, on the far side of the bailey near some outbuildings, because he could see that the door was open and light was coming from inside. The soldiers that Jareth had left behind on the day they'd brought the ill Lady Andia to Lockwood were still around, but there was so little for them to do that they mostly stayed to the troop house, especially at night. There was no real reason for them to be on the wall or on patrol. However, Stefan wanted to retire for the night, so he was thinking about summoning a few of them to man the gatehouse overnight when there was a shout from the other side of the gate. Curious, Stefan mounted the wall to see who was there.

It was a messenger.

"What do you want?" Stefan yelled. "And speak up so I can hear you!"

The man reined his horse in Stefan's direction, and Stefan could see that he was wearing the scarlet tunic of golden lions representing the House of Plantagenet.

A royal messenger.

"I have a missive for Sir Torran de Serreaux," the man shouted in return. "Is he here?"

Stefan held up a hand to the man, silently bidding him to remain where he was, before taking the steps down to the gate and disengaging the bolts. The left gate remained anchored into the ground as Stefan pulled open the right gate.

"Torran is here," he told the messenger. "Who sent the missive?"

"Lord Cheltenham."

Stephen stood back, indicating for the man to enter, before closing the gate again and engaging the bolts. The messenger paused inside the gate, handing over the missive and waiting for Stefan to direct him, and Stefan indicated the stables against the west side. The messenger dismounted and headed to the stables to tend to his horse as Stefan headed to the manor house.

Other than a fire in the hearth in the solar, with the door open, there was very little light coming into the dark and shadowed entry. Stefan took the steps up to the second level where he knew Torran and Andia were. He went up to the chamber and rapped on the door. He didn't hesitate. Then he backed away, trying not to think of the fact that he might have interrupted something.

Gaze averted, he waited for the door to open.

About a minute later, it did. Torran appeared, dressed only in his breeches, and Stefan came through the door and shut it quietly.

"I am sorry to disturb you, Torran," he said softly. "But this arrived from the Earl of Cheltenham just now by royal messenger."

He held up the folded, sealed missive and Torran took it from him, frowning. "That seems odd," he said as he moved into the chamber adjacent to the one where his new wife was sleeping. He began fumbling around for a taper. "Look over by the hearth to see if there is a flint and stone."

Stefan did, coming up with the requested items just as Torran found an old taper. Stefan lit it as Torran snapped open the seal and unfolded the vellum. As Stefan held the taper up, Torran read the missive that described a visit from Lord Dudwell, who was, in fact, Andia and Aeron's uncle. The missive went on to state that Lord Dudwell eagerly wanted to see his niece and nephew and to keep the pair sequestered at Lockwood until further notice.

"That's damn curious," Torran muttered as he lowered the vellum.

"What did you say?" Stefan asked.

Torran handed him the missive. Stefan read it quickly, looking at Torran with confusion as he returned it.

"What does it all mean?" he asked.

Torran raked his fingers through his dark hair in a pensive gesture. "Please do not repeat what I am to tell you," he said. "But it could mean trouble. You see, we were informed yesterday of a possible assassination plot against Henry. The man seeking to kill Henry is a Frenchman, but one of the Executioner Knights got the man drunk and Lord Dudwell was mentioned as part of the plot. We didn't know why, or what the connection was to Henry, but now we find out that Dudwell is my wife's uncle."

My wife.

That reference wasn't lost on Stefan, who tried to pretend like the mention didn't hurt him. He struggled to focus on the subject at hand. "Then the plot thickens," he said. "Dudwell wants to meet his niece and nephew? For what purpose?"

Torran shrugged. "That is the question, isn't it?" he said. "It's all very strange."

"Cheltenham wouldn't have told the man where they are, would he?"

Torran shook his head, lifting the missive. "Very doubtful," he said. "De Lohr says to keep both of them sequestered at Lockwood. That tells me that he is concerned that Dudwell might be out looking for them."

"I would agree with that."

Torran scratched his chin, moving to the window that overlooked part of the yard and a partial view of the river beyond. The security at Lockwood, with the moat, had always been secure, but that didn't mean a man who was determined couldn't make it over the wall.

That concerned him.

"How many men do we have in the troop house?" he asked.

"Twenty very bored souls."

Torran turned to him. "Put them on the walls," he said. "If Dudwell is looking for Andia and Aeron, he could try to discover all he can about where they might be. Servants are always good for information with a few coins pressed into their palms, and the fact that I have taken charge of both Andia and Aeron might come up. It is no secret that Lockwood is a Bexhill property and I am the heir, so the man might put the pieces of the puzzle together and end up here."

Stefan nodded. "A remote chance, but a chance nonetheless."

Torran cast him a long look. "Vigilance is the better part of valor, I think," he said. "Especially with a man who was mentioned in an assassination plot against Henry. I don't like the fact that Dudwell was poking around today, so I think I'll spend the night on the wall with you. In fact… where is the messenger? Did he return to London?"

Stefan shook his head. "Not yet," he said. "Why?"

Torran cocked an eyebrow. "Send him back tonight," he said. "Tell him to fetch the Six. There was to be a feast tonight, as Henry's allies are still in London, so they will be roaming the great hall. Tell the messenger to find Jareth and give him the message that the Six must come to Lockwood immediately. I can't explain why, but I have a bad feeling about this, Stefan. I want the Six here, with us, at least until morning."

Stefan nodded, in full agreement. As he headed down the stairs, Torran returned to the darkened chamber where Andia was still snoring. Only this time, she was on her back, in the middle of the bed, with both arms flung out and one leg hanging over the side of the mattress. Arms and legs were askew. Torran started to laugh at the sight, hand over his mouth so he wouldn't make any noise, as he went about locating his clothing. He'd just bent over to pick up his tunic when Andia suddenly kicked all of the covers off, snorting in her sleep as she did so. Now she was spread out all over the bed, head off the pillow and very nearly sideways.

It was all Torran could do not to laugh out loud.

Silently snickering at his new wife's sleeping habits, he went over to the bed and collected the covers, carefully trying to cover her back up again, but it was truly a shame. Her nude, delicious body was a feast for his eyes and, with tunic in hand, he sighed heavily because he could feel himself becoming aroused. He looked at the chamber door, an indication that he knew what he needed to do, but his gaze moved back to the bed and that glorious body before him.

He also knew what he *wanted* to do.

To hell with it.

Tossing the tunic back on the ground, he loomed over her on the bed, very carefully pushing her hair out of the way so he could get to her breasts. They were calling to him, like a siren's song, and he couldn't resist. Very gently, he began to suckle her, first one breast and then the other, thinking he could keep it very soft and tender so she wouldn't wake up. Truthfully, this was for him. He needed this, like he needed air to breathe. But suckling her wasn't enough.

He wanted more.

Sliding his breeches off, he climbed back into bed with her, at least as much as he could considering she was spread out all over the mattress. But her legs were apart, wide apart, and he wedged his big body down between them, his hands and mouth going to her torso. When he began to fondle her, no longer being gentle about it, Andia awoke. Eyes rolling open, it took her a moment to realize where she was and an even longer moment to become aware of what was happening. Seeing Torran on top of her, feeding on her flesh, she groaned with pleasure.

Her arms went around him.

"Oh… Torran," she said sleepily.

Joining Stefan down in the courtyard was going to have to wait.

CHAPTER EIGHTEEN

L OCKWOOD WAS A big place with a big moat.

That might be a problem.

It was raining, but not too terribly, as Donnel, Gaubert, and Styx stood on the road about a quarter of a mile from the manse. Styx had already done some scouting and come back to announce that there was one way in and one way out unless they were keen on swimming the moat.

No one was.

It presented a bit of a logistical problem. The manse, for the most part, wasn't a large structure, but the moat made it one of the most fortified homes in the area.

The moat changed everything.

It hadn't been difficult to find Lockwood. All they'd had to do was ask someone in London, who thought it might have been near Rochester. So they crossed the river and asked for directions from the first tavern they came to, and that tavernkeep knew exactly where it was. On the south side of the Thames, there weren't many homes, as most of them tended to be to the west and on the north side of the river. But Lockwood was on the south side of the river, to the east, and it sat amongst heavy trees and swampy fields. It did, however, have a commanding view of the river from the east, and even though it wasn't particularly imposing, it did present a problem.

A problem that they had to solve.

Something in their favor was the fact that there were no soldiers that anybody could see. The manse looked vacant except that when the sun went down and the storm rolled in, they could see points of light moving on the upper floors. Tapers, held by the occupants, were staving off the storm and the darkness inside the old stone walls.

That meant someone was there.

Perhaps even a certain niece and nephew.

Bolstering that opinion was the fact that just after sunset, while they were watching tapers in windows, a man departed the manse on a small palfrey. As they watched through dripping leaves, they could see that it was a priest because he was dressed in the robes of the cloister. If that wasn't strange enough, the royal messenger finally arrived. How on earth they beat the messenger to Lockwood was a mystery, but they had. Styx suggested that the messenger must have stopped somewhere for food and drink. Perhaps he had even visited friends. Whatever the case, the man had delayed his arrival to Lockwood, so that they saw him go in and they clearly saw him come out.

That was when Gaubert came up with an idea.

"Listen to me," he hissed from his hiding place behind a birch tree. "We will ambush the man, steal his clothing, and then go back and ask for admittance. Of course they will open the gate because they will think it is the messenger returned."

"Get in?" Donnel whispered loudly. "But we cannot see who is inside. We must have more time to determine what we are facing."

Gaubert waved him off. "We must kill whoever opens the gate to silence them," he said. "Then we find Ashford's children and depart."

Donnel, with rain dripping off his eyelashes, was watching the messenger draw closer as he plodded down the road. "I think it is reckless to gain entry so soon," he said. "We do not know who is inside. We do not even know who is at the gate. Mayhap only a servant, because we certainly have not seen any soldiers. I have difficulty believing the place is so poorly guarded."

"Look at it," Gaubert said, gesturing. "With that moat, they do not need soldiers. No one can get across that moat, so this may be our only opportunity, Donnel. We are foolish if we do not take it."

Donnel was still hesitant. "I am not certain," he said. "Just because we have not seen soldiers does not mean there are not any."

"Do you want your niece and nephew or don't you?"

"Of course I do."

"Then how else do you propose to get in?"

Donnel didn't have an answer, but that also made him defensive. "Do I have to think of everything?" he said. "*I* discovered where my niece and nephew were taken. *I* paid the man back in Southwark to tell us where this place was. I am even the one who will gain you entrance to Westminster so you can seek Henry when the time is right. I have done everything so far and you have done nothing. We are in this together, Gaubert. I suggest you start thinking of ways to contribute to the success of our plan."

Gaubert eyed the man unhappily. This entire venture was Donnel's idea. Well, for the most part, he didn't appreciate being scolded like he was so much baggage while Donnel was the brains. That was hardly the truth. As the messenger drew closer, Gaubert leaned in Styx's direction.

"Take the messenger," he muttered, indicating the rider. "We want his horse and his clothing."

Styx took off, using the heavy foliage as a shield. He remained on the very edge of the road, hidden in the bramble, as the messenger passed by. Then Styx launched himself at the messenger and the horse, plowing into the messenger and sending the man crashing off the other side of the horse. As Gaubert went after the startled animal, Styx descended on the messenger and smashed the man into the wet road, holding his face down into a dirty puddle of water.

It didn't take long for the messenger to stop moving.

Styx hauled the body over to the side of the road and began to strip him as Gaubert returned with the horse. Donnel bolted across the road where Styx was pulling the clothes from the messenger, and the three of them quickly realized that Gaubert was the only one who could possibly fit into the clothing. He was tall and thinner than either Styx or Donnel, so he began pulling off his clothing in haste.

"I will ride to the gate," he said, peering off into the distance even as he donned the scarlet and gold royal tunic. "But you two must remain concealed. I will dispatch whoever answers the gate and then you must come in a hurry. Do not delay once I summon you."

Donnel was helping Styx with the messenger. "This will work provided there are not a hundred soldiers inside that yard we cannot see," he said. "I still say that we must be cautious."

Gaubert put a big dagger in the belt of the tunic before pulling on the messenger's helm. "We have been watching that place for a few hours now and it is dead," he said flatly. "There are no soldiers inside."

"The walls are tall. They could be concealing them."

"I will ask you again—do you want your niece and nephew or not?"

Donnel did. He just didn't like that they couldn't see much of the manse in the distance. The night was dark and the rain, though light, hindered the view even more.

But they had to take the chance.

"I do," he said in resignation. "Styx and I will stay just inside the trees until you gain admittance. We will ride swiftly once you give us a signal and join you."

As Donnel darted back across the road for the mounts, Gaubert made sure the messenger's too-small helm fit well enough to cover his facial features. At least until he gained admittance. He mounted the man's skittish horse and began to trot down the road as Styx went to help Donnel collect all of the horses.

As agreed, the pair remained in the trees, watching Gaubert approach the gatehouse. The rain was beginning to let up a bit and the clouds were moving out, revealing a silver moon in the sky when they parted. It was much easier to see that way. And they saw, clearly, when Gaubert approached the gatehouse and shouted to whoever was inside.

With great anticipation, they waited.

CHAPTER NINETEEN

H E DIDN'T WANT to go to bed.

His sister was off with her new husband, a man who had spanked him no less, and Aeron wasn't haven't a good day. Things had changed so drastically for him, in truth, that he was feeling increasingly disoriented. His father was gone, his home was destroyed, and his sister had been married, all within days, and the events were enough to bewilder him. Though Aeron was young, his life had always been planned out for him. He knew what was expected of him and had always been determined to be the best Earl of Ashford that he could be. But now...

Now he didn't know what he was going to be.

After a priest came and blessed his sister's new marriage, reading prayer after dull prayer, Andia had sent Aeron with Emile and the cook to the kitchens, where the cook proceeded to feed him rabbit stew. It had chunks of carrots in it, and celery, and he liked it a great deal, but there he was, sitting in a kitchen with people he hardly knew, in a house he didn't know, while his sister went with her husband. It was the cook who had told him to go to bed, but he hadn't. He'd stayed up, watching the courtyard below before leaving his chamber and going across the landing to the other chamber where he could see the river meander by.

It gave him time to think about his future, which had seemed so certain once.

Not anymore.

Restless, Aeron wandered outside, shuffling around in the dark, looking for Emile and hoping he was in the stable. But the stable was dark and quiet at this hour and he'd been forced to hide when a man wearing a red tunic with gold lions entered to water his horse. Aeron had remained tucked back in the shadows, watching, wondering who the man was. He couldn't leave until the man did, so he settled down to wait him out, hoping the dusty hay wouldn't cause him to sneeze.

Then Stefan appeared.

Aeron didn't know what was going on, exactly, but Stefan told the man to return to London with another message. The man headed out, as did Stefan, and Aeron was able to come out of his hiding place. Slipping out of the stable unseen, he climbed onto a wet pile of hay, onto an outbuilding's stone roof, and then onto the wall walk.

He could see everything from here.

Overhead, the sky was starting to clear a little and he found himself starting skyward, watching the stars, wondering if his father was looking down upon him. He'd always been told that when people went to heaven, they went up in the sky. Maybe his mother was up there, too, a woman he'd never even met. He felt like he knew her because his father had told him about her often, but he heard his father say once that Andia looked just like her mother. That was why his father had never paid his sister much attention.

Because she looked like Genevieve and it was just too painful.

One thing Aeron knew was that there were a lot of mysteries in this world, things he was trying to figure out. Down below, he saw Stefan near the armory and his thoughts turned to the big, brawny knight who seemed determined to be cruel to him. Stefan said he was trying to teach Aeron a lesson, but Aeron wasn't sure why he needed lessons. He already knew everything his father taught him. But secretly, Aeron was curious about Stefan because he was a real knight. He was big and strong and brave, much like Torran was, but the difference was that Stefan hadn't threatened him. Yet, anyway.

There was still time.

Stefan ducked into the armory and Aeron was left bored again, looking up at the sky, wondering if he should just run away and go back home, only there wasn't much of a home to go to. He remembered getting a good look at it as they left Kennington. The walls were smashed and there were piles of debris and bodies everywhere. That had been his first taste of battle, and he had to admit he didn't like it. Dropping pots on the heads of knights aside, it had been a frightening experience.

Perhaps he couldn't go back after all.

Then what would become of him?

Aeron was pondering that very idea when he saw Stefan emerge from the armory again. Pressing himself back against the wall, he could see Stefan plainly as the man moved in the dim light of the courtyard. There were a few lit torches placed strategically by Emile, designed to illuminate the courtyard just enough to see by. They were burning fat, so the greasy smell was heavy in the air. As Aeron continued to watch, he heard a voice from the gates. Stefan continued walking, but a second, louder call caught his attention. He seemed to pause as if confused, but then he charged up the steps leading to the wall walk just above the gates and looked down. After some reciprocal shouting, Stefan went back down to the gate and threw the bolts.

Curious as to who would be coming in so late at night, Aeron came away from his position on the wall to see who had arrived.

He was just in time to catch sight of the visitor ramming a dagger into Stefan's torso.

CB

WHEN TORRAN DIDN'T make it down to the yard in a reasonable amount of time, Stefan guessed what had happened. He probably had a worried bride up in that chamber and had remained to soothe her. Not that Stefan blamed him, because he would have done the exact same thing.

And he would have done it gladly.

After sending the messenger back to London with a verbal message for Jareth, Stefan went to the armory, where Aeron's dusty spears were lined up against the wall, because that was where he kept his armor. He'd spent all of his time on the walls, or even patrolling outside the walls, on that tiny sliver of land before it sloped down into the moat, so it was simply a matter of convenience to keep his armor close. Donning almost everything but his broadsword, he exited the armory and looked to the troop house, noticing that the door was shut, meaning the men had gone to bed. Since Torran hadn't come down yet, Stefan was wondering if that was where he belonged, too.

In bed.

Not out here in the night, alone.

But he remained by the gate, dutifully intending to rouse the troop house, when he heard shouting again. Or at least he thought he did. It might have been the weather as the rain started to ease up and the clouds blew west, revealing patches of sky and a big silver moon. Curious, he paused because he wasn't sure what he'd heard, so he rushed up the steps that led to the wall walk over the gate. In the darkness, he caught a glimpse of a man on a horse wearing the royal scarlet and gold tunic.

The messenger had returned.

"What is it?" he called down. "Why have you returned?"

The messenger was coughing, almost violently. "May I enter, m'lord?"

The voice was raspy as the man continued to cough. Since Stefan had already seen the man a short time ago, he didn't think anything about going down to the gate and throwing the big bolts. He threw the final bolt and opened the gate, stepping back as the man, now on foot, entered leading his horse. But the moment he came within close proximity of Stefan, he plunged a dagger into Stefan's torso.

Grunting with pain and shock, Stefan stumbled back. A thousand things rolled through his mind at that moment, not the least of which was the fact that he wasn't armed yet. His sword was still in the armory. He'd come out half dressed, with the intention of summoning some of the soldiers for the wall, when the messenger had come.

But it wasn't the messenger.

It was someone else.

Self-preservation kicked in.

When the messenger withdrew the dagger and kicked him, hard, in the gut, he fell backward and feigned unconsciousness. He wasn't sure how bad his wound was and wasn't sure how much of a fight he could put up if the man was armed and he was losing blood, so he kept his eyes closed and prayed the messenger didn't try to stab him again. As he lay there on his left side, he could hear faint footsteps. He thought he might have heard another shout. Hissing, perhaps? He wasn't sure. But after a minute or two, he began to hear whispering.

There's more than one of them.

Stefan peeped an eye open. There were three that he could see. Robbers? Bandits? Assassins? God only knew who they were, but they wanted in and they'd gotten what they had wanted. The problem was that Stefan couldn't fight off three of them, not in his present condition. He suspected he was bleeding fairly heavily because he was starting to feel some tingling in his extremities as his blood drained away. If he made a move, they would probably kill him, so he had to lie still. At least at the moment. But once they started to move away from him, he intended to act.

That was his plan, anyway.

But he passed out before he could take charge.

ᘓ

THEY WERE IN.

"What about the knight?" Donnel asked, pointing to the bleeding man on the ground. "Did he put up a fight?"

"Nay," Gaubert said, looking around nervously. "But he is dying, if not dead already. We must move swiftly before we're seen."

"Then we go to the house," Donnel said, pointing to the big, gloomy manse. "If Andia and Aeron are here, surely they are in the house."

"Then we move," Gaubert said, but not before he turned to Styx. "Secure the horses outside of the gate. We will have to leave swiftly."

Styx nodded, watching the pair of them rush for the house. He waited until they were halfway across the muddy yard before he turned for the gate, glancing at the big knight on the ground. He was going to walk past him until he realized that the knight was wearing the colors of the Earl of Canterbury.

Daniel de Lohr.

That puzzled him. It also concerned him. Glancing over his shoulder to see where Gaubert and Donnel were, he swiftly knelt beside the knight, rolling the man onto his back. A quick examination showed that he'd been stabbed on the left side of his torso, underneath the ribcage as far as he could tell. Not low enough to puncture his guts, or high enough to hit his lungs, but it was in an area that could bleed a lot. The knight stirred a little, and Styx leaned over him, slapping him lightly on the cheek.

"You," he said. "Wake up. Open your eyes."

The knight did. He blinked. When he realized there was a man hovering over him, an enormous fist came up and Styx barely managed to duck it. He put his hands on the knight to ease him and also to prevent him from trying to strike him again.

"I am not here to harm you, I swear it," he whispered sternly. "You serve de Lohr?"

The knight grunted. "What did you say?"

Styx raised his voice. "I asked if you served de Lohr."

"I *am* a de Lohr," the knight said, trying to pull away. "If you're going to kill me, I'll not make it easy for you."

Styx looked behind him to make sure Gaubert and Donnel were still heading for the house before he continued.

"I am not going to kill you," he muttered. "Come on—we must get you to safety before they come back."

Stefan was struggling, trying to roll away from him. "Who are they?" he demanded. "And who in the hell are you?"

Styx was trying to help the man up, but Stefan didn't want his help. It became like a wrestling match.

"There's no time for explanations," Styx said. "I am an ally, I swear it. De Dere is the name. My father is a friend of your father and grandfather."

Somehow, Stefan miraculously made it to a sitting position, but that was all he could do at the moment. "You… you're *what?*" he said, confused and in pain. "Who in the hell is your father?"

"Achilles de Dere."

"Who?"

"Achilles de Dere."

He said it louder, and Stefan heard him that time. Strangely, that seemed to calm him down. He was pale and trembling as he faced off against the intruder. "Achilles de…" he muttered. "*He* is your father?"

"He is."

"But I do not know you."

"Nor I you," Styx said. "But we must trust one another or there will be serious trouble tonight. Can you walk?"

Stefan seemed uncertain. "I think so," he said. "But—"

He was cut off when there was a loud thump and the man who identified himself as a de Dere suddenly fell forward, face first into the dirt. Shocked, Stefan looked up to see Aeron standing behind the man with a hammer in his hand.

And he'd used it.

"I'm going to kill him!" Aeron declared. "He tried to kill you, but I am going to kill him!"

Stefan had never been so glad to see that annoying pest in his life. He had no idea where the boy had come from, but he didn't care. When Aeron lifted the hammer to hit Styx in the head again, Stefan wrenched it out of his hands and pointed to the troop house.

"Go," he commanded. "Sound the alarm. Tell the soldiers we have intruders and they tried to kill me. Tell most of them to spread out on the perimeter and make sure no one else enters, but send a couple to me. *Hurry!*"

Disappointed he wasn't going to get to kill yet another knight, Aeron ran for the troop house as ordered. As Stefan sat there, trying find the strength to stand and head to the keep to help Torran, he caught sight of a figure coming in through the gate. He was preparing to use the hammer he'd just taken off the boy when the figure came into view.

"Jesus, Stefan!" Kent exclaimed. "What in the hell is going on here?"

Yet another shock to Stefan. He didn't know why Kent had suddenly appeared, but he didn't question it. He jabbed a finger toward the keep.

"Intruders," he said. "Help Torran, Kent. Hurry!"

Kent could see the blood all over Stefan's torso. "You're bleeding," he said, greatly concerned. "Let me help you."

"Nay!" Stefan said. "Go—the lady needs help. Torran is going to have his hands full, so go on. Help him!"

Kent hesitated. "Are you sure?

"I am."

"How many of them?"

"Two, as far as I know," Stefan said. "Hurry, Kent. Time is wasting."

Leaving his horse standing near Stefan, Kent unsheathed his weapon—Insurrection—and charged toward the keep.

And Insurrection was hungry for blood.

CHAPTER TWENTY

"**D**ON'T LOOK AT me like that or I'll never make it outside."

Andia had just finished pulling on a sleeping shift because the room had grown cold for lack of stoking the fire. She had been watching Torran dress, smiling dreamily at him, and he'd just told her not to.

She ignored him.

"Can I not look at the man I have married?" she asked. "Can I not gaze upon his handsomeness and feel proud? You belong to me, Torran. Can I not marvel at my good fortune?"

He was standing over by the bed, securing his tunic. "Cease," he said without force. "You are going to swell my head."

"Good," she said, going to the dressing table near the hearth and picking up a horsehair brush belonging to Torran's mother. "I hope I do. I hope you understand how very fortunate I feel. I hope you know that your touch, as new as it is to me, feels as if I have always known it. As if it was meant to be."

He stopped fussing with the belt and looked at her. "That is a very flattering thing to say," he said. "I feel the same way, but you are better at putting it into words."

Andia smiled as she began to brush her long hair. "We will always feel this way."

"Are you certain?"

"Of course," she said. "We shall never grow weary of one another. Not today, not tomorrow, not ever."

He heard his words reflected in her sentiment and grinned, resuming with the belt. "I pray that is forever true, my dearest," he said softly. "For certain, I could have never imagined this day, considering the rough start we had."

Andia turned to look in the mirror as she brushed. "Odd how our paths of life come together," she said. "Be it fate or divine intervention, I do not care what it is. All I care about is the fact that our paths *have* come together. Now we walk the same road."

He smiled as he sat down on the bed to pull his boots on. "You are poetic," he said. "I like to think that God has brought us together. I've thought about this situation we find ourselves in and it came when we both needed it. You needed it because your dreams had been crushed by a careless father and a demanding brother. But me... I've spent much of my life trying to discover who, and what, I am. I've killed and I've sinned and I've wandered, but now I find myself in the very place I was looking for. As if you are the absolution for a life I've lived and the promise of what is to come."

She looked at him, mid-brush. "I am your absolution?"

He nodded. "It has several meanings," he said. "Forgiveness... release... freedom. You give me the freedom to be who I was meant to be, Andie."

A soft knock on the door caught their attention. "I think *you* are very poetic," Andia said, tilting her head in the direction of the door. "If we ignore the knocking, will they go away?"

He grinned. "Probably not."

"Shall I answer it?"

Torran nodded with resignation. "It will be Stefan, wondering what is keeping me."

Andia fought off a smirk as she made her way to the door. "Will you tell him?"

"Nay," Torran said firmly before she even finished her question. When he saw her giggle, he shook his head at her. "And you will not, either. What we do… That is for us and us alone."

She was snorting as she put her hand on the latch. "I will not say a word, I promise," she said. "I would never do such a thing."

He winked at her, going back to his other book, as she opened the door.

What occurred after that happened in a matter of seconds.

Someone reached out and grabbed her, yanking her out of the chamber. By the time Torran rushed to the door, he could see two men on the landing, one of them holding Andia against him with an already-bloodied dagger to her throat.

"What is your name, woman?" the man with a heavy French accent demanded. "Name!"

He was shouting in her ear, and Andia screamed in terror. "Andia!" she cried out.

"Let her go," Torran boomed, his voice echoing off the stone walls. "If you value your lives, you will let her go!"

But the man didn't let her go. He had his hand on her throat as he held her against him, that horrible dagger tip pointed right at her jaw. He was backing away to the stairs as his companion put himself between Andia and Torran.

"Stop where you are, big man," he said calmly. "She is coming with me."

Torran didn't say a word. He disappeared for about two seconds before reappearing in the doorway with Absolution in his hand. That enormous, wicked-looking broadsword caught the light, glinting malevolently.

"I told you to release her," Torran said, his voice steely. "Let her go now and I will not harm you. Fail to comply and I will make sure your death is as painful as possible."

The man between Torran and Andia shook his head. "My apologies, but you shall not keep your whore," he said. "How dare you take her as your whore? That is a finely bred woman you keep to your bed."

The man holding Andia took the first step on the stairs, but she failed to navigate it because she couldn't see where he was going. She ended up slipping and shrieking, terrified she was going to fall down the stairs. Enraged, Torran came out of the chamber as the man holding the dagger jabbed her in the jaw with it.

Blood began to stream.

"That was a warning, big man," the Frenchman said. "She comes with us."

Torran's instinct was to cut the man down in front of him and then deal with the Frenchman who held Andia, but he had no doubt that the man could sink that dagger into her neck faster than he could get to her.

It was a struggle to calm his rage and speak rationally.

"She is not my whore, but my wife," he said evenly. "You have no right to take my wife."

The man standing between him and the Frenchman looked puzzled. "Wife?" he repeated. "She… she is married?"

Over with the Frenchman, Andia burst into soft tears. She was terrified and the prick to her jaw bloody well hurt. "Please," she begged softly. "Please let me go."

The man between her and Torran looked at her. "Answer me," he barked. "You have married?"

Andia had no idea who the man was, asking such questions. "Aye," she said. "I am married. Please let me go!"

The man stared at her a moment before scratching his head in an oddly casual gesture. "This was not conveyed to me," he said. "Where is the boy?"

Andia looked at him in confusion. "What boy?"

"Your brother. Where is he?"

Now she was incredibly confused, and the tears started to fade. "My *brother*?" she said. "Who are you? Why do you ask such questions?"

"Is Aeron here?"

Andia looked at Torran, who nodded his head faintly. Struggling to swallow her tears, she nodded as much as she could with a hand around her throat and a dagger pointed at her face.

"Aye," she said. "He is here. Who *are* you? What is this about?"

The man gazed at her a moment longer before motioning to the man who held her. "Take her downstairs," he said. "I do not like this confined space. It is dangerous for all of us. Go."

The man began to drag Andia down the stairs, and she panicked because she was afraid of falling. Torran followed, sword in hand, watching the man drag his wife down the stairs, holding her tightly, until they reached the entry level of the manse.

All the while, Torran was stalking them like a hunter. He was seriously wondering where in the hell Stefan was, and both answers were disturbing—either he had been disabled by these men or he hadn't heard them. Mayhap he was in a place where the sights or sounds of a break-in hadn't reached him. Torran wasn't sure how he could alert him without endangering Andia, which he wasn't willing to do.

Therefore, all he could do was stalk them.

Wait.

And pray.

"I would suggest you let her go," he said as they reached the bottom of the stairs. "She is of no value to you. Tell me what you want and I will ensure that you get it, but only if you release her."

Before the man could reply, the entry door slammed back on its hinges and Kent appeared. Before Torran could call him off, he charged the man holding Andia, who had enough time to turn around and present Andia as a human shield. It was enough of a distraction for both intruders that Torran could finally act. He had no choice. He came off the stairs, goring the man who had been standing between him and his wife. The man screamed, falling to the ground, as Torran leapt over him and attacked the man holding Andia from behind.

Unable to defend on two fronts with a woman held against him, the man shoved Andia to the ground, but not before his dagger cut her on her neck and shoulder. On the ground, she quickly crawled away from the fight just as Aeron came running through the door with one of those awful, rusty spears. One look at his bloodied sister and the boy went mad with rage.

"I'll kill you!" he shouted, aiming for the injured man on the ground. "You hurt my sister!"

The man on the ground was in a bad way. Torran had sliced his belly deeply and his innards were starting to spill out. He screamed, holding out a hand against Aeron, who used the man like a pincushion. He stabbed him at least four times before the sight of blood got to him and made him sick. The spear clattered to the floor and he ran to Andia, pulling her away from the battle as much as he was able.

But it was a short battle, indeed.

The Frenchman was very good, but not good enough against two of the Guard of Six. In four or five moves, Kent cut the man in the back of the knee, severing a major tendon and rendering him unable to walk, and Torran sliced his chest and belly wide open. Guts and blood gushed out over the floor. As the Frenchman pitched forward, onto his face, a man Andia didn't recognize appeared in the doorway, armed, and she screamed. Torran and Kent turned to the source of her terror and the swords went up. As they started to charge, the man in the doorway immediately dropped his weapon and put up his hands in surrender.

"Nay!" he said urgently. "I am an ally! Peter de Lohr is my commander!"

That brought Torran and Kent to an immediate, yet confused, halt. "De Lohr?" Torran repeated. "Explain yourself or I'll gut you where you stand."

The man looked at the two bleeding corpses on the ground before speaking. "My name is Cormac de Dere," he said as calmly as he could. "I am an Executioner Knight. I was assigned to this mission to prevent the assassination of the king."

Torran looked at him in shock for a moment. "You... You're *what*?" he gasped. "An Executioner Knight?"

Cormac nodded steadily. "I am an ally, I swear it," he said. Then he pointed to the face-down body. "That is Gaubert Chambery. He is plotting to assassinate Henry, so I have been shadowing him."

Suddenly, everything Roi had told Torran came rushing back and he lowered his sword, his eyes wide in disbelief. "The agent," he said as the situation became clear. "*You* are the agent Cheltenham told us about, the one the Frenchman had solicited as an assassin."

"Exactly, my lord. That is me."

When he realized that they weren't about to engage in another battle, Torran's relief knew no bounds. But just as quickly, his attention turned in Andia's direction. She was covered in blood, from her jaw to her waist, and he rushed to her side, setting Absolution to the ground as he moved to help her.

"Christ," he muttered, his voice trembling. "Let me see what they've done to you."

Andia was pale, quivering, and still terrified as Torran pulled her hair back to get a look at the wound.

"Are you well?" she asked, running her hands over his left arm and chest. "You were not injured, were you?"

Torran looked at her, startled by her question, and tears filled his eyes. Here she was, bleeding all over herself, and she was only concerned about him. He honestly couldn't answer her, but he didn't have to. Kent and Cormac were suddenly beside him, and Cormac took hold of the sleeve of her sleeping shift and began to tear off pieces of it.

Kent took them.

"Let me see where she is wounded," Kent said because Torran had tears streaming down his face. He could see the bloody slice by her collarbone. "It does not look too serious, Torran. She's not going to die."

As Torran nearly fell apart attempting to comfort Andia, Kent put the pieces of material from her shift over the wound on her neck and collarbone, applying pressure to stop the bleeding. Beside him, Cormac tore a few more pieces from the hem of her shift.

"There is a wounded knight outside," Cormac said. "He needs a physic."

Torran's features became washed with concern. "Stefan," he muttered, quickly wiping at his face. "I knew something had happened to him. He would have never let anyone enter had they not disabled him. Is it bad?"

Cormac stood up, torn pieces of hem in his hand. "Bad enough, but I think he'll live," he said. "If anything vital had been hit, he would have bled to death by now. The last I saw of him, some soldiers were helping him. I'll be back."

He started to move away, but Aeron stopped him.

"I want to help," he insisted. There wasn't much he could do for his sister, but Stefan was hurt and he wanted to help the knight who was both the bane of his young existence and someone he admired. "Should I get something for him? Wine?"

Cormac nodded. "That would be very helpful, little man," he said. "Go get some wine and bring it back here."

Aeron took off for the kitchens as Cormac slipped out into the darkness. The entry was suddenly still, with Torran struggling to regain his composure and Kent pressing the linen against Andia's collarbone.

"Go and help Stefan," Torran said hoarsely. "I'll take care of Andia, but you must send someone for the physic. There is one in London, on Candlewick Street, the same one who tended Andie when she was ill with fever."

Kent turned everything over to Torran as the man took a deep breath, steadied himself, and focused on his wife's care. Truthfully, he'd never seen Torran react like he had to Andia's injury. The Torran he knew was like a rock—immovable, unemotional in battle. Nothing disturbed him. But his breakdown when he saw that his wife was injured told Kent that, perhaps, Torran wasn't as against this marriage as he and Jareth had speculated.

Perhaps not against it at all.

He let his gaze linger on Torran for a moment, with perhaps a bit of a smile at the realization he might actually be happy about the marriage, before he rushed out into the darkness to help Stefan.

That left Torran alone with Andia.

"It doesn't look too bad," he reassured her softly. "The physic may need to stitch it, but you will heal completely."

Andia looked at her pale, shaken husband and lifted her right hand, putting it against his face. "I am not worried," she said. "I will be quite well by tomorrow, even. But you did not answer me."

"About what?"

"Are you well? You were not injured in the fight?"

He had been looking at her shoulder and neck. When she asked him that, he seemed to freeze. He was still staring at her shoulder when big, fat tears popped out of his eyes and onto Andia. Startled, she began to caress his face.

"What is it?" she begged softly. "Why do you weep?"

He blinked furiously. "I... I do not know," he said. "All I know is that you are bleeding and injured, yet you are only concerned with me.

I've never had anyone concerned about me, not like that. Not someone who meant so much to me. Someone like you. I… I cannot explain it more than that."

Her thumb stroked his stubbled cheek. "Do you not wish for me to be concerned?"

He met her eye then. "I do," he whispered. "But it is the strangest thing. It makes me feel vulnerable, yet in the same breath, it makes me feel like the strongest man in the world."

She grinned at the bewildered man. "You had better decide how you feel about this because I am certain it will not be the last time I inquire as to your health," she said. "It is not a weakness to allow someone to care for you, Torran. I do care and I will always care. Today, tomorrow, and forever."

He smiled weakly. "That sounds like it is to be our battle cry."

"What?"

"Today, tomorrow, and forever."

"I think it aptly describes you and me. It is the most beautiful sentiment in the world."

He kissed her, so incredibly grateful that she was alive and would heal. He kissed her again, eyes closed, before taking a close look at her wound, which was clotting nicely. As he thought about moving her into the solar where there was a leather chair she could more comfortably sit in, Kent and Cormac appeared, carrying Stefan between them.

Stefan was conscious but pale. However, he took one look at Andia, with blood all over her, and he very nearly walked to her himself without assistance.

"What happened?" he demanded. "How badly hurt is she?"

"It is a serious cut, but she will heal," Torran said as they sat Stefan down next to Andia. "And you? How badly hurt are you?"

Stefan had to lie back on the floor. He was too weak to sit up. Aeron appeared with a pitcher of wine that was spilling over the sides as he walked. Emile came in behind him, eyes wide with the carnage, but he'd come to help Aeron with whatever was needed. Aeron handed the wine over to Kent before going back to the rusty spear he'd dropped. Picking it up, he went to Stefan and sat down beside him, prepared to protect the downed knight. Stefan might have thought it was rather sweet had he not felt so weak.

"I was caught off guard when they came through the gate," he said after a moment, looking over to the two bodies on the ground several feet away. "That man in the royal tunic stabbed me. He is dressed like the messenger who was just here delivering Cheltenham's missive, so I thought the messenger had returned. I had no sooner opened the gate than he thrust a dagger into my side."

"I've sent a couple of soldiers for the physic, Torran," Kent said quietly. "I told them to hurry."

"Good," Torran said. But then he found himself looking at the dead men behind him. "Does anyone know what has happened? Who *are* these men? Cormac? You came with them, did you not?"

Cormac nodded. "I can explain," he said. "As I said before, the man in the royal tunic is Gaubert Chambery. He is a cousin to Queen Eleanor. The other man is Donnel de Meudon, Lord Dudwell."

Torran was the first to react. "Dudwell!" he exclaimed as he looked at Stefan. "We were correct to be on our guard, weren't we? He *did* put the pieces of the puzzle together. Somehow… Damnation, I knew he would."

As Stefan nodded to the revelation, Andia looked at Cormac in surprise. "Donnel?" she repeated. "Uncle Donnel?"

Torran looked at her, brow furrowed. "Who is Uncle Donnel?"

Distressed, Andia was peering around Torran, trying to get a look at the dead men on the floor. "Lord Dudwell is my mother's brother," she said. "Donnel de Meudon. My father stopped speaking to him after my mother passed away because he said all Uncle Donnel wanted was money. I think he actually stole from my father, though my father never told me that directly. Whatever happened, my father and Uncle Donnel stopped speaking and I've not seen him in years. I did not even recognize him."

"He wanted guardianship over you and your brother, my lady," Cormac said. "I heard the plans. God knows, Donnel and Gaubert were full of plans. From what I understand, it started when Donnel was outraged because Henry sacked Kennington. He wanted to seek guardianship of you and your brother, and by doing so, he wanted to control the Ashford fortune."

Torran shook his head in disgust. "That is exactly what we suspected," he said to Andia, to the others. "It was speculation, of course, but reasonable speculation. But what about Gaubert? How does he fit into this?"

Cormac cocked an eyebrow. "That is where it becomes muddled," he said. "It was Donnel, as far as I understand, that suggested the death of Henry. Gaubert, who is a cousin to Eleanor, evidently does not like Henry, so he agreed to find an assassin for the king. He went to The Pox, of all places, and I happened to be there. When I realized what he wanted, I sent word to Cheltenham because I knew he was at Westminster. Even though his brother commands the Executioner Knights, I knew Cheltenham would want to know. He was also much closer than his brother, who is at Ludlow Castle, in case I needed direction on how to proceed."

It all made sense, so far, and Torran nodded as he digested the entire sordid situation. But there had to be more to it.

"But what was in it for Gaubert?" Torran asked. "Other than his hatred for Henry, why did he become involved?"

"Money," Cormac said. "Donnel promised him money from Ashford. This entire circumstance is about money, my lord. Greed does terrible things to men. Those two ended up here because Donnel was able to discover where his niece and nephew were being held. It was not difficult to find the property once we knew the name. At that point, I though I'd better stay close and be prepared to assist whoever was holding the lady and her brother. Knowing those two were out for blood, I was fairly certain they would try to kill whoever was guarding them."

Everything was becoming clear. Now, at least Torran and the others knew who their attackers were and what it was all about. A greedy uncle and an opportunist, and an incendiary situation was born. As Cormac had said, greed did terrible things to men.

"It could have been worse," Torran finally said. "How they made it into the house, I do not know, but it could have been worse. All things considered, I think we escaped relatively unscathed."

"They got into the house because the door was not bolted when I left you earlier this evening," Stefan said quietly. He had been listening to the entire sordid tale, at least as much as he could, and caught the gist of Torran's statement. "When they caught me unaware at the gate, I was unable to stop them. Cormac came to my aid and probably could have stopped them had young Aeron not hit him in the head with a hammer because he thought Cormac was trying to harm me. That was a brave thing, Aeron. I am appreciative."

Sitting with his dirty spear, Aeron had no idea how to respond. He was so used to fighting with the knights that appreciation wasn't something he could quite comprehend. Everyone looked at him, and, seeing the attention, he turned red.

"I... I still do not want to clean all of these spears," he said to Stefan. "Do I have to? Still?"

Everyone started chuckling, especially Stefan. Leave it to Aeron to impress upon them what was *truly* important in his world—not cleaning those damn rusty spears.

Torran was the one who answered.

"Mayhap a reward, Stefan?" he said, tilting his head in the direction of the boy. "He *did* try to save you."

"True," Stefan said. He cast a long look at Aeron, studying the boy for a moment. "I will return your shepherd's sling to you. I will not make you clean the spears for it. By trying to help me, I believe you have earned it back."

Aeron leapt to his feet. "Where is it?" he asked eagerly.

Stefan grinned as Torran waved the boy off. "Not now," he told him. "At the moment, we must get your sister back into her chamber and then find a clean bed for Sir Stefan so the physic can tend them both. Then we can discuss your shepherd's sling."

"But—!"

"Later, Aeron."

The boy shut his mouth, rising to his feet with that rusty spear as Cormac and Kent helped Stefan to stand. As Aeron and Emile rushed up the stairs to find a proper bed for Stefan, Torran scooped Andia up into his arms and the group of them, ignoring the two corpses still in the entry, headed up the stairs to find beds, rest, healing, and the prospect of a better tomorrow. Andia, in particular, was grateful for this moment because five minutes earlier, she wasn't sure she would ever see it.

She'd thought her dreams might be lost all over again.

Fortunately for Andia and Torran, the lady of lost dreams was lost no more.

And neither was her husband.

EPILOGUE

Five years later
Kennington Castle

"I THOUGHT THAT was you, my lord," Andia said, beaming as she lifted her hand to shield her eyes from the sun. "Welcome to Kennington."

Daniel dismounted his steed and handed it over to Emile, who was now the horse master at Kennington. Daniel gave his torso a twist, stretching out stiff muscles, surrounded by the dust and noise of the bailey in the midst of what had been a warm, dry summer. In fact, he was red around the cheeks because of the heat, and he smiled pleasantly at Andia.

"You are looking well, Lady de Serreaux," he said.

"Thank you, my lord."

"And how is your brood?"

She grinned. "I am not entirely sure," she said. "Mayhap you should ask Lady Penden?"

Daniel chuckled. "Is she still here?"

"Still? She has not been home to Rochester in years!"

Daniel was still grinning. "Can you blame her?" he said. "Inviting her for your eldest child's baptism was the start. Once the children started coming, how could she resist?"

"That is true," Andia said. "Especially when I named our first daughter Olivia, after her."

"And then you named your second daughter Desiderata," Daniel said. "God's Bones, that name is a mouthful."

Andia giggled. "It is a beautiful mouthful," she said. "Just as my new daughter is beautiful. She looks just like her father."

"Speaking of Torran, where is the man?"

"In London," she said, her smile fading as she looped her arm companionably in his, leading him toward the great hall. "That is not surprising. He has spent most of the past six months there, ever since the passing of Henry, as you know."

"I *do* know," Daniel said. "I know that the Earl of Ashford has been one of Prince Edward's most trusted advisors. Some say Edward will hardly make a move without him."

Andia puffed up proudly. "Torran is a great man," she said. "But you would know if that statement is true. You put just as much time there."

Daniel shook his head. "Not lately," he said. "Chad does. Stefan does, of course. But me? I am in my winter years, Andie. I would rather spend time with my wife at Canterbury. She has had to share me with the monarchy all these years. She does not want to share me anymore."

Andia understood. "I do not blame her," she said. "But that is the burden for women who marry important men. They must share them."

"You are quite generous with Torran."

She shrugged. "He tries to come home at least once a month, for a few days, but the travel has been wearing on him, so we are moving back to London for the time being."

"To the new townhome?"

"Have you seen it?" she said, incredulous. "It's a glorious monstrosity, one insisted upon by Edward. The thing rivals Westminster in its grandeur."

Daniel laughed softly. "It is quite grand, I agree," he said. "When will you leave?"

"Soon," she said. "We could not move before because of my pregnancy, but the baby is three months old now and she can travel."

"With Lady Penden standing guard, no doubt."

"Probably," Andia said. Then she shrugged. "Lady Penden's son has not yet married and she has no grandchildren, so tending to my children brings her great joy. Her husband even comes to visit her once in a while. I am not exactly sure about the state of their marriage that he would let his wife leave to go live with another family and tend their children, but he tolerates it and she is very happy. My children love her and I am grateful for her nurturing."

"Then I am happy for her and for you," Daniel said. "Speaking of children, however, I've come with news about your brother."

"Is that what has brought you all the way to Kennington?"

He shrugged. "Truthfully, I was traveling home from a gathering at Dover," he said. "But I wanted to stop and tell you that I am sending Aeron north to Castle Questing, seat of William de Wolfe. It is time for him to enrich his education, and Castle Questing, and the entire de Wolfe empire, is very active. He'll learn a good deal about the Scots and about warfare. He's eager to learn, Andie. This will be good for him."

Andia pondered her little brother, now verging on the cusp of manhood. "Are you sure he is old enough?" she said. "I have heard about the House of de Wolfe. They are a warring house."

"No more than de Lohr is, although they do have the Scots to deal with," he said. "But Aeron has excelled at everything we've taught him. I cannot teach the lad any more, so it's best that he go somewhere to learn new things."

Her smile returned. "I am so grateful he has had you to teach him all of these years," she said. "You took a child my father had practically ruined and turned him into something that we can all be proud of."

Daniel thought about the boy who was once fond of shepherd's slings and shouting out rude commands. "Much of that was Stefan's doing," he said. "Even though Stefan has gone on to be part of the Six, he's still gone out of his way to mentor Aeron. Even as his hearing has failed him almost completely, I think in some way, Aeron has kept him from being completely desolate about it. Your brother gave him something to focus on."

Andia nodded in agreement. "It goes both ways," she said. "Stefan has helped Aeron so much. It's like he's not even the same boy I knew."

"That is a good thing."

"Aye, it is."

"What does Torran intend to do with him once he's knighted? He'll be a good one, you know."

She nodded. "I hope so," she said. "Torran intends to send him to Etchingham, the castle that used to belong to my uncle. It's an Ashford property these days. I think that Torran wants to give it over to Aeron, with Edward's permission, so he'll have something of his own. A new legacy for him."

"Does he ever say anything about losing the Ashford title?"

"Not really," she said. "I often thought it was strange that he hasn't, but Torran seems to think he simply doesn't want to be reminded of his past. He only wants to move forward."

"What do *you* think?"

She chuckled. "I think he is grateful to a sister who had the foresight to hide the family coin from Henry's men," she said. "He may not have the Ashford name, but he has the Ashford fortune waiting for him once he is knighted. That's enough legacy for any man, wouldn't you say?"

They were nearly to the great hall at this point, but the sounds of the sentries alerted them that there was a new arrival at the gatehouse. They both paused, turning to see who it might be, when Torran rode through the gatehouse astride his big black and white horse.

Andia let out of shriek of surprise.

Leaving Daniel standing near the great hall, she rushed in Torran's direction as the man came to a halt. He'd barely had time to dismount before his wife was hurling herself at him, and he found himself engulfed in the embrace he lived for. Even though it had been five years since their marriage, there wasn't anything he craved more than this. In his world, there was nothing more important than Andia's touch, her warmth, and her love.

Her lips slanted over his and, for a brief moment, he was lost.

Like always.

"You've come home," she finally gasped, kissing him again. "Why did you not send word ahead?"

He grinned. "Because I do not get a reaction like this if I do," he said, watching her laugh. "I like catching you by surprise. 'Tis much more fun that way."

Andia hugged him again, tightly. "I'm so happy you're here," she said. "I've missed you."

"I hope so," he said, holding her against him but also noticing the tall, white-haired man over by the hall. "What's this? Canterbury is here?"

Andia loosened her grip on him. "He just arrived," she said. "He said he was coming from a gathering in Dover and stopped to tell me that Aeron will be going to the Scots border to train with William de Wolfe. Did you know about that?"

Torran put her on her feet. "Nay," he said. "But I approve. It is time for Aeron to expand his training."

"That is what Daniel said."

"I'll talk to him about it," Torran said as he put his arm around her waist and began to head toward the hall. "But first, tell me about things around here. How have you been? Well, I hope. How is our growing litter of children?"

Andia snorted. "Your eldest is doing quite well," she said. "Sebastien takes after you in every way, Torran. It's truly remarkable."

"And Tavin?"

"He's more like Aeron every day."

Torran rolled his eyes. "God," he groaned. "Say not so."

Andia fought off a grin. "Olivia is an angel, of course, like me," she said. "And little Desi is the happiest baby. She's such a joy."

"I'm sure she's grown tremendously since I last saw her," he said. "Let me speak with Daniel first and then I will see to the children."

"Of course," Andia said. "Do you wish to speak with him alone?"

He hesitated. "Do you mind?" he said. "Political business. Things that wouldn't interest you. Just for a little while, if I may."

Andia understood. This was standard for her life, married to a king's advisor as she was. Torran was still the leader of the Guard of Six, of course, but his duties had taken on dimension over the years. Even if his father still didn't have much communication with him, it didn't really matter because Torran had the kind of wife and children that most men would kill, or die, for. A life he had created on his own that had turned into the best life possible.

Andia understood that.

And so did Torran.

He kissed Andia once more and watched her head off toward the keep where their young brood was waiting with their adoptive grandmother. Every time he saw his wife, his love for her grew. So did the disbelief that she was his, and this was their life, and it was the most amazing life he could have ever imagined. He was extremely busy in his professional life, still guarding the king, now also advising the man, but the name Torran de Serreaux stood for something. It stood for resilience, for loyalty, for responsibility, but most of all, it stood for the Earl of Ashford and the new legacy he was making for himself and his family. A legacy that embodied everything good and true and worthwhile.

Words that described his wife, as well.

Good, true, and worthwhile.

That was Andia.

Once his wife reached the keep, Torran turned his focus to Daniel, lifting a hand in greeting to the man. As he did so, he happened to catch a glimpse of the standards on the roof of the hall, snapping in the breeze. They were his standards, combining the old Ashford colors of red and silver with the de Serreaux black and blue to create a three-point shield of black and silver with rearing white horse in the center.

Hodie Cras et in Saecula was the motto.

Today, tomorrow, and forever.

On the day Torran married Andia, he meant every word of it.

And he always would.

☙ THE END ❧

Children of Torran and Andia:

Sebastien

Tavin

Olivia

Desiderata "Desi"

Yancey

Jasper

Alen

Maxim

Juliana

Stefan

KATHRYN LE VEQUE NOVELS

Medieval Romance:

De Wolfe Pack Series:
Warwolfe
The Wolfe
Nighthawk
ShadowWolfe
DarkWolfe
A Joyous de Wolfe Christmas
BlackWolfe
Serpent
A Wolfe Among Dragons
Scorpion
StormWolfe
Dark Destroyer
The Lion of the North
Walls of Babylon
The Best Is Yet To Be
BattleWolfe
Castle of Bones

De Wolfe Pack Generations:
WolfeHeart
WolfeStrike
WolfeSword
WolfeBlade
WolfeLord
WolfeShield
Nevermore
WolfeAx
WolfeBorn

The Executioner Knights:
By the Unholy Hand

The Mountain Dark
Starless
A Time of End
Winter of Solace
Lord of the Sky
The Splendid Hour
The Whispering Night
Netherworld
Lord of the Shadows
Of Mortal Fury
'Twas the Executioner Knight Before
Christmas
Crimson Shield
The Black Dragon

The de Russe Legacy:
The Falls of Erith
Lord of War: Black Angel
The Iron Knight
Beast
The Dark One: Dark Knight
The White Lord of Wellesbourne
Dark Moon
Dark Steel
A de Russe Christmas Miracle
Dark Warrior

The de Lohr Dynasty:
While Angels Slept
Rise of the Defender
Steelheart
Shadowmoor
Silversword
Spectre of the Sword
Unending Love

Sons of Poseidon:
The Immortal Sea

Pirates of Britannia Series (with Eliza Knight):

Savage of the Sea by Eliza Knight
Leader of Titans by Kathryn Le Veque
The Sea Devil by Eliza Knight
Sea Wolfe by Kathryn Le Veque

Note: All Kathryn's novels are designed to be read as stand-alones, although many have cross-over characters or cross-over family groups. Novels that are grouped together have related characters or family groups. You will notice that some series have the same books; that is because they are cross-overs. A hero in one book may be the secondary character in another.

There is NO reading order except by chronology, but even in that case, you can still read the books as stand-alones. No novel is connected to another by a cliff hanger, and every book has an HEA.

Series are clearly marked. All series contain the same characters or family groups except the American Heroes Series, which is an anthology with unrelated characters.

For more information, find it in **A Reader's Guide to the Medieval World of Le Veque.**

ABOUT KATHRYN LE VEQUE

Bringing the Medieval to Romance

KATHRYN LE VEQUE is a critically acclaimed, multiple USA TODAY Bestselling author, an Indie Reader bestseller, a charter Amazon All-Star author, and a #1 bestselling, award-winning, multi-published author in Medieval Historical Romance with over 100 published novels.

Kathryn is a multiple award nominee and winner, including the winner of Uncaged Book Reviews Magazine 2017 and 2018 "Raven Award" for Favorite Medieval Romance. Kathryn is also a multiple RONE nominee (InD'Tale Magazine), holding a record for the number of nominations. In 2018, her novel WARWOLFE was the winner in the Romance category of the Book Excellence Award and in 2019, her novel A WOLFE AMONG DRAGONS won the prestigious RONE award for best pre-16th century romance.

Kathryn is considered one of the top Indie authors in the world with over 2M copies in circulation, and her novels have been translated into several languages. Kathryn recently signed with Sourcebooks

Casablanca for a Medieval Fight Club series, first published in 2020.

In addition to her own published works, Kathryn is also the President/CEO of Dragonblade Publishing, a boutique publishing house specializing in Historical Romance. Dragonblade's success has seen it rise in the ranks to become Amazon's #1 e-book publisher of Historical Romance (K-Lytics report July 2020).

Kathryn loves to hear from her readers. Please find Kathryn on Facebook at Kathryn Le Veque, Author, or join her on Twitter @kathrynleveque. Sign up for Kathryn's blog at www.kathryn leveque.com for the latest news and sales.